"THE ONLY THING I REALLY WANT TO DO IS TO KISS YOU. NOW."

Before Cheyenne could utter a word of protest, Quinn lowered his lips to hers. Caught by surprise, all she could do was give a quick little gasp before his mouth captured hers.

The kiss was as hot and hungry as the look she'd seen in his eyes just moments before. A kiss that was all fire and flash and sizzle. The mere touch of his lips on hers had sparks igniting between them. They moved slowly, deliberately, on hers, engaging her fully before she was even aware of what she was doing.

The arms that held her were so strong she couldn't have resisted if she'd tried. Not that she wanted to resist. Not when there was so much pleasure here in Quinn's embrace...

Raves for R. C. Ryan's Novels

Montana Glory

"The child adds a lovely emotional element to the story, the secondary romance is enjoyable, and all loose ends are nicely tied up."　　　　　　　　—*RT Book Reviews*

"[The Montana trilogy] is a good series of hunky cowboys and nail-biting mystery. Zane and Riley have great chemistry and are a read that you can't put down."
　　　　　　　—*Parkersburg News and Sentinel* (WV)

"These not-to-be-missed books are guaranteed to warm your heart!" —FreshFiction.com

"Ms. Ryan did an amazing job keeping the story line at a perfect pace... A stand-alone novel, but I would definitely recommend you grab the other two... because I promise you will love them, too!... I, for one, definitely want to visit my friends at the McCord ranch again!" —TheRomanceReadersConnection.com

"Wonderful romantic suspense tale starring a courageous heroine who is a lioness protecting her cub and a reluctant knight in shining armor... a terrific taut thriller." —GenreGoRoundReviews.blogspot.com

"I love romantic westerns, and this book fit the bill to a T. The characters were very well developed... The chemistry between Zane and Riley was electric. If you enjoy a great romance with a bit of suspense and mystery, then you are going to love this book... I do want to go back and read the first two, because this story was just that good!" —KittyCrochetTwo.blogspot.com

"The story line was magnificent, the characters were intriguing, and the climax kept me flipping the pages... I [loved] the flow of the story and plan to read more work by this author. Romance junkies will love this one." —RexRobotReviews.com

"Tender and sweet...Ms. Ryan did a great job of unfolding Riley's story line at just the right pace...This book was definitely a balm for my 'cowboy itch'...I actually went out and bought the first two books in the series because I wanted more of these delightful characters."

—BookAddictPatti.com

"Wonderful, exciting...an explosive conclusion to the McCord family trilogy...I would highly recommend this book, especially if you enjoy love, ranch life, mystery, and sweet romance.

—MyBookAddictionandMore.wordpress.com

"A sweet story with a breathtaking setting!...The author made you feel like you were actually witnessing life on a working ranch...The characters were charming, and I enjoyed the quirky locals...The sexual tension between Riley and Zane was intense. Major chemistry alert!... Check this one out if you have a thing for sexy cowboys or want a romance story that will leave you smiling."

—TheFictionEnthusiast.blogspot.com

Montana Destiny

"5 Stars! Watching this wild rebel and independent woman attempt to coexist was so much fun...The author, R. C. Ryan, delivers an ongoing, tantalizing mystery suspense with heartwarming romance. Sinfully yummy!"

—HuntressReviews.com

"Ryan's amazing genius at creating characters with heartfelt emotions, wit, and passion is awe inspiring. I can't wait until *Montana Glory* comes out...so that I can revisit the McCord family!"

—TheRomanceReadersConnection.com

"The series continues to intrigue, and each page brings you closer to finding the treasure. Another terrific story from R. C. Ryan." —SingleTitles.com

"Sure to entertain. Enjoy." —FreshFiction.com

"[A] wonderful series...The characters are extremely well developed...I couldn't put this book down. I can't wait until Zane's story comes out."

—NightOwlReviews.com

Montana Legacy

A *Cosmopolitan* "Red Hot Read"

"A captivating start to a new series." —*BookPage*

"Heart-melting sensuality...this engaging story skillfully refreshes a classic trilogy pattern and sets the stage for the stories to come." —*Library Journal*

"Fabulous...a well-written story with fully developed characters that I easily came to care for."

—HuntressReviews.com

"Delightful...Jesse and Amy are a breath of fresh air, and R. C. Ryan beautifully translates the intense feelings they stir in one another. I look forward to the next in the series." —SingleTitles.com

"Enjoyable...solid secondary protagonists and a wonderful lead pair." —*Midwest Book Review*

"A fresh, entertaining tale that will keep you wanting to read more...We only get tantalizing hints of Wyatt and Zane, but I can't wait to read their stories." —RomRevToday.com

QUINN

R.C. RYAN

FOREVER

NEW YORK   BOSTON

Forever
Hachette Book Group
237 Park Avenue
New York, NY 10017

Printed in the United States of America

978-1-61793-656-2

Forever is an imprint of Grand Central Publishing.
The Forever name and logo are trademarks of Hachette Book Group, Inc.

*For families everywhere, who love, laugh,
and work to make the future brighter for
those who follow.*

And for Tom, who cherishes his family above all else.

QUINN

PROLOGUE

---◆◆◆---

Wyoming—1996

Get in." The rusted old Ford truck rolled to a stop beside the back door of the Conway ranch house, and Big Jim Conway, patriarch of the family, pointed to the passenger side as he barked commands. His voice had the rasp of a rusty nail. "Quinn, help your little brother."

Quinn, at ten the oldest of Big Jim's three grandsons, grabbed hold of little Jake's hand. "Come on."

As always, five-year-old Jake jerked his hand free, resenting any hint that he couldn't keep up with his two older brothers. "Don't need any help."

"Don't sass, boyo, or you'll answer to me." As always, whenever his temper heated, the trace of Irish brogue in Big Jim's voice deepened.

Jake climbed up beside his grandfather, followed by seven-year-old Josh. Quinn climbed in last and pulled the door shut.

Quinn, the practical one, reached around his brothers. "There aren't enough seat belts."

"Double buckle."

At the impatient command he stretched the seat belt as far as it would go. The truck was already speeding along the curving driveway of their ranch, leaving a trail of gravel in its wake.

"Where're we going, Big Jim?" little Jake asked.

The three boys had never called their grandfather anything but Big Jim. No soft, cuddly nicknames like Gramps or Grandpa would suit this tough bear of an Irishman.

"We're heading to town, boyo." Big Jim couldn't keep the frustration from creeping into his voice.

"Why?" Jake demanded.

"'Cause your pa needs some time alone."

"He's not alone." The little boy's tone was matter-of-fact. "The police chief is with him."

Josh dug an elbow into Jake's ribs to quiet him.

He turned on his brother. "Hey. That hurt."

Big Jim shot a quelling look at his middle grandson, and Josh, always the rebel, hunched his shoulders in defiance. "Your pa and Chief Fletcher just need to talk."

It had become a weekly ritual. Ever since their mother disappeared without a trace, Chief Everett Fletcher would stop by to fill in Cole and Big Jim on the latest details of the police investigation, which seemed to be going nowhere. No trail to follow. No witness to her disappearance. No strangers spotted in the vicinity. No rhyme or reason to the mystery. No solution. No closure. No end to the pain. Though they never spoke about it, Quinn could tell by their sad, mad faces that the news wasn't good.

When he would leave, Big Jim would mutter and

swear and take the boys away while Cole would go off to one of the barns and work off his frustration and grief in a frenzy of chores.

To discourage any further questions, Big Jim turned up the volume on the radio. They drove the rest of the way serenaded by Patsy Cline and Buck Owens until they reached the town of Paintbrush, more than an hour from their ranch. Along the main street they drove past Thibalt Baxter's Paint and Hardware, the Odds N Ends shop with the slogan "If we don't have it, you don't need it" painted across the top of the building, and came to a halt outside Flora's Diner, announced in gaudy pink and purple letters.

Big Jim handed Quinn some money. "While I'm picking up supplies at Homer's Grain and Seed, you three can have some lunch at Flora's."

The three boys vibrated with excitement as they climbed down from the truck and walked inside.

"Why, look who's here." Flora, white hair looking like the cotton balls their mother used to remove her makeup, her angular face creased with a warm smile, came out from behind the kitchen as soon as she caught sight of them walking up to the shiny stools at the counter. Ordinarily she left the waitress duties to her daughter, Dora, a younger, wider version. But Dora was busy with the other tables. Besides, these customers were special in Flora's eyes. The whole town was buzzing about the mysterious disappearance of their mama, Seraphine. "What'll you boys have?"

"Burgers and fries." Quinn spoke for the three of them.

"How about some milk shakes to go with that? On me, of course."

Three heads bobbed up and down and she hurried

away. When she returned, she passed around plates and tall soda-fountain glasses with thick chocolate shakes.

Flora's burgers were the big, greasy kind that oozed mustard and ketchup. She always added extra fries and made their milk shakes so thick they had to use spoons. The whole time she served their food, she kept making soothing little noises about the poor, motherless boys.

They didn't much care for the words or the fact that she sounded like she was cooing at a couple of babies, but they figured it was a small price to pay for the special food they never got to taste back at the ranch.

When she finally walked away to wait on a table, her voice lowered to a raspy whisper so she wouldn't be over-heard by the three boys at the counter. Unfortunately, Quinn could hear every word.

"Them's the Conway boys. Their daddy and grand-daddy are legends in this part of Wyoming."

There wasn't anything Flora didn't know about any-body within a couple hundred miles of Paintbrush. The only thing she liked better than cooking was sharing what she knew with anybody willing to listen. If anybody wanted the latest news, they didn't have to wait for the weekly newspaper. They just dropped by Flora's Diner.

Quinn saw some people turn to stare and was grate-ful that Josh and Jake didn't notice. They were too busy slurping their milk shakes.

At one table was Thibalt Baxter, who owned the paint and hardware store. He was the skinniest man Quinn had ever seen. So skinny, he had to wear both a belt and sus-penders to hold up his pants.

Across from him was Dr. April Walton, whose father had been a doctor when Big Jim first came to Wyoming.

Dr. April always boasted that she had a granddaughter just about Quinn's age. At another table was Reverend Cornell, pastor of the Paintbrush Church, sitting with Judge Kirby Bolton and Randall Morton, who ran the fairgrounds where the annual rodeo was held.

Flora was having herself a good time relaying all she knew about the boys to a couple of customers, who were obviously new to town. "Their grandfather, Big Jim, carved their ranch out of pure wilderness, with a hundred head of cattle he herded from Saskatchewan, Canada, clear across Montana to the plot of land he'd inherited from an unknown uncle on his mother's side. That herd has grown into more than a hundred thousand head of some of the finest beef cattle in the world, and he's continued to add to his land. Now his ranch is the biggest in the state."

"You don't say." The young cowboy shot another glance at the three boys. "Lucky kids."

"Ranching's just the beginning," Thibalt Baxter added. "Big Jim's land is rich in coal and oil."

Flora nodded, eager to take back control of the conversation. "Which he leases to oil companies and mining companies for a whole lot of money. I've heard they produce enough gas and oil to fuel the entire state."

"Big Jim's a generous man," Reverend Cornell put in quickly. "There isn't a man or woman in this town who hasn't benefited from his generosity at one time or another."

"Including me," Flora insisted. "When I couldn't keep up the payments on this place, Big Jim loaned me the money and told me to pay it back whenever I could. You don't find 'em any better'n that." Her voice lowered. "But

Big Jim paid a high price for all that success. He lost the great love of his life, Clementine, at an early age. A pretty little thing. I knew her when we were girls. She gave him five sons, and not one survived past his first birthday. But then Colby, their sixth boy, was born, and he was the strongest, healthiest child you'd ever see. Big Jim figured his string of bad luck was broken, until that winter when Clementine was found dead in a snowdrift after one of the worst snowstorms trapped her between the barn and the house, while Big Jim was up in high country with the herd."

The strangers, spellbound by all they were hearing, shook their heads.

"Now that's tough," the cowboy muttered. "That kind of thing would break most men."

Flora was enjoying herself, relaying a tale that had become bigger than a legend in these parts. "Big Jim Conway isn't most men. He did what he had to. With a ranch to run and a baby to tend, he strapped the baby to his back and took him everywhere. Even after Big Jim hired a full-blooded Arapaho woman named Ela to tend to the kitchen and household chores, he kept that boy with him. By the time Cole Conway, their daddy"—Flora nodded toward the three boys slurping their milk shakes—"was old enough to walk, he could handle the reins of a horse. By the age of eight he could drive a tractor loaded with feed for a stranded herd while his father tended far-off ranch chores. I've heard it said that Cole Conway can chart a trail by studying the stars, survive a blizzard with nothing but a few evergreen branches for cover, and can bag a deer or a rabbit for his dinner with a single toss of his knife."

"Now you're making him sound like some kind of superhero," Thibalt Baxter protested.

Flora laughed like a girl as she turned to the others for confirmation. "I guess that's how most of us around here see Cole Conway. I still remember him coming to town with his daddy. By the time he was sixteen or so, women of all ages found him irresistible. Of course, that can be both a blessing and a curse. I bet there isn't a female in this town who hasn't fallen under the spell of Cole Conway at one time or another."

"Lucky guy." The cowboy shook his head from side to side.

"Or cursed." Flora lowered her voice as though revealing a state secret. "His wife Seraphine's gone missing without a trace. The police and the private investigators that Cole and Big Jim hired have all come up empty."

Across the room Quinn couldn't hear what was being said, but the sudden silence in the diner had his food sticking in his throat like a boulder and he sensed the keen interest of the other diners.

Everyone, it seemed, had something to say about his family. Everyone except the people directly involved.

He and his brothers had learned to avoid all mention of their mother or risk their father's stony silence or, worse, his embarrassing, unexpected, heart-wrenching grief. Given a choice, they would prefer silence to grief. It went completely against the grain to see their strong, stoic father crushed by the weight of his loss, his eyes red rimmed, his spirit broken for days and weeks at a time.

And so they had adopted a code of silence.

Quinn had a sudden itch to breathe fresh air.

"Come on." He shoved away from the counter, and his younger brothers looked up in surprise.

"I'm not done," Jake said.

"Bring it with you."

The little boy shoved the last of his fries into his mouth and began sucking down the dregs of his shake before sliding off the stool to follow his brother.

Josh, determined to flaunt his independence, took his time, dipping his fries in ketchup and eating every last one before following the other two.

"Bye, now, you sweet things," Flora called. "You be sure and bring your daddy and granddaddy with you next time you come calling."

"Yes, ma'am." As usual, Quinn spoke for all of them.

Once outside, Quinn spotted his grandfather's truck at the end of the street. Without a word he started toward it, with the other two trailing slowly behind, stopping to peer in the windows of the Odds N Ends shop, the barbershop, and even the doctor's office.

Quinn kept his head down. The last thing he needed was to run into any more busybodies wanting to cluck over the poor, motherless boys.

His mother's absence had left a terrible hole in their family. A hole none of them knew how to fill.

The ride back to the ranch was even more subdued than the ride to town had been. Big Jim pulled up next to the barn and spotted Cole inside, mucking stalls like a man possessed.

"You boys might want to take the horses out for a while," Big Jim said. "Give your daddy more time."

Quinn didn't need any coaxing.

As he saddled the big brown gelding, Quinn's grandfather said, "You keep an eye on your brothers, you hear, boyo?"

"Yes, sir."

A short time later, after Quinn and Josh helped Jake saddle the spotted mare, the three boys headed into the hills.

"I'm tired. Why are we riding way out here?" Jake's high-pitched voice broke through the stillness.

Quinn reined in his mount and looked over his shoulder. " 'Cause Pa's not ready for company."

"We're not company."

Quinn rolled his eyes and urged his horse into a run, with the others following.

Behind them, the rusted gate leading to their ranch was swinging back and forth, creaking and moaning in the wind. Burned into the wooden arch above it was the letter *C* for *Conway*, though Big Jim often joked that the ranch should really be called Devil's Wasteland. That's what he thought he'd entered when he'd first come upon this wild, primitive place.

Their horses moved single file along the sage-covered meadow. Though it was mid-May, here in the Wyoming wilderness there were still patches of snow beneath some of the bushes in the higher elevations.

"Come on, Jake. Keep up." Quinn kept looking back at Jake, riding between him and Josh. Not that Jake needed tending. Despite his young age, their little brother was absolutely fearless. A fact that caused Quinn endless trouble.

As Quinn's horse came up over a rise he caught a slight movement out of the corner of his eye. Curious, he slid from the saddle and led his horse toward a fallen log. Even before Quinn reached it, a tiny black and tan wolf pup gave a welcoming yip and bounded toward him.

Jake and Josh, following Quinn's lead, dropped to their knees beside the pup. At once three more wolf pups emerged and began climbing playfully among the children.

"Oh, look. Aren't they cute?" Jake was clearly enchanted by their antics.

"I wonder where their mama is?" Josh couldn't resist picking up one of the pups, which began licking his face.

"Maybe she's gone, like Ma."

At Jake's words Quinn felt the hair at the back of his neck rise. Eager to deny it, he shook his head and gathered a wriggling pup into his arms. "She's probably off hunting food while these little guys are supposed to be sleeping."

The three children were soon laughing out loud as the pups tumbled over one another vying for their attention.

Jake looked over at his big brother. "Maybe that's where Ma went. To hunt some food for us."

Quinn's smile was wiped away at another sudden, wrenching reminder of their loss. Would it never end?

"That's dumb."

"Why?" Jake stared at him with all the innocence of a five-year-old.

"'Cause there's enough beef in the freezer to feed us for years."

"Maybe she wanted to ride into town and buy us something special."

"Like what?" Josh picked up two yipping pups and tucked them inside his vest to warm them.

"I don't know. Cookies, maybe. Or a birthday cake. Ma knew I was turning five."

"You don't know anything." Josh's voice trembled, and

he tried to cover the quick flash of pain by burying his face in the pup's fur.

"Do, too." Jake stuck out his chin in an eerie imitation of their grandfather. "Ela says Ma was taken by evil spirits, but we're not 'posed to say so in front of Pa, 'cause it makes him sad."

"Why would evil spirits want to take away our ma?" Josh demanded.

The little boy gave an expressive shrug. "I don't know."

"There are no evil spirits." Quinn's eyes flashed.

"How would you know?" Jake challenged. "Ela says—"

"Come on." With a snarl, Quinn deposited the pup on the ground and got to his feet, wiping his hands down his pant legs.

Whenever they started talking about their mother he got this terrible empty feeling inside, as though nothing in the world would ever be enough to fill the hole. Maybe this was how their dad felt when he went off to the barn and worked like a devil was after him.

"Time for us to head home."

Despite their reluctance, the other two set down the pups they'd been petting and pulled themselves into their saddles. It never occurred to them to question Quinn's authority.

As they turned away, Quinn pointed to a blur of shadow in the woods. "Just in time. There's their ma now, heading home with their dinner. Let's not spook her." He wheeled his mount and the others did the same.

As they rode away they kept looking back, relieved that the mother wolf had returned to her pups.

For Quinn, it was a sign of hope. Maybe, by the time they got home, their own ma would be back, too.

Just as they topped a ridge they heard a single gunshot and the high, sharp cry of something wild, followed by a volley of gunshots that echoed and reechoed like thunder through the still air.

With the hairs at the back of his neck bristling, Quinn tugged on the reins, wheeling his mount, and the other two followed, urging their horses into a run as they raced back to the wolf den.

A neighboring rancher, Porter Stanford, was standing over the bodies of the female and her pups sprawled around her.

It was a grisly scene, the ground already stained with blood, the bodies twisted and still where only moments earlier they'd been filled with life.

The children stared in stunned silence as Porter spit a wad of tobacco. "Lucky I got here when I did. I just saved my herd and yours from these filthy predators."

"But they didn't—" At Jake's protest Quinn reached over and covered his mouth, stifling anything more.

He saw the flash of fury in their neighbor's eyes as he looked up at them, still seated on their horses.

"You got anything to say?" he demanded of Quinn.

"No, sir."

"Good. Glad your daddy taught you to respect your elders." He looked back at the wolves. "Murdering bastards got no right to live."

With a muttered oath the man swung away and pulled himself heavily into the saddle. He dug in his heels and his horse took off with a flurry of hooves.

Without a word Quinn slid from the saddle and bent to cradle one of the dead pups. Despite its eerie stillness, the tiny body was still warm.

He knelt and set it gently inside the den.

Seeing what he intended, Jake and Josh did the same, placing the pups side by side in the hollowed-out earth.

It took all three of the children, sighing and straining, to lift the female's body, which they placed on top of her pups. By the time they were finished, their clothes were stained with blood and dirt.

"Should we say a prayer?" Jake asked.

Though his brothers looked uncomfortable, they nodded, and Quinn murmured the words from one of the familiar nighttime prayers their mother had always insisted on, while the other two echoed his words.

They remained there for long, silent moments, bound together by their shared pain.

As they mounted their horses and started away, Quinn could no longer hold back his tears. Of rage. Of frustration. Of a deep, unexplained pain at the loss of beautiful creatures that had been so alive, so vibrant, just a short time ago. They didn't deserve this cruel fate. They deserved to live, to grow, to play, and to howl at the moon. To mate, and have pups of their own.

Instead, their lives had been cut short by the whims of one man.

This cruel act was so final. So wrong and unfair.

As wrong and unfair as the twist of fate that had stolen a mother from the family that needed her.

As Quinn worked frantically to stem his tears, his fingers left filthy streaks of mud and dirt on his cheeks, like the war paint Ela had described to them when telling them about her Arapaho heritage.

The sight of Quinn's tears had Jake nudging his mount closer to Josh for comfort.

Despite all that their family had been through, these two had never seen their older brother cry. Not even when they'd learned of their mother's mysterious, unexplained disappearance.

The sight of their brave brother, his heart broken and raging against the injustice they'd been forced to witness, was an image they would carry with them for a lifetime.

And for Quinn Conway this mother wolf and her pups seemed connected in some strange way to his own mother, and to her sudden, wrenching loss.

This single incident was the germ of a passion, a wild longing in his heart that would forever set his feet on the path to his future.

CHAPTER ONE

❖

Grand Tetons—Present Day

In the predawn darkness storm clouds hovered, threatening more snow. A ribbon of pale pink rimmed the horizon.

Red sky in the morning, sailors' warning.

The childhood rhyme played through Quinn Conway's mind as he stretched his long, lanky frame and slipped from his bedroll. As if to prove the wisdom of the words, the first fat snowflakes began dusting his hair, tickling his face. It may be springtime in Wyoming, but here in high country drifts were still waist deep.

For Quinn, the weather wasn't even a distraction. He kept his attention focused on the wolf pack as they began emerging from their den. He could tell, by their happy yips and yaps, that they were content to be back on their home turf, after days of hunting and travel. These wild creatures could typically travel forty or more miles in a twenty-four-hour period while hunting food. And when he was tracking them, he traveled the same route, keeping them always in his sight and grabbing his sleep whenever they did.

This was his pack. The one he'd been studying for more than five years. When the young male had been little more than a pup and Quinn an eager graduate student, he had implanted a tracking device under the animal's skin that allowed him to monitor every movement. When the wolf matured and became an alpha male with his own pack, he'd become the perfect subject for a scientific study. The publication of Quinn's papers chronicling the behavior of the pack had made him one of the preeminent naturalists in the country. His advice was often sought by scientists and ranchers in search of the latest up-to-the-minute information regarding wolves in the wild.

Now, with his latest wilderness trek behind him, Quinn gathered his notes, securing them inside his backpack along with his bedroll. He ran a hand through the growth of beard that darkened his face. With any luck he would be home in time to help with some of the ranch chores before breakfast. Afterward, he intended to take a long, hot bath before tackling this beard.

The thought of a hot meal and a steaming tub had him moving out at a fast pace.

The sun had been up for nearly an hour when Quinn paused at the top of the hill to gaze down at the ranch that was home to three generations of Conways. It was a sight that always stirred his blood. The house and outbuildings of weathered wood and stone looked as though they had been here as long as the mountains. The hills and valleys dotted with lowing cattle. The horses in the corral, tossing their heads and occasionally running full out, as though daring the others to race them.

A smile of contentment creased his face as he approached the horse barn and saw the big door standing open. A sure sign that his father was already hard at work mucking stalls.

Quinn stepped inside and waited a moment for his eyes to adjust to the dim light.

"Pa."

When there was no reply, he turned toward the stall of his father's favorite gelding, Scout.

The horse was standing very still, head down, as though watching something in the corner of his stall.

Quinn paused to run a hand along the gelding's muzzle. "Hey, big fellow..."

It took a moment for the dark form slumped in the corner of the stall to register in Quinn's brain. In that first second, as he took in the familiar parka, the solid, sturdy figure of his beloved father, Quinn's mind rejected the truth, even while the natural instinct for survival kicked into high gear.

"Pa." He was down on his knees in an instant, his hand at his father's throat.

Eyes fierce, he studied the sickly pale flesh, so cold to the touch.

At last, finding a faint pulse, he sucked in a breath and reached for his cell phone.

Alive. Alive.

For now, for this one moment, it was all that mattered. It meant that they still had a fighting chance.

At the voice on the other end he said tersely, "Quinn Conway. I need a medevac at the Conway ranch right away."

He listened, then replied, "Not a ranch accident. He's on the ground. Weak pulse. No response. Possible heart attack."

He rang off, before dialing the number up at the house.

He heard the voice of old Ela, who had been with the family for as long as Quinn could recall. "Ela. I'm out in the barn. I need Big Jim."

He listened, then swore under his breath when he learned that his grandfather was in high country with the wranglers. "Have Phoebe come out to the barn right away."

Phoebe Hogan had been twenty-three when her cowboy husband had died in a flaming truck accident, leaving her the impossible task of running their hardscrabble ranch alone. She'd been hired as a temporary housekeeper and surrogate mother shortly after Seraphine went missing and stayed on, easing three boys through the loss of their mother, helping them navigate the minefield of awkward teen years. As the months had turned into years, Phoebe had sold her own ranch and remained with the Conways, serving the family with absolute devotion.

Minutes later she stepped into the barn, holding the lapels of the oversize parka she'd grabbed from a hook in the mudroom.

"Welcome home, Quinn. What do you need?"

As she spoke, she stepped closer and gasped at the sight of Cole lying deathly still in the hay, wrapped in Quinn's parka for warmth.

Her hand flew to her mouth as she knelt beside Cole. She looked up at Quinn. "What...?" It was all she could manage.

"I found him in Scout's stall. I've already phoned for a

medevac. I need you to contact Big Jim and my brothers. As soon as I get word from the doctors in Jackson Hole, I'll call." Quinn's tone was gruff. "I'll leave it to you to tell Ela."

"I'll take care of it. You take care of him." She nodded toward Cole and took hold of his hands, squeezing gently before getting to her feet.

Quinn was grateful for her quiet acceptance. Some women might have wept or asked a dozen questions, none of which he could answer. Phoebe, though she was as stunned by all this as he was, could be counted on to hold things together and do whatever necessary until this thing was resolved.

This thing. The very thought of what might have taken his father down had Quinn's nerves quivering.

When the helicopter arrived to ferry Cole Conway to the hospital, Quinn helped the medics lift his father onto the gurney and remained by his side throughout the long flight.

As he sat beside the eerily still figure of his father, grasping his cold hand in both of his, Quinn was reminded once again of the incredible strength Cole Conway had found while drowning in despair. The strength to continue working the land, raising his boys, while grieving the loss of the only woman he'd ever loved. And now, Quinn could feel that strength slowly ebbing.

Quinn leaned close to whisper, "Stay with me, Pa."

Had there been a flicker of movement behind those closed lids?

Quinn pressed his mouth to Cole's ear. "We need you, Pa. I need you to stay strong."

Cole's fingers flexed, moved, and Quinn gave a long,

deep sigh as the helicopter began its descent. "Hang on, Pa. We're almost there."

As he moved along beside the medics rushing his father into the emergency room of the hospital, Quinn was stopped at the door by a young woman who hurried from behind her nurse's station.

"You can't go in there. Only medical personnel go beyond these..."

Her words trailed off. Maybe it was the size of the man, who stood easily six and a half feet tall. More imposing than his size, however, was his appearance. Even in this remote part of the country, it wasn't often that she saw a man who resembled a grizzly. Thick, dark hair curled over the collar of a frayed wool shirt. His eyes, narrowed on her with fierce determination, were so gray and piercing, they reminded her of a feral animal.

Quinn brushed past her as though she were invisible. Once inside, as a team of doctors and nurses began working over his father, Quinn thought about the dark cloud that seemed to cast its pall over his family and this land, and braced himself for whatever was to come.

He'd never had a chance to say good-bye to his mother. Fate couldn't be cruel enough to hand him a repeat of that heartbreak. Not that he had any illusions about life being fair. He was a man who believed in charting his own course in life while playing the cards dealt him.

Still, he wasn't about to leave his father's side until Cole was able to walk out of this place under his own steam.

"Good job, as always, Josh." Henry Townsend, a burly medic with AMT, Air Medical Transport, shook Josh

Conway's hand before slogging through waist-deep snow to the waiting helicopter.

Within minutes the blades of the copter were spraying blinding snow with all the force of a blizzard as the vehicle lifted high above the mountain.

Josh Conway shaded the sun from his eyes and watched until the helicopter dipped out of sight.

He was bone tired. He'd spent the past forty hours crawling around snow-covered Gannett Peak in the Wind River Mountain Range searching for a lost climber. He'd found the man, a member of a six-man team who had been climbing the summit and had been separated from his friends, wedged between two high, sheer cliffs.

It had taken another six hours for a helicopter crew to arrive and cut the man free of his icy prison.

Now, with the noise of the copter fading in the distance, Josh wanted nothing more than to return to his family ranch, take a long, hot shower, and fall into a real bed.

Not that he minded the work. Though he was a rancher, he was also one of a select few climbers who knew these mountains well enough to be trusted to traverse them in any weather. When the usual rescue crews failed, they turned to Josh to do the impossible. He rarely failed in his mission.

Tall, athletic, and, best of all, fearless, he was perfectly suited to pit his skills against the fickle mountains that had been his playground for his entire life. Because of his success rate in persevering when others gave up, Josh Conway had become something of a legend in this part of the country.

By the time he reached his vehicle parked at a base in the foothills, his stomach was grumbling, reminding him that he hadn't eaten a thing since the previous night.

He climbed inside his truck and tipped up a bottle of water. He'd left his phone here, knowing the storm on the mountains rendered service useless. As he began scrolling through the missed calls on his phone, there was only one message he bothered to play.

When he heard Big Jim's voice, he rewound and played it again.

"Boyo, I know you're somewhere in the mountains, but as soon as you get this message, hurry to the hospital in Jackson Hole. That's where they've airlifted your father."

That's where they've airlifted your father.

Those words, and the tone in which they were spoken, had his blood freezing in his veins.

Cole Conway had never, as far as Josh could recall, been to the hospital.

Josh put his truck in gear and headed toward the town hundreds of miles from here. With every mile he found himself praying that he would get there in time.

In time for what? He refused to allow himself to think about the possibilities. For now, he would drive like the devil was chasing him. In truth, it was a devil. A devil in the form of an icy band of fear that was tightening around his heart with every mile.

Jake Conway stepped out of Lambert Hall, where he'd just spent the past two hours in an intense study session led by Dr. Chason, preparing for the grueling exams that would begin in another week.

He glanced up at the fragrant pink buds of the apple trees that lined the walkway. After his years here at Michigan State, studying veterinary medicine, he was constantly amazed by how quickly springtime arrived in the

Midwest. Back home there would still be snow on much of the ground.

He waved to friends as he made his way across the campus. Even to the casual observer, he never gave the appearance of being just another college student. Maybe it was the lean, rugged, rancher's body encased in well-worn jeans. Or the ever-present cowboy boots. Or the wide-brimmed Western hat worn as comfortably as his friends wore their baseball caps.

To his professors, he'd proven himself to be a natural in his chosen field of study. As a working rancher, he was comfortable with the life-and-death cycle of animals large and small. The pain and mess associated with birth, which often distracted first-year students, had been second nature to Jake Conway. As for administering antibiotics to bawling heifers, he'd been doing that since he was ten.

Now that he was free of the study session, he reached into his shirt pocket and turned on his phone. Dr. Chason had threatened murder and mayhem to anyone whose phone dared to interrupt a single word of his lecture.

Jake smiled as the numbers began to scroll and was about to return the call from his roommate when he spotted the call from home.

He was crossing the street, but as the message began he stopped dead in his tracks.

Pa. In the hospital.

The sound of a horn, followed by the screech of brakes, had him looking up in confusion.

He hastily retreated to the sidewalk, then played the message a second time.

His frantic call home was answered by a machine. That had him dashing back to his apartment in a fog. It took hours to book a flight to Wyoming, drive to the airport, and then wait. And worry. And pray.

Quinn had been awake for more than twenty hours, refusing food or the offer of a room in a nearby inn. Instead he remained at his father's bedside while monitors buzzed and beeped, doctors poked and probed, and nurses silently entered to check vital signs before slipping away to write their reports.

When Cole Conway finally opened his eyes, the first person he saw was his oldest son.

"Where the hell am I?"

"Hospital. In Jackson Hole."

"How'd I get here?"

"Medevac. I came home from the hills and found you slumped over in Scout's stall."

Cole let that sink in a moment before saying, "I don't remember. But it sounds serious. I hope I don't look as bad as you."

That had Quinn smiling. "You look good, Pa."

"And you look like hell. What's that damnable noise?"

"A heart monitor."

"Yours? Or mine?"

Quinn laughed out loud. Oh, it felt so good to be able to laugh. "Yours. The doctors tell me you had a heart attack."

"Liars. The whole pack of 'em."

"That's what I told them. I said you were just lying in Scout's stall taking a catnap."

The two men shared a quick grin.

Cole closed his eyes and took in a long, deep breath. "Think I'll take another quick nap."

"Go ahead. I'll be here when you wake up, Pa." Quinn

took his father's hand and watched the steady rise and fall of his chest, willing him to continue to breathe.

It was Quinn's last coherent thought before he tilted his head back in the chair and slept.

Quinn awoke to his brothers, Josh and Jake, standing on either side of a hospital bed. The minute he lifted his head they hurried over.

His arm was punched fiercely by Jake. His shoulder slapped by Josh with enough strength to stagger most men.

He looked beyond them. "Where's Big Jim?"

"At the airport." Josh grinned. "He was here and talked to the doctors. Now he's going over our plane with the mechanic, so he can fly Pa home whenever the doc releases him."

Jake nodded toward their father. "What's the verdict?" His voice was little more than a whisper.

"The patient will live," came the gravelly voice from the bed.

Seeing that their father was awake and alert, they hurried over to grasp his hand.

Cole Conway managed a weak smile. "What took you so long?"

"Sorry, Pa." Josh shot his father a grin. "I was up in high country. Took me some time to make my way down. At least, once I got within range, I was able to learn why you were here. What'd the doctor say?"

"You can ask him yourself." Cole nodded toward the doorway and his three sons turned as the white-coated physician strode across the room.

"Dr. Whittacre, you met Quinn, but you haven't yet met my other two sons. Josh and Jake."

The three exchanged handshakes.

"Dr. Whittacre's the finest cardio surgeon in Wyoming." Cole's eyes twinkled. "Or so everyone on this floor tells me."

"From your lips." The young surgeon, with soft hands and an engaging smile, moved to the foot of the bed. "The test results are in. You suffered a mild myocardial infarction. In layman's terms, a heart attack, which always results in some damage. But since you were lucky to get in as quickly as you did, the damage seems minimal."

"Great. When can I leave?" Cole was already swinging his legs over the side of the bed.

"Hold on." The young doctor moved quickly to lay a hand on Cole's arm, restraining him. "You'll be released. But not until you meet with my associate, Dr. Bradley, who will give you a list of things you'll need to do going forward."

"Do? Hell, just tell me when I can get back on a horse, drive my tractor, and when I can fly my plane again."

"It's a lot more complicated than that, Mr. Conway. There's diet, and exercise, and—"

Cole swore and glanced at his sons. "See why I avoid doctors and hospitals?" He looked over at the doctor. "I have a ranch to run. A herd to see to. Ranch hands depending on me to pay them. Several international companies that depend upon my land to remain in business. And some young intern fresh out of medical school is going to talk to me about what I should eat and how many push-ups I need to do every day? I don't have time for this."

"I'm sure you don't." Dr. Whittacre kept his easy smile in place. "But if you don't follow orders, Mr. Conway, you may find yourself with all the time in the world.

You could find yourself sitting in an easy chair, drooling into your bib, and trying to tell your family what you want, which won't be easy after you've suffered a major stroke."

Cole fell back against the pillows as though he'd been slapped.

Jake's protective instinct kicked in and he draped an arm around his father's shoulders before giving the doctor a steely look. "That's some bedside manner, Doctor. Do you really think that was necessary?"

"Sometimes my patients just don't understand the gravity of what they've come through." He spoke directly to Cole. "You were lucky, Mr. Conway. This time. But your heart can't be pushed like a string of horses on a roundup. If it wears out, you can't saddle up a spare. So you need to take better care of the one you have, from this day on. After you've spoken with Dr. Bradley, who, by the way, has been out of med school for a number of years and is a much-respected professional, I'll have your discharge papers ready. And I'll want you to set up an appointment to see Dr. April Walton in Paintbrush in four weeks. By then I'll have all your data sent to her, and we'll come up with a plan that you can live with. Can I count on you to follow through on this?"

"You've got my word on it," Cole said gruffly.

The doctor shook hands with Josh and Quinn and reached across the bed to shake Jake's hand before walking away.

"That arrogant—"

Before Jake could finish, Quinn grinned at his father. "That's the first time I've ever seen you cave in so easily."

Their father shrugged. "Gotta know when to hold 'em

and when to fold 'em. I figure he's holding all the aces on this one."

The four men tossed back their heads and laughed.

Jake gave a shake of his head. "I guess some things never change. While Rome is burning, the Conway men make jokes to cover the seriousness of the situation."

"It's better than crying." Cole turned from his angry youngest to study his firstborn. "You look rough. Have you slept at all?"

Quinn realized that his father was eager to change the subject. Cole had never been one to bare his soul, and knowing his father so well, Quinn figured the old man was more embarrassed at having been felled by a heart condition than worried about the consequences of it.

Quinn chuckled. "There'll be time enough for sleep later. Right now, all that matters is that you're going home."

Something flared in Cole's eyes and he blinked quickly before looking away. "Okay. Why don't you three go find something to eat while I wait for Dr. Bradley? When I'm through with him, I'd like to get out of here."

Jake clapped a hand on his father's shoulder. "It can't be too soon for me."

Quinn turned away and the other two followed, eager to learn whatever knowledge he'd gleaned that would fill in the gaps of their limited information about their father's shocking medical crisis.

CHAPTER TWO

---❖---

As soon as the room emptied, Cole Conway gave a long, deep sigh.

Until this moment, he hadn't realized just how much he'd missed having his three sons around him.

This event—he refused to allow himself to even think the words *heart attack*—had left him stunned and reeling.

What if Quinn hadn't come home when he did? How long could he have survived alone?

His last clear memory before waking in the hospital was working out in the main barn, mucking out the stall of his favorite gelding, Scout. Cole had been doing the same down-and-dirty chores since he'd been a kid, and the last thing he'd expected was to be flattened by hard work.

Or had this event been caused by something else?

Stress? The doctors kept mentioning that word, but wasn't the life of every rancher filled with stress?

While mucking the stall he'd been thinking about his sons. About how proud he was of them. Not only were they able to pursue their own distinct interests, but they did so while managing to pitch in and help keep the ranch running smoothly.

Take Quinn. He'd carved out an amazing career as a wildlife expert, yet he was always around when he was most needed. Despite his frequent treks in the wilderness chasing after his pack, he always returned renewed and energized.

And there was Josh, back from climbing somewhere in the Wind River Mountain Range, searching for another careless climber who'd gotten himself lost. It was always Josh those rangers called when they ran out of hope. As though he had nothing better to do than leave a dozen ranch chores unfinished while he traipsed off in search of the lost. Cole felt a thrill of pride at the knowledge that his middle son was as comfortable hiking in the treacherous snow-covered mountains as a city kid would be walking to a neighborhood park. He supposed, to Josh, it was like a walk in the park. His neighborhood. His childhood home. His comfort zone. Spread over thousands of acres of the most desolate mountains in the West.

Cole sighed. And then there was Jake. Pursuing veterinary medicine. Cole shook his head in amazement. Who would have believed that the wild, fearless boy would suddenly settle down and decide that what their ranch needed most was a veterinarian? What was even more amazing to Cole was the fact that his youngest son had aced every test and had gotten himself into one of the toughest veterinary programs in the country.

Thinking of Jake always had Cole thinking of Jake's

mother. He had been so young when Seraphine had disappeared. Did the lad have any memory of her at all? Of her laughing eyes? Her fabulous hair, which she'd dyed every color imaginable. Black. Red. Platinum. As though she couldn't decide who she wanted to be—earth mother or seductress. Not that it ever mattered to Cole. He'd loved her no matter what part she was playing. He'd loved everything about her. That fine porcelain complexion. Those green eyes, all fire and ice. That lithe dancer's body. He swore under his breath. And that hardheaded attitude that Cole found both endearing and infuriating.

Cole suddenly frowned. He remembered something else that had flashed through his mind just before the incident. He'd been worried about the fact that sometimes he couldn't remember Seraphine as clearly as in years gone by.

Was she slipping away from him? Was he letting her slip away?

Drained by too many memories and lulled by the steady drip of the intravenous in his arm, Cole slept and dreamed of home.

"That beef stew hit the spot." Cole, seated at the head of the table, mopped up the last of the gravy with a biscuit and sat back, glancing around at the others.

Though he appeared as rugged and rock steady as ever, with that rogue smile and handsome, Irish countenance, there was a weariness in his eyes that he couldn't hide.

Big Jim, an older mirror of his son, except for the white in his full head of hair, was seated at the opposite end of the table. Both father and son were lean and muscled, eyes crinkled at the corners as much by laughter as by the effects of a lifetime squinting into wind and sun.

Big Jim drained his mug of coffee and nodded. "I bet you didn't get food like this at the hospital."

Cole shared a smile with his father. "I have to say, it wasn't half-bad. But then, all I remember having is some broth and some mashed potatoes."

"Saving your appetite for the homecoming, were you?"

The two men laughed. Around the table, the others joined in.

As they had been for years, Quinn and Josh were seated to the left of Big Jim, with Jake and Phoebe and Ela on his right.

Phoebe wasn't exactly seated. During the meal she'd been up and down half a dozen times, fetching a forgotten pitcher of water, then a batch of biscuits from the counter, and later the freshly baked apple pies that had been cooling in the kitchen. There had also been refills of coffee, a tray of mugs, along with cream and sugar, and, finally, extra plates for the dessert.

All of these would have ordinarily been handled by old Ela, who, it was whispered, had been old when Big Jim hired her to cook and clean for him and his infant son more than fifty years ago. No one was sure of her age, but she was still going strong. She was barely five feet tall and nearly as round. Her constant attire was a shapeless native dress of doeskin and, over that, a crisp white apron. Her gray hair was braided and pinned up like a crown around a face so deeply lined it resembled aged parchment.

"Where's your mind today, woman?" Big Jim studied her as Phoebe was forced to retrieve yet another forgotten part of their meal, Cole's favorite tall glass of foaming milk with his dessert.

Ela pretended not to hear while Phoebe's cheeks

turned pink. "We're both just a little distracted. But we're so glad to see our patient home where he belongs."

"Amen to that." Cole studied the stingy slice of pie she passed him. "What's this?"

"The dietitian's list warned about excess sugar."

Cole's lips thinned. But before he could explode, Jake intervened. "Remember, Pa, the doctor also said that you have to be your own advocate. Don't put this on Phoebe's shoulders, or on Ela's. You know what's good for you, and it's up to you to do the right thing."

Cole glowered at his youngest. "I don't need you to tell me—"

"That's right. You don't." Jake turned to Phoebe. "Just so you know, it's not your responsibility to be Pa's nursemaid. He doesn't need to be coddled right now. What he needs is to step up to his responsibilities and do the right thing."

Phoebe couldn't hide the impish grin that tugged at the corners of her lips. "Thanks, Dr. Jake. I'll keep that in mind."

Quinn and Josh shared a smile before Quinn decided to change the subject. It was obvious that their father was getting close to his boiling point.

Quinn turned to his grandfather. "Josh tells me one of the herds is snowbound up in the hills."

Big Jim nodded. "They may be there until spring thaw. I'll be heading back up there at first light with a truck full of feed."

Quinn glanced out the window, where snow fell like a thick, hazy curtain. "That's a mountain of feed to disperse. Do you have wranglers to lend a hand?"

"I do, boyo." Big Jim smiled. "And don't think about

volunteering. You look like you need about a week of sleep to catch up."

Quinn touched a hand to his freshly shaved face. "At least I don't look like a grizzly."

"Or smell like one," Jake added.

Around the table, everyone joined in the laughter.

Cole looked over at his oldest son. "You thinking about leaving again soon?"

Quinn shot a glance at his brothers. The three of them had come up with a strategy of sorts. They would try to see that one of them was always around to handle the toughest chores without letting their father know what they were doing. If he had even a hint of what they were planning, he'd have their hides.

"Not for a few weeks."

Cole fixed his middle son with a look. "What about you, Josh?"

Josh shrugged. "My job is done for now. I found the lost hiker I was searching for, and the rangers have assured me he's doing fine in the hospital. So I have plenty of time to lend a hand."

Cole visibly relaxed. "Good." He swiveled his head. "What about you, Jacob? Got time for your old man? Or are you heading out, too?"

The use of his full name was a signal to his family that Cole was battling his emotions. One look at his face told him that they'd guessed correctly that Cole was craving sympathy and attention from his long-absent family.

"We'll be in finals all next week. But I have my laptop and can study everything I need right here. I won't have to fly out until the weekend."

Now Cole smiled broadly, and the last of his tension

seemed to melt away. "That's good news." He looked down the table. "Right, Big Jim?"

The older man nodded. "Great news, boyo." He tucked into his dessert, which Ela had topped off with a mound of vanilla ice cream.

Seeing it, Cole's eyes narrowed for a moment. Then, seeing his family watching him, he pushed aside his own dessert and drained his glass of milk.

He'd be damned if he'd whine about having to give up desserts. For now, for tonight, he had his family around him. That was sweet enough for him.

"What do you think?" Josh settled himself into a chair pulled close to the fireplace in the great room, where a roaring fire blazed.

Quinn shrugged. "His color's good. He seems tired, but that's to be expected, I'd say."

Both men turned toward Jake, who walked in carrying a tray of longnecks.

After passing them around, he set aside the tray and took a long pull on his drink before dropping down on one of the hearth cushions.

Having overheard them, Jake picked up on the thread of their conversation. "I think this heart attack has rocked Pa's world. He never saw it coming."

"Neither did I." Quinn leaned a hip against the arm of a sofa. "He's the strongest man I know."

"Next to Big Jim," Josh put in.

"Yeah." The two shared a look.

Jake looked over at his brothers. "This doesn't have anything to do with strength, physical or mental. This is about stress to the heart. And we all know Pa's had enough of that in his life. I see a sadness in Pa that I haven't seen in years. Not since..."

His words trailed off, as they always did when he started thinking about their mother. After a lifetime, it was second nature to avoid all mention of Seraphine. Even now, after all these years, the loss was still a source of real anguish to Cole Conway. A lingering wound that continued to fester and drain the joy from his life.

Jake cleared his throat. "Maybe Pa's sadness is just a natural side effect of his heart trauma. Or maybe he just wants some attention, and sees this as a way to get it. Whatever the cause, I've decided to put off leaving as long as I can."

"You said you're in finals. You plan on just dropping out and forgetting about graduating?"

At Josh's question Jake shook his head. "I did give it some thought. But I've worked too hard, studied too long, to quit now. I'll fly back and turn in my last papers and take whatever exams and complete any procedures that are necessary. And then I'm heading home for good."

Quinn drained his beer and idly tapped the empty bottle against his thigh while he digested his youngest brother's words. "I plan on staying put for now. I can't think about leaving Pa when he looks so..."—he struggled for words—"...so crushed. But sooner or later I'll have to go. This weather won't wait. If I don't get back to that pack soon, they'll be lost to me until summer and, with them, years of work down the drain."

Josh stood and slapped his brother on the back. "You don't need to explain to us. I know Pa understands."

"I hope so." Quinn turned back to Jake. "I'm glad you're hanging around for a couple of days more. That ought to take some of the sting out of my departure whenever I decide to go."

The two brothers shared a backslap, the closest thing they'd ever had to a hug between them.

As they stepped apart Jake couldn't help laughing aloud. "You realize, of course, that staying a few more days will make me Pa's favorite."

"Wow. What a concept," Josh deadpanned. "The baby of the family a favorite."

His two brothers broke into gales of laughter while Jake shot them each a smug look.

"Not that you're jealous or anything. But I am, after all, his baby forever."

Josh chuckled. "I'm sure glad my babysitting days are over."

"You." Quinn shook his head. "What about me?" His voice took on a perfect imitation of their grandfather's growl. " 'Quinn, take your little brother along. Don't let him out of your sight, boyo. Did you let Jake ride that ornery stallion? Shame on you, boyo.' " He chuckled. "I'm surprised he and Pa didn't ask me to take you along on my dates."

"You went on dates? With girls?" Jake pretended to be shocked.

Josh and Quinn shared a laugh.

Josh nudged his brother. "You had him fooled, Bro." He turned to Jake. "I bet you thought he was tracking wolves whenever he slipped away after dark."

"And just who were you seeing?" Jake demanded.

Quinn put a finger to his lips. "Some things are better left a secret, little bro. But I will tell you this: Francine Hurly may be one of the best kissers in all of Wyoming."

"Fancy Francie? You actually dated her?"

"I don't know if you could call it a date. But whenever we met in her daddy's barn, we used to melt the snow for a hundred yards or more in all directions."

After sharing a laugh, Jake shook his head. "And I thought I was the only one Francie ever kissed."

"Francie kissed every guy in this part of Wyoming. But what about your wild fling with that flame-haired niece of Flora's when you were sixteen?"

Jake's smile faded, as he remembered his first mad crush. "She was dating three guys in town and telling me I was her one true love."

"As I recall, Bro, you moped around for days after you found out about the other guys."

Quinn nodded. "And when Phoebe found us teasing you, she ordered us out of the room so she could have a little talk with you about life."

Jake's frown turned into a smile at the memory. "And Phoebe became some kind of mama grizzly, even ordering Pa and Big Jim out of the house, as well. And the next thing I knew, I was telling her everything. And she told me that I'd just experienced an important life lesson. Hearts, she told me, were very resilient organs. They could be broken again and again and, given enough time, would eventually heal."

"Good for Phoebe." Quinn put a hand to his heart. "I wonder why she didn't tell me the same thing when Francie dumped me for one of her daddy's ranch hands?"

"Maybe because you never bothered to confide in her." Jake looked over at his oldest brother. "Did Francie break your heart?"

Quinn grinned. "The only thing she wounded was my

ego. It wasn't very cool to be dumped for a guy who was missing some teeth and a few brains, as well."

The three shared a laugh.

"Anyway, I survived without Phoebe's sage advice."

"And moved on to college girls," Josh added.

"Well, they did take the sting out of my bruised ego."

While the fire burned low the three brothers continued nursing their beer and reminiscing together until at last, drained by the emotional events of the past few days, they were forced to give in to the need to sleep.

Quinn climbed the stairs to his old suite of rooms on the second floor.

Inside he kicked off his boots and stripped off his clothes before turning down the bed linens.

Before he could climb into bed he heard the distinct howl of a wolf. Low and mournful, it carried on the night air.

The sound always had the same effect on him. It shivered through his veins and seemed to touch his very soul.

He crossed to the window and leaned against the sill, watching the darkened silhouette against the snow on a distant hill. The very sight of the wild creature sent a thrill coursing along his spine.

He loved his family. There was no place he'd rather be than here on his ranch. But when he wasn't needed here, there was no doubt where he would be found. Out there. On the trail with his pack.

CHAPTER THREE

Quinn framed the wolf in his long-range viewfinder and snapped off a couple of quick photos. The male's coat, thick and shaggy, was matted with snow from the blizzard that had been raging now for three days.

After Quinn had left the ranch and returned to the mountain, it had taken considerable skill to locate the pack, despite the homing device implanted in the male. Cut off from their den by the storm and with the alpha female about to give birth, the pack had hunkered down in the shelter of some rocks near the top of a nearby hill. Since there'd been no sighting of the female, Quinn was fairly certain there would be a litter of pups before morning. That would create a problem for the leader of the pack, whose hunting ground had been narrowed considerably by the unexpected spring snowstorm. The alpha male would have to provide food and shelter for his pack, and all would have to wait out the storm before returning to their den.

Quinn saw the male's attention fixed on something in the distance. Using his binoculars, Quinn studied the terrain. When he spied a small herd of deer nearly hidden in a stand of trees, he understood what had snagged the wolf's interest.

The springtime blizzard had caught all of nature by surprise, it would seem. As Quinn watched, a doe dropped her newborn into the snow and began licking it clean of afterbirth.

Sadly, the doe and her fawn, in such a vulnerable state, would be the perfect mark for a hungry pack of wolves desperate for food during their own confinement.

The male wolf took up a predator position, dropping low as he crept slowly up the hill until he reached the very peak. For a moment he remained as still as a statue, gazing into the distance.

Quinn watched, transfixed. Even though he knew this would end in the bloody death of a helpless newborn fawn, he also knew that it would mean the difference between life and death for the pack of wolves unable to go forward until their own newborns were strong enough to travel. Their strength, their survival, depended upon sustenance. The female, too weak at the moment to hunt, would trust her leader to provide fresh meat while she nursed her young.

Quinn felt again the familiar thrill as he saw the alpha male rise up and begin to run full speed across the rim of the hill. The raw power, the fierce determination of this animal, never failed to touch a chord deep inside him.

The wolf dipped below the rim of the hill and was lost from sight.

Quinn experienced a rush of annoyance. He wanted to record the kill for his journal. But something had caused the wolf to veer off-course at the last moment. Snatching up his camera, Quinn was on his feet, racing up the hill, half-blinded by the curtain of snow that stung his face like shrapnel.

He was halfway up the hill when he heard the unmistakable sound of a rifle shot echo and reecho across the hills. It reverberated in his chest like a thunderous pulse.

Heart pounding, he ran full speed the rest of the distance.

When he came to the spot where the male had fallen, Quinn stared at the crimson snow, the beautiful body now silent and still, and felt a mingling of pain and rage rising up inside, clogging his throat, tightening a band around his heart until he had to struggle for each breath.

How dare anyone end such a magnificent life. Why?

He studied the prints left in the snow made by a single horse.

Far off in the distance, barely visible through the falling snow, was a tiny beam of light.

An isolated ranch house, it would seem.

Clouds scudded across the rising moon, leaving the countryside in near darkness.

Quinn knew that he needed to return to his campsite soon and settle in for the night or risk freezing. But he was determined to confront the rancher who had just robbed Quinn's pack of its leader. A cruel act that had not only left the vulnerable female and her newborn pups without a guardian but had also cut short the scholarly research that had consumed the past five years of Quinn's life.

With a heavy heart he turned away, knowing that by morning scavengers would have swept the area clean of any trace of carnage. It was the way of nature.

Even if he were so inclined, there wasn't time to dispose of the wolf's body. Quinn needed to follow the tracks in the snow before the storm obliterated them completely. Already the surrounding countryside had fallen under the mantle of darkness.

He returned to his campsite and began to pack up his meager supplies. As he did so, anger rose up like bile, burning the back of his throat and eyes.

All attempts at scholarly disinterest were swept away in a tide of fury at the loss of the wolf Quinn had come to love.

He could no longer hide behind a professional wall of anonymity.

This was personal.

He needed, for his own satisfaction, to confront the rancher who had snuffed out the life of the creature that had consumed every minute of every day of his life for the past five years.

As he shouldered his supplies and began the trek in the darkness he found his thoughts turning to his father. There was no comparison between this despicable act and the horrible trauma Cole had suffered at losing Seraphine. Still, the loss was so deeply felt that it connected Quinn to Cole Conway in a way that nothing else ever had.

Was this how Cole had felt when he'd faced the greatest loss of his life? Had he been swamped with this helpless, hopeless sense that everything that he'd worked for had just been swept away by some cruel whim of fate?

Cole had been, in those early days, inconsolable. A man so grief stricken, even the love for his children and his father, Big Jim, hadn't been able to lift him out of the depths of hell. Cole's only coping mechanism had been to throw himself into every hard, physically demanding chore he could find around the ranch, many of which would have broken a less determined man.

Right this minute, Quinn would welcome any challenge that would lift him out of his own private hell.

Quinn moved through the waist-high drifts, keeping the light of the distant ranch house always in his sight.

Someone would answer for this vicious deed.

Someone would pay.

As Quinn drew close enough to peer through the falling snow, he could make out the sprawling ranch house and, some distance away, the first of several barns and outbuildings.

He was turning toward the house when he caught the glint of light in the barn. Pausing just outside the open door, he watched the rancher forking hay into a stall, where a horse stomped, blowing and snorting, as though winding down from a hard ride. The snow that coated the rancher's parka and wide-brimmed hat was further proof that he'd just retreated from the blizzard that raged beyond these walls.

Quinn stepped inside, holding his rifle loosely at his side. It wasn't his intention to threaten the rancher, merely to confront him. But right this minute, Quinn relished the thought of a good knock-down, drag-out fight. For one tiny instant he was that helpless boy again, confronting the rancher Porter Stanford as he'd gloated over the needless deaths of a wolf and her pups. Then Quinn snapped back to the present, though the thought of that long-ago scene had his voice lowering to a growl.

"I'm tracking a wolf-hating rancher. Looks like I found him."

The figure whirled.

Quinn continued to keep his rifle pointed at the ground, though his finger tightened reflexively on the trigger when he caught the glint of metal as the rancher lifted the pitchfork in a menacing gesture.

"Who the hell do you think you are?"

Quinn blinked. The voice didn't match the image he'd had of a tough Wyoming rancher. It was obviously female. Soft. Throaty. Breathless, as though she'd been running hard.

"My name is Quinn Conway. My spread's about fifty miles east of here. And you'd be . . . ?"

"Don't act coy with me. You know who I am. You're trespassing on my land. I'll give you one minute to turn tail and leave, or you'll answer to this."

Quinn realized that, though her left hand continued to hold the pitchfork aloft, her right hand had dipped into the pocket of her parka and she was holding a very small, very shiny pistol aimed at his chest.

He lifted a hand, palm up. "I didn't come here to hurt you."

"Oh, sure. That's why you burst into my barn holding a rifle?"

"I'm here to get some answers."

"Sorry. I'm fresh out." She tossed aside the pitchfork and in one quick motion pocketed the pistol and grabbed a rifle leaning against the wall. Taking careful aim, she hissed, "Now get, whoever you are. And tell Deke I have no intention of changing my mind. If he thinks he can send some bully—"

Quinn reacted so quickly she didn't have time to blink. He kicked aside her rifle, sending it flying into the air. Before it landed in the hay he'd leaped at her, taking her down and pinning her arms and legs with such force beneath him that she was helpless to move anything except her head.

She let loose with a stream of oaths that would have withered a seasoned cowboy. That merely reinforced Quinn's determination to pin her down until her fury ran its course.

In the process, his own anger seemed to intensify. He'd come here to confront a cold-blooded wolf killer. What he'd found was a crazy woman.

"Let me up." Teeth clenched, she bucked and shuddered with impotent rage.

"Not until..." His breath was coming hard and fast and he found himself having to use every ounce of his strength to keep her pinned. In the process, he became aware of the soft curves beneath the parka, and the fresh, clean evergreen scent of her hair and clothes. "...you agree to give me some answers."

"Go to hell."

Damn her. He wanted to end this tussle, but she wasn't going to make it easy for him. And the longer he lay on top of her, the more aware he became of the woman and less of the enemy he'd come here to confront. "You're not going to cooperate?"

When she made no response he dug in, using his size and weight to intimidate. "You shot a wolf out there on the trail. I want to know why."

"A wolf?" She stopped fighting him.

He absorbed a small measure of relief that she seemed to be relenting.

She was clearly out of breath. "What business is this of yours?"

"That wolf is my business."

He saw her eyes go wide. "This is really about the wolf?"

"What did you think it was about?"

He saw the way she was studying him beneath half-lowered lashes and realized how he must look, hair wild and tangled, his face heavily bearded from his days on the trail.

He decided to take a calculated risk. Moving quickly, he got to his feet and held out a hand.

Ignoring his offer of help, she rolled aside and got her bearings before turning to face him.

Her hand went to the pocket where she'd stowed her pistol but didn't dip inside, remaining instead where he could see it.

"Let's start over." He fought to keep the anger from his voice. "My name is Quinn Conway. I study the life cycle of wolves. I was tracking my pack when the alpha male was shot. I followed the shooter here. Now I want to know why a rancher would kill a wolf that was only hunting food for his pack."

When she held her silence he arched a brow. "It's your turn to introduce yourself and say... 'My name is... I shot the wolf because...' "

"My name isn't important, but the wolf is. It was threatening my herd. That's what wolves do. And what smart ranchers do is shoot them before they can rip open a helpless calf."

"My wolf was stalking a herd of deer."

"Your wolf?" She eyed him suspiciously. "I didn't realize he was a pet."

"He isn't. Wasn't," Quinn corrected. "He was, in fact, the object of years of scholarly research."

"Uh-huh." She shot him a look guaranteed to freeze a man's heart at a hundred paces. "I wouldn't know anything about scholarly research, but common sense told me he was about to take out one of my calves. And I got him before he could get to my herd. Now if you don't mind..." She turned away.

Before she could reach for her rifle Quinn caught her arm. "I don't believe you. I saw the herd of deer."

She yanked herself free of his grasp. "I don't give a damn what you believe. I know what I saw."

"Prove it."

Her head came up sharply. "I don't have to prove anything to you."

"You already have. The fact that you're a liar."

Her eyes narrowed on him. "Look. I don't care what you call me. I know what I saw."

But even as she spoke, he could see the wheels turning as she cast a glance at the snow swirling in the darkness just beyond the barn. Neither of them was eager to face the blizzard. But neither of them was willing to concede that fact.

She took in a breath. "You can saddle up the mare over there."

Without another word she turned away and began saddling the big roan stallion she'd been tending.

Quinn crossed to the other stall and began saddling the spotted mare.

When both horses were saddled and ready, Quinn and the woman moved out single file, into the stinging snow and darkness of night.

Each of them was carrying a rifle.

Neither of them was willing to give an inch until this trek was over.

In Quinn's mind, it would end with this crazy woman admitting her mistake and apologizing for the wrong she'd done. Not that it would make anything right. The wolf would still be dead and his pack left without a leader. But for Quinn this was all about justice.

Once again he flashed back to that incident in his boyhood. He hadn't been able to do anything about that female wolf and her pups. But things were different now. This time, he would have the satisfaction of knowing he'd done all he could to persuade at least one angry rancher to give the wolves of this world a fighting chance to survive.

CHAPTER FOUR

———◆◆◆———

They rode the entire distance in silence. Quinn noted that the woman, riding ahead of him, was paying very careful attention to her surroundings. As though expecting at any moment to be attacked. By wolves? he wondered. Or by the person she'd named during their scuffle?

Deke.

Quinn tucked that away in the back of his mind. For now, he intended to get this over with as quickly as possible. He'd prove to her that the wolf pack had every right to kill a deer for survival, and then he'd accept her apology and move on.

The night had turned bitter. Between the raw wind flinging snow into their faces and the horses stirring up fresh snow with every step, Quinn was soon numb with cold.

He glanced at the woman, hunched into her parka, head down against the assault, and felt a brief wave of remorse. If not for him she would have been snug and warm in her ranch house by now and probably enjoying a hot meal. Instead, she had to be every bit as cold as he was.

Still, he reminded himself, it was her deliberate act that had forced his hand and had them both out on this frigid night. He was convinced that there was nothing she could say or do that would absolve her of her guilt.

As they drew near the snow-covered hill, she reined in her mount and glanced back at Quinn. They studied the wolf's carcass that had bled into the snow, turning the killing site crimson.

After a brief pause, Quinn urged the mare up the hill and pointed to the stand of trees where earlier the herd of deer had taken shelter.

"That's where the wolf was headed. I saw a doe giving birth. The scent of it would have alerted any predator in the area to the doe's location. He was about to provide food for his pack when your bullet stopped him."

She shot Quinn a look of disdain. "Now let me show you what your wolf was really after."

She flicked the reins and descended the hill before pointing.

In the darkness were several darker shapes, visible against the white snow. As they rode closer Quinn was able to make out a number of cows and their calves that had been isolated from the herd by the blizzard. Standing beside their mothers were several newborns, and one so new it was still lying in the snow, with its nervous mother standing guard.

Quinn couldn't hide his surprise. And then he had a flash of memory. Of the wolf veering off-course. At the time Quinn had wondered about that strange behavior. Now it made perfect sense. A herd of deer could scatter and run, making a predator's job difficult. The cows, however, not as agile as animals in the wild, were practically immobile in this heavy snow, making them ideal targets.

"Sorry." He held up a hand. "I know that my apology doesn't make up for what I called you. But I honestly didn't see these cows here. After spotting the deer, I really believed that the wolf was headed toward them."

The woman barely acknowledged his words. Distracted, she slid from the saddle to lift the head of the newborn.

"He's freezing. He's too weak and cold to even stand. He'll never survive the night out here."

Quinn was beside her in an instant. "We'd better take him to your barn."

He lifted the shivering animal in his arms as though it weighed little more than a puppy, before nodding toward the cow. "If you rope her and tie her between our two horses, we can probably tow her through the worst of the drifts so she can nurse her calf in the barn."

The woman nodded and looped a rope over the neck of the cow, and then a second rope, which she tossed to Quinn before pulling herself into the saddle.

With snow slapping their faces and the weary cow bawling and fighting every step of the way, they headed into the raw wind once more. If the journey to the hill had been bitterly cold, the return trek facing into the wind was almost unbearable. They were forced to bend low and tuck their heads almost to their chests to escape the stinging bite of icy crystals.

At last they were back in the safety of the barn. There

they settled the cow and her newborn into a stall with plenty of hay and water before unsaddling their mounts and tending to their needs, rubbing them down and filling their troughs.

Quinn stowed the pitchfork and turned toward his gear, lying near the door where he'd dropped it.

Seeing what he intended, the woman walked over and extended her hand. "I never introduced myself. Cheyenne O'Brien. If you hadn't goaded me into going back out there, I'd have lost this calf. I never thought I'd be saying this after the way you behaved before, but... thanks for your help."

He arched a brow in surprise before giving her a quick, charming grin. "You're welcome. It's the least I could do after heaping all that blame on you."

She struggled to ignore his unexpected smile and glanced at the blizzard still raging outside the door. "You're welcome to spend the night before moving on."

Quinn didn't need any coaxing. The thought of a warm, dry bed after such a long time on the trail was irresistible. "Thanks. I'll take you up on that."

She led the way across the snow-covered yard that separated the barn from the house. They stepped into a utility room with a row of hooks along the wall holding a variety of coats, scarves, and work gloves.

Cheyenne eased off her boots and parka and hung her wide-brimmed hat on a hook before giving her head a shake, revealing a mass of thick, dark, tangled curls that glistened with snowflakes. Without the heavy parka, her body was surprisingly slender.

Quinn followed her lead, hanging his sodden outerwear and hat beside hers.

They stepped into a kitchen that was filled with the most mouthwatering fragrances. Bread baking. Stew simmering in a heavy skillet on the stove. Cinnamon coffee cake, fresh from the oven, cooling by the window.

It was enough to make a grown man weep.

He glanced at the woman, lifting lids and sniffing the air. "Don't tell me you threw all this together before heading into that storm."

She laughed. A clear, joyous sound that had him relaxing even more.

"I can't take credit for anything that goes on in the kitchen. I leave that to Micah."

"Your husband?"

She laughed again. "Micah's better than any husband. He's my cook, housekeeper, and all-around caretaker of everything on this ranch."

She looked up as a door opened and an old man hobbled in. His hair was the color and texture of cotton— thick, white, and curled around the ruddy face of a gnarled cherub. Despite the pronounced limp and the three-pronged cane held tightly in his right hand, there was a childlike twinkle in his dark eyes. Eyes that were fixed on Quinn with curiosity.

"Hey, cowboy. What're you doing so far off the beaten track? The storm blow you off-course?"

Quinn stuck out a hand. "Quinn Conway. Cheyenne invited me to stay the night."

"Micah Horn. I hope you brought your appetite." The old man began ladling stew into big bowls.

When they were filled, Cheyenne carried them to the table and indicated the opposite side. "Sit. Enjoy."

"I'd be a fool to refuse." Quinn watched as she removed

a square of linen from a basket to reveal a loaf of freshly baked bread still warm to the touch. After slicing several thick slabs and taking one for herself she passed the basket to Quinn.

He slathered butter on the bread and took a big bite, then closed his eyes. "I didn't think anybody could outdo Phoebe when it comes to baking bread, but this just might top it."

"Your wife?" Cheyenne asked.

Quinn shook his head, taking his time to enjoy every morsel. "Housekeeper at our ranch. She could make old leather taste good."

The old man chuckled. "Sounds like my kind of woman. Where's this ranch of yours?"

"About fifty miles east of here."

"East?" Cheyenne's brow lifted. "The Conway ranch?" Her eyes widened as the truth dawned. "Of course. I guess I had other things on my mind. You're one of those Conways?"

"Yeah." Quinn looked up. "You've heard of our place?"

"Anybody who's lived in Wyoming knows of it."

Micah nodded in agreement. "I even worked it a time or two in my cowboy days. I used to lend a hand bringing the cattle down from the high country. I know Big Jim and his son, Cole."

"My grandfather and father," Quinn said.

"Good men. Both of 'em."

That had Quinn smiling. "I can't argue with that. They're the best."

Seeing his bowl empty, the old man nodded toward the stove as he sat down and reached for the pipe in his breast pocket. "Help yourself to more stew."

"Thanks. I don't even remember eating this."

Micah tamped tobacco into the bowl of his pipe and held a match to it, sucking until he drew smoke into his lungs and exhaled it into a wreath that circled his head in a rich, aromatic cloud. "When's the last time you ate?"

Quinn crossed the room and filled his bowl before returning to the table. "I had some dried jerky this morning. Dawn, I guess."

"Jerky." Micah chuckled, shaking his head from side to side. "That saved my life more times than I can count. There were plenty of times on the trail that all I had for a week or more was jerky and melted snow to stave off starvation."

Cheyenne laughed. "I believe you refer to them as the good old days, right?"

The old man's eyes twinkled. "That's right. And I honestly wouldn't trade them for a month on some island paradise with half-naked females serving me rum punch."

"That's good," Cheyenne said with a laugh. "Because I can't possibly spare you for a week, let alone a month."

"You better not try." Micah leaned back and regarded the young woman through his smoke. "What were you two doing out on the trail on a night like this?"

"Rescuing a newborn calf."

At her explanation he saw the way Quinn's brow lifted.

The old man chuckled. "I think there's a story in there somewhere, but maybe you ought to save it until you've finished that stew."

"Good idea." Quinn tucked into his food, mopping up the last of the gravy with a slice of warm bread.

While he ate, Cheyenne drained a tall glass of milk

before turning to the old man. "Quinn was trailing a pack of wolves."

"What for?" Micah poured himself a mug of coffee.

"He says he studies wolves."

The old man shook his head. "Takes all kinds."

Quinn was too busy eating to explain. At the moment he didn't feel the need to defend himself.

"Anyway, I shot one, when I saw him about to attack one of my herd, and by the time Quinn trailed me to the barn, he'd worked himself into believing I was some kind of crazed wolf killer." Cheyenne glanced over at Quinn. "That is what you called me, isn't it?"

He shrugged and continued eating. Between bites he said, "You're doing a fine job of explaining. I'll leave you to it."

She winked at Micah. "You know how I can't ignore a challenge..."

At that the old man burst into raucous laughter.

She went on as though she hadn't heard it. "...so when this deranged cowboy insisted that I'd killed a poor, misunderstood wolf, I had to prove him wrong." She shot Quinn a triumphant smile. "And I did. Turns out his wolf wasn't so innocent."

"That so?" Micah turned to Quinn. "So now what? Do you pick another wolf to study?"

"Yeah. But not right away. First I'll have some papers to write."

"Papers? Like newspapers?"

Quinn shook his head. "More like journals documenting the wolf pack's hunting grounds, habits, mating rituals, habitat. That sort of thing."

The old man studied Quinn more closely. "You some kind of wolf whisperer?"

That had Quinn chuckling. "I haven't had a chance to get close enough to whisper to them, but I've been tracking them long enough to understand why they do the things they do."

"So you're not out to change them?"

Quinn gave a quick shake of his head. "I'm out to change people's attitudes about them. Wolves are a whole lot more than just predators who feast on a rancher's herd. They're smart and clever and loyal and courageous, and sometimes they do really stupid, silly things, just like people."

"That's a pretty passionate speech." Cheyenne was studying him with new interest. "From the tone of your voice, I'd say this is a whole lot more than just a job."

"It's been my passion since I was a kid. I hope to spend my life learning everything I can about wolves." While he talked he pushed aside his empty bowl and sat back, sipping strong, hot coffee.

"Why?" She was blatantly staring.

He shrugged. "Everything about them calls to me. The fact that they've had to adapt after being nearly extinct. The fact that they're smart, clever hunters who are being hunted by ranchers. And I like the fact that they're fiercely loyal to their family."

Cheyenne shivered at the passion in his tone.

Quinn could feel his energy flagging. For hours he'd been going on nothing but adrenaline, and now the long days on the trail were catching up with him. He recognized that he'd been running on empty and now, with his stomach full and his body warm, he was desperate for sleep.

Cheyenne stifled a yawn. "If I don't head up to bed

soon, I'll never make it." She pointed to the stairs. "Follow me and I'll show you where you can bunk."

Quinn crossed to the room off the kitchen and picked up his gear before following Cheyenne to the foot of the stairs.

Once there he turned. "Thanks for the grub, Micah. It was a lifesaver."

"You're welcome, wolf whisperer." The old man spoke around the stem of his pipe. "I'll see you in the morning."

Quinn followed Cheyenne up the stairs and tried not to stare at her trim backside.

She paused and shoved open a door. Inside was a big, sturdy bed and on the far side of the room a desk and chair.

When she turned, he was standing so close, she could feel his warm breath on her cheek. Startled, her gaze darted up into that sun-bronzed face before settling on his mouth.

A mistake, she realized. Just looking at him had her throat going dry.

To fill the uncomfortable silence she said, "This used to be my brother's. I think you'll be comfortable here."

He shot her a grin. "I appreciate it. But at this point I could probably fall asleep on the floor and never know the difference."

"Suit yourself." She returned his smile. "But if I were you, I'd give the bed a try."

He couldn't help laughing at her delightful sense of humor. "All right. Thanks for the advice."

He stepped aside to allow her to pass. As she did, their bodies brushed. It was the merest touch, but enough to have his eyes narrowing on her. "Good night."

She moved quickly, eager to put some distance between them.

As she headed toward the bedroom down the hallway she called, "You can wash up in there." She pointed toward the bathroom, situated between their two rooms, which they would apparently share. "There's plenty of hot water, and a supply of towels. Last one to use the shower gets to wipe down the tile and mirrors. First one gets the hottest water. I intend to be first." She was laughing as she closed the door to her bedroom.

As Quinn tossed aside his gear and began unbuttoning his shirt, he was grinning. Having Cheyenne O'Brien share his shower might not be a bad way to start a new day.

What a fascinating woman. She had a smile that would light up a room. And from what he'd seen of her so far, she also definitely had mind of her own. Something he'd always admired in a woman.

When he'd stripped naked he climbed under the covers and was asleep as soon as his head hit the pillow.

CHAPTER FIVE

———◆———

Quinn studied the scene outside the window. Thin ribbons of pink and mauve colored the horizon. Snow fell in a hazy curtain.

Just below his window the flat roof of the utility room lay covered in a thick blanket of white.

He'd slept like the dead before waking at dawn, as was his custom. Not wanting to wake the others, he'd managed to fill the early hours by working on his journal.

He stared at his notes with a frown.

Despite the loss of his alpha male, Quinn wouldn't take back a single minute of the five years he'd spent trudging through waist-high drifts of snow in places so isolated, he was certain no human had ever before trod there. He had slept in hollowed-out logs, in caves, and often in the open air, with the ripple of a stream the only sound to break the silence, under an ever-changing sky. At times it was leaden and gray with snow or rain. At other times filled with stars so bright and big they looked close enough to touch. And always, always, lulled by the sound that owned his heart. The howling of his wolf pack.

They had lived, hunted, mated, procreated, and thrived freely, ruled only by the laws of nature. And though he'd loved them, he'd remained an objective observer. He'd allowed himself to cheer their accomplishments and to share their adventures, though he had never permitted himself to intervene, even when the safety of the pack had been threatened. He'd been there merely to study, to observe, and to record their life cycle. And yesterday was no exception. He'd watched. He'd recorded. And he'd been forced to witness the death of the beautiful creature that had been the object of his scholarly studies for the past five years.

At the moment he was feeling adrift. Cut off from the life he'd so carefully built for himself. Not that he wouldn't be happy to step back into his life as a rancher. He'd always known that the two went hand in hand. Ranching was what he'd been born to do. Studying wolves was something special that he'd chosen to do just for himself. It filled a real need in him to be one with nature.

Now, with his longtime alpha male gone, Quinn had some decisions to make. He could tag one of the pups in his pack and begin again. It made perfect sense. He knew the habits of most of the pack, and by following them and their new leader Quinn could continue the saga.

A part of him argued that, since everything happened for a reason, he might want to spend some time with his father before taking on another pack. It had been years since Quinn had had nothing more challenging than ranch chores and family matters.

He looked up and realized he'd been lost in his thoughts.

Now, with sounds of activity downstairs and the wonderful aroma of fresh coffee drifting into his room, he decided he could use the shower without feeling guilty about waking anybody.

Barefoot, his jeans unsnapped at the waist, he picked up his gear before heading down the hall. He paused outside the door of the bathroom. Hearing no sound, he let himself in. And found himself staring at a sight that stole his breath away.

Cheyenne, wearing nothing but a towel that barely covered her from torso to hips, was brushing out her long, wet hair. The instant the door opened she froze, her head coming up sharply to meet his gaze in the steamy mirror.

"You could've knocked."

"I didn't hear the water running, and figured you were already downstairs."

When she said nothing in her defense he added, "Hey. You did brag that you'd be first in here, didn't you? I thought you'd be long gone."

"Yeah." She picked up a tote filled with her bath supplies and turned away.

"Wait. Take your time. No need to rush on my—" Without thinking Quinn put a hand on her bare shoulder. At the intimate contact the rest of his words died in his throat as heat spiraled through him.

"No. I..." Equally flustered, Cheyenne felt the tote slip from her hand and drop to the floor, spilling the contents everywhere.

Reflexively they both dropped to their knees and bent to retrieve the tubes and bottles and jars, nearly butting heads as they did.

Laughing, they moved slightly apart and continued to pick up the articles, setting them in the tote.

Quinn held up a tube and read the label. " 'Frizz control.' " He chuckled. "I'll never understand why someone blessed with perfectly natural curly hair would want to make it straight."

"We're just slaves to fashion, I guess."

He grinned. "Think the cows like you better with fashionable hair?"

"Definitely." Feeling her towel dropping dangerously low, she tugged it upward.

When she looked over and found Quinn staring at her, she felt her cheeks grow hot.

She got quickly to her feet. "Okay. I'm out of here. It's your turn."

Before she could make the quick exit she'd planned, he tugged on a strand of her wet hair. "Let's start over. You deal with your hair and, when you're done, knock on my door before you head downstairs."

"No. I..." She turned and found him entirely too close for comfort. His eyes, smoke gray, were fixed on her with such intensity, she couldn't look away. With nothing but a towel for cover, she was even more aware of his size, his strength, his potent maleness. Suddenly the room felt too small, too confining, with him beside her.

"I can do this in my bedroom." She moved as quickly as possible toward the door.

He couldn't resist teasing. "Sure you don't want to stay and scrub my back?"

"A really lame, tired old line, Conway."

He shot her a heart-stopping grin. "Sorry. I haven't had much practice lately. But if you want to stay, I'm sure I can come up with something better."

"I just bet you can. You're on your own, cowboy."

Once inside her own room, Cheyenne dropped down on the edge of the mattress and told herself to breathe in and out until her pulse rate returned to normal.

Without his bulky parka and heavy shirt, Quinn Conway had a fantastic body. All those sculpted muscles and that hair-roughened chest had left her tongue-tied.

If he hadn't looked as surprised as she'd been, she would suspect him of deliberately barging in, shirtless and with those jeans unsnapped, just to tempt her. But the look on his face told her that he'd honestly expected to find the bathroom empty.

It was a good thing he was leaving right after breakfast. Even with a tired line, this guy was entirely too sexy for his own good. Or hers.

Quinn stared at the closed door and grinned foolishly. Cheyenne O'Brien was an altogether different person without the rancher's attire. In jeans and woolen shirt, she gave off vibes of single-minded efficiency. In nothing but a towel, she offered a glimpse of a heart-stopping figure and a vulnerability that was endearing. In this steamy bathroom she'd been all woman. And downright delicious to look at. The kind of woman a man wanted to devour, bite by tasty bite.

He gave a shake of his head at the direction of his thoughts.

He shaved off the beard that had been allowed to grow while on the trail. Stripping, he turned on the shower and stepped under the spray. He soaped himself before pressing his hands to the tile wall and lifting his face to the water. As it spilled over him he gave a sigh of pure pleasure. Now this was heaven.

As he stepped out and toweled himself dry he was chuckling. *Not a bad way to start the day*, he mused. A hot shower and a view of a hot babe, all before breakfast. Now if Micah's cooking lived up to last night's promise, the day would be just about perfect.

Wrapping the towel around his waist, he returned to the bedroom and dressed quickly before packing up his gear and heading for the stairs.

Micah stood at the stove flipping flapjacks. Sausage sizzled in a blackened skillet. Another skillet was filled with fried onions and potatoes. It was the sort of hearty ranch breakfast that was familiar to Quinn and his family.

Hearing Quinn's footsteps on the stairs, the old man looked up. " 'Morning. Help yourself to coffee."

"Thanks." Quinn filled a mug and walked to the window, watching as, in the distance, Cheyenne leaned her weight against the barn door until she'd managed to close it against the wind. With her head down against the snow that was being whipped by the wind, she made her way to the house.

He listened to the sound of the outer door being opened and closed and turned to watch as she stepped into the kitchen. For a moment their gazes met and held, and he thought he detected the slightest hint of excess color on her cheeks before she turned away. For some perverse reason, he liked knowing that he made her uncomfortable.

"Freezing out there," she muttered to no one in particular.

Though she didn't look at Quinn, she was acutely aware of him sitting at the table. His presence filled the room, just as he'd filled the doorway of Buddy's bedroom last night, and the bathroom this morning. Despite her best efforts, this wasn't a man she could ignore. It wasn't just that toned body, or the handsome face with those hypnotic eyes and the teasing grin. It was the man himself. Down-to-earth, direct, and sexy as hell.

"Yeah." Micah filled a platter with a mound of flapjacks and carried it in one hand to the table, managing to balance it gracefully while using his cane with the other hand. "I promised Wes and the boys I'd deliver enough grub to hold 'em for a week or more."

Cheyenne paused in the act of filling her coffee mug. "You think it's wise to go up in the hills today?"

The old man shrugged. "They've been stuck up in that bunkhouse for more'n a week now. That spring snowstorm caught everybody by surprise. I figure they're about to go stir-crazy unless they get some fresh, hot food to take their minds off the herd."

Quinn drained his mug and poured more coffee. "There's snow in those clouds. From the looks of them, there's a big storm blowing in. You head up in the hills, you may be stuck there for a week yourself."

Micah merely laughed. "That's springtime in Wyoming. If I've got to be stuck somewhere, it may as well be with wranglers who appreciate my cooking."

Cheyenne's head swiveled. "You don't think I appreciate you?"

"Now, Cheyenne, honey, I never said that. But cooking for one's not nearly the challenge as cooking for a dozen hungry cowboys. Whenever I get the chance to go up in the hills to cook for the ranch hands, I'm in hog heaven."

She smiled. "I know. But I worry about you. Like Quinn said, there's snow coming."

He patted her shoulder, then turned away to stir

something simmering in a huge kettle. "Stop treating me like I'm some helpless old man and eat your breakfast."

"Yes, sir." She winked at Quinn across the table, and the two of them dug into the food.

When Micah returned the lid, Cheyenne breathed in the steam from the kettle. "You made your chili."

"I wouldn't dare show my face up in the hills without a pot of my chili. Those cowboys would have my hide."

"I hope you plan on leaving some here for me."

"Yes, ma'am. A big pot of it, so even if I get snowed in, you'll have plenty of food until I get back."

She touched a hand to her heart. "My hero."

"And don't you forget it." He nibbled a sausage while he limped around the kitchen, wrapping loaves of freshly baked bread in plastic bags, filling giant containers with coffee, packing everything carefully on a wheeled cart that had been cleverly designed with shelves and drawers to keep from rolling around while being hauled in the back of a truck.

"You going to be okay alone here?" Micah glanced over at Cheyenne.

"And why wouldn't I be?"

When he opened his mouth she held up a hand to stop him. "I said I'd be fine."

"Uh-huh. And I told your daddy at his grave that I'd look out for you."

"I know that. And you do. But you didn't promise to be a nursemaid, holding my hand every minute of the day."

"All the same, I wish this place wasn't so far away from civilization."

"Wishing won't change things. Besides, maybe being isolated is a good thing."

The old man paused in his work. "What's that supposed to mean?"

She merely smiled. "Being this far off the beaten track, it isn't easy for someone to just happen to be passing through."

Quinn looked up. "I did last night."

"That's different." Annoyed, Cheyenne stabbed another pancake and smothered it in syrup.

"Different?" Quinn glanced from Cheyenne to Micah. "What're we talking about here?"

"Nothing." Cheyenne's eyes narrowed on the old man, as though issuing a warning.

Micah shrugged. "I have a right to worry. I've known her since she was a runny-nosed kid."

She huffed out a breath. "My nose never ran."

"But your mouth did. Still does. You think you know it all, but you've still got a lot to learn. Who taught you to ride? To rope? To birth a calf?"

"You did."

"That gives me the right to worry."

She shoved back her chair and crossed the room to brush a kiss over his weathered cheek. "Yes, it does. And I appreciate it, Micah. Really I do. But I'll be just fine here."

"I know. Just don't go taking any chances." He stuck out his hand to Quinn. "Nice meeting you, wolf whisperer."

"It was nice meeting you, too, Micah. Thanks for the fine food."

"Any time." After patting his pocket to assure that he had his pipe and tobacco, the old man headed toward the door, shoving the wheeled cart ahead of him, before pausing to turn to Cheyenne. "If the weather holds, I could be back by sundown."

"Wishful thinking." She lifted a hand to wave him off before pouring another cup of coffee.

At the sound of the truck leaving Quinn carried his empty dishes to the sink, where he began to rinse them and set them in the dishwasher.

He glanced over. "Is there some reason why Micah is worried about leaving you alone?"

"Of course not." She turned away, avoiding his eyes.

"Last night you suggested that I was someone's bully. Would you care to explain?"

His question was met with complete silence.

He studied her for a moment before giving a slight nod of his head. "Well then, I'd better be leaving, too, and let you get to your chores."

"Wait." She crossed her arms over her chest and leaned a hip against the counter. "Sorry. You deserve an explanation. There was an . . . incident some time ago with a neighbor. I think it's left me spooked."

"You think you're in danger?"

She shook her head. "Not really. But when I saw you in the barn holding that rifle, Deke was the only one I could think of."

"That's what you said. One of Deke's bullies."

"I guess he's been on my mind. I hate the fact that a longtime friend and neighbor could let me down."

Quinn shrugged. "People have a way of doing that."

She nodded. "Yeah." She looked up. "Are you heading home to family?"

"Yeah."

"A wife and kids?" She'd wanted to ask that sooner,

but there had never been a time that seemed right. Now, she realized, she was holding her breath as she waited for his answer.

"No wife. No kids. But I've got a father, grandfather, and two brothers."

She let out a long, slow breath. "Tell me about them."

He arched a brow, realizing that she was trying to draw out their good-bye. In a way it was flattering. He really would have enjoyed spending more time with her.

He leaned a hip against the counter. "Right about now my youngest brother, Jake, is taking his final exams at Michigan State University's school of veterinary medicine."

"He's a vet?"

He nodded. "Or will be when he gets that piece of sheepskin that says it's so. It's perfect for Jake. He's been doctoring the herd since he was a kid. Big Jim always says he's assisted at more births than an obstetrician."

"Big Jim?"

"My grandfather."

Her tone was warm with sarcasm. "I guess it would be too easy to call him Grandpa like other kids."

"Yeah." Quinn chuckled. "He's always been Big Jim. Always will be."

Cheyenne laughed. "I think I'd like your grandfather and your little brother."

"I know you would. Then there's my father, who's tougher than a grizzly, with a temper to match, and my brother Josh, who's a rancher like the rest of us when he isn't off rescuing missing hikers on the mountain."

"That's a pretty impressive family. And everybody lives together on your family ranch?"

"Yeah. Live together, eat together, fight together." While he was talking he dried his hands on a kitchen towel and wondered at the fact that he was being so chatty. It wasn't at all his style, but she'd asked and he'd sensed her need to keep him talking. "Now it's time I let you get to your ranch chores." He offered a handshake and a smile. "Thanks for the hospitality, Cheyenne. After the way I behaved last night, it was more than I deserved, but much appreciated."

She returned the handshake and the smile. "My pleasure, Quinn Conway. I hope you find a new wolf to track."

"I'm sure I will. In time." He made his way to the utility room and pulled on his parka before snatching up his gear.

She followed him and slipped into her own parka. "I'll walk you out. I'm heading to the barn."

As they walked outside she studied his heavy gear. "You've got a lot of miles to haul that. If my wranglers weren't up in the hills with all my trucks, I'd loan you one. But how about taking one of my horses?"

He arched a brow. "I'd be grateful. As long as you have one to spare."

"More than one." She crossed the distance from the house to the barn, with Quinn following.

Once inside she pointed to the various stalls. "You can take the spotted mare over there. Or the gray mustang."

Quinn shrugged. "You choose."

"The mustang." She was laughing as she opened the stall and stepped inside. "He was tough as nails when we first caught and tamed him, but now he's only skittish when it storms. I'll just—"

The blow from the mustang's hoof came out of

nowhere. One minute Cheyenne was reaching for the saddle blanket tossed over the rail. The next she was thrown against the rail with such force she could feel her world going black.

In that same instant Quinn dropped his gear and raced into the stall. Seeing the mustang's eyes wild and terrified as he danced nervously around the tiny space, Quinn knew he had to get the horse out of there before Cheyenne was trampled.

In one quick movement Quinn scooped up the saddle blanket and covered her horse's head before leading him into a nearby stall. Quinn hurried to kneel beside Cheyenne, who gave a low moan of pain.

"Lie still and I'll see if anything's broken."

Her breath was coming hard and fast as she struggled to speak. "He's never done anything like that before."

"Shh." Quinn took his time, checking for any breaks, but even though he found none, he could see the pain etched on her face. "I'm going to carry you back to the house. Think you can hold on?"

She nodded. "I think I can walk."

At once Quinn had his arm around her, helping her to sit up before easing her to her feet.

She was moving slowly, her right arm gripped firmly around her left to keep it as still as possible. The slightest movement had her wincing and moaning.

Once inside the kitchen Quinn led her to a chair and unzipped her parka. "Let's have a look at that arm."

She was gritting her teeth as he removed the bulky coat. It was plain that even that slight movement caused her excruciating pain.

After a thorough examination he sat back on his heels.

"Not broken. But I'd lay money that you've dislocated your shoulder."

She sucked in a breath. "I helped my dad treat my brother for that once. I think I'd rather have a break."

"Yeah." Quinn's mind was working overtime.

They were too far from town to call a doctor. And since Quinn had had an intimate contact with a dislocation, he knew the pain she was suffering, and the even greater pain he would have to inflict on her in order to get that shoulder back into place.

"Got any whiskey?"

She nodded. "In the cupboard over the fridge."

He crossed the room and located the bottle. Filling a tumbler to the top, he carried it to her and muttered, "Drink it. All of it. And then"—his voice lowered—"we'll have to get on with it."

Get on with it.

Cheyenne closed her eyes against the wave of pain, knowing there was more to come.

CHAPTER SIX

———◆———

Cheyenne sipped the whiskey and made a face. "Ugh. I've never figured out how people can stand to drink this without something to soften the taste."

"Don't think of it as medicine. The trick is to just drink it down without tasting it."

"Easy for you to say." She took a big gulp and felt herself gag. Even the fumes of the whiskey made her stomach queasy.

Quinn saw the way she held the liquid in her mouth while she considered whether to drink it down or spit it in the glass. "Swallow it or you'll be wearing it."

Though she could feel herself gagging, she managed to swallow down the entire tumbler of whiskey.

When she lowered the glass she sniffed. "I smell like a brewery."

"Trust me. In a couple of minutes, that'll be the last thing you'll be worried about."

"Yeah." She gritted her teeth, aware that her head was already swimming. "Okay. I'm ready, Doctor. Do what you have to."

He was grateful that there was nothing small or frail about this woman. She was a rancher, whose body was toned and healthy from the million and one ranch chores she tended to each day. But from his own experience, Quinn knew that even in the best of health, the manipulation needed to treat a dislocation could cause the most unbearable pain.

"Maybe you ought to consider another glass of whiskey."

"At this point, Conway, I haven't decided which would be worse. Another drink of that poison, or having to deal with the pain I know is coming. Besides, the whiskey is doing the job. My eyes are crossing. I'm seeing two of you."

"That's good, I think. I was just trying to warn you."

"Yeah. Thanks." She gritted her teeth. "I think you're just putting off the inevitable."

Knowing she was right, he took in a breath. "Want to stay in this chair, or lie on the floor?"

She paused for only a moment. "Floor. That way, if I faint, I won't have so far to fall."

He helped her from the chair and eased her gently to the kitchen floor.

"I could get a pillow."

"No pillow." Her words were slightly slurred as the alcohol began to numb her brain. "I'm ready."

Kneeling over her, he took hold of her arm. "I've done this a couple of times, and the quickest way seems to be to rotate the arm. But—"

She held up a hand to stop him. "I know. It's also the most painful."

"No matter what I do, it's going to be painful. I just want you to be warned."

"Enough stalling. Get on with it, Conway."

"Right."

He'd already decided that speed was of the essence. The minute he grasped her elbow and began rotating her arm, he heard her gasp of shock and pain. Her eyes went wide, and a low moan escaped her lips.

On the second rotation he felt the head of the upper arm bone slide smoothly back into the socket.

"Done." He knew he sounded triumphant, but he'd been prepared for a much longer ordeal and was thrilled to have it over with.

He glanced down at her with a smile, but the smile faded when he realized that she wasn't responding.

"Cheyenne." He brought his face close to hers.

She was out cold.

He picked her up and carried her through the doorway and into a formal dining room. Beyond that he spotted a great room, with comfortable sofas arranged around a huge fireplace. He deposited her on one of the sofas and covered her with an afghan he found folded over the arm.

Finding a log already in place on the grate, he added kindling from a basket and got a fire started. Content that the room was comfortably warm, he crossed to the sofa and sat on the edge, rubbing her hands.

He saw her lids flicker, then open.

For a fraction of a second she appeared confused. Then her eyes rounded and focused on him.

"Is it over?" Her words were slurred.

"Yeah. Can you move your arm?"

Very carefully she flexed her arm. "Ouch. It's tender."

"Sorry. It may take a while before the last of the pain is gone. I hope it's not as bad as the dislocation."

She gave a slight shake of her head, as though speaking took too much effort. "Not so ... bad now."

"Good. That's a start. If it doesn't improve within a few hours, you might want to think about going to town to have Dr. Walton look at it."

"The town's a good ... two hours from here."

"Yeah. But I'm no doctor. I think I'd feel better if—"

"Quinn." She lifted her left hand to his mouth to still his words. A dreamy smile played on her lips. Her head was still spinning. She was, she realized, pleasantly drunk. At some other time she might have been embarrassed. Right now, it made her want to giggle. "Thanks for what you did."

"You're welcome." At the touch of her fingertips he felt the sudden jolt to his system. He absorbed a rush of heat and blamed it on the fire. "But I didn't do much. You were the one suffering."

"It's not just what you did for my shoulder." Her palm moved over his cheek, then upward to brush a strand of hair from his forehead. "You saved my life."

He went still, enjoying the curl of pleasure down his spine at her simple touch. "Now how do you figure that?"

"That mustang." Her voice softened to a dreamy sigh. "If I'd have been caught in that stall alone, I could have been trampled. Nobody would have found me. I could have died."

"Don't let yourself think about that."

"Okay." She smiled up into his eyes. "I'll think about you instead. My hero." Her hand cupped his head and she began drawing him closer. "Have I told you that you're easy to look at?"

He grinned. "No. I guess you forgot."

"Pretty hard to forget you." She gave a long, deep sigh. "Hold me, Quinn."

"I don't think I'd better do that. You'll regret it later."

"Nuh-uh. No regrets." She gave a deep, throaty laugh. "Come on. Hold me, Quinn."

He didn't need any coaxing. His arms were already closing around her. But only because he wanted to soothe. At least that was the excuse he gave himself.

"I didn't tell you." She paused, trying to remember what she wanted to tell him.

"Tell me what?"

"Hmm? Oh. That I knew about you. Well, not exactly about you. I didn't recognize you when you first said your name. But I'd heard about the dreamy, sexy Conway men."

"Yeah?" His grin was quick and amused.

"Who hasn't heard? Your family owns the biggest ranch in Wyoming. You're cattle and oil barons."

"Yeah. That's us." He gave a dry laugh. "The barons of Wyoming."

She shared a laugh with him before focusing on his mouth with a sultry look that could burn a man's heart like a laser. "Kiss me, Quinn."

"That wouldn't be wise in your condition."

"My condition is perfect, thanks to you. All right." She drew his head down slowly. "If you won't kiss me, I'll just have to kiss you."

She brushed her lips over his.

He thought about drawing away, but it was already too late. The taste of her was far too tempting to ignore. And though he hadn't planned to, it seemed the most natural thing in the world to return the kiss with one of his own.

The warmth of her, the sweetness of her, poured into him, leaving him stunned and reeling.

Her lips were made for kissing. So soft. So perfectly formed. So welcoming.

She felt so good in his arms.

"Again," she muttered.

His lips moved over hers, at first soothing, caressing. Until the atmosphere changed between them and he absorbed a shocking, sexual jolt.

He'd meant only to play along with her little tipsy game. But now that he was kissing her, holding her, it was no game. This was so much more. So real, he couldn't turn away if he wanted to.

In the back of his mind, he knew he was taking advantage of her weakness. Chugging a tall glass of whiskey would turn most brains to mush and would certainly weaken a woman's resistance. But he had no such excuse, and still he couldn't seem to stop. With each touch, each taste, he could feel himself sinking into her. Into all that sweetness. All that strength. And wanting more.

He would stop, he promised himself. In just a minute. At least that's what he fully intended. But with each passing second, with each unsteady beat of his heart, he couldn't find the strength to pull away. *Just a minute more*, he thought as his pulse began racing and he could feel his temperature climbing. One more kiss. One quick press of that perfectly honed body to his. But instead of ending it, the kiss spun on and on until he began wondering which of them was really drunk. Her kiss was like a powerful drug, and he wanted more. He wanted all.

At last, gathering his willpower, he managed to lift his head and fill his lungs with several deep breaths.

He looked down at her. "You all right?"

"Fantastic. Amazing. I'm floating. Ummm." Her eyelids fluttered and closed.

Quinn sat watching the steady rise and fall of her chest. Her hair, long and loose, spilled over her shoulder. He brushed a strand from her cheek. Soft. Her hair and skin were as soft as a newborn calf.

Her eyes opened and he realized he'd been caught staring.

She gave a lazy cat smile. "Did I tell you that I like you better without the beard? You look...really sexy." Again her hand lifted to his cheek. "And you're a really great kisser, Quinn Conway."

Her hand dropped like a stone.

He managed a dry laugh as he absorbed a sudden rush of adrenaline. "Thanks." He got to his feet. "I think you'd better rest awhile."

"I never...take naps. Besides..."—her words were badly slurred—"...after that amazing kiss, I'm too keyed up to sleep."

"Right." His grin was quick. "Trust me. You'll sleep."

"I never—"

Her eyes were closed before he left the room.

Quinn's first order of business was to check on the mustang. The horse, though still skittish, had settled down as though the incident had never happened.

Quinn saddled Cheyenne's mare and rode out to check on the wolf den.

Along the trail he had plenty of time to think. And though he'd hoped to concentrate on scholarly things, his mind kept circling back to Cheyenne.

And that kiss.

It hadn't been so much a kiss as an earthquake. A storm that had left his whole world tilted out of sync. What was wrong with him? Maybe he'd been alone in the wilderness too long. The first pretty woman to flatter him had his head spinning like some lovesick teen's. But there was no denying that kiss. He'd been caught completely off-guard. At first he'd thought he was being so chivalrous. He shook his head, just thinking about his reaction. One minute he was offering her comfort, and the next he was so caught up in kissing her that a herd of mustangs could have stampeded through the house and he wouldn't have taken any notice at all.

When he arrived at the wolf den, he blinked and realized he'd ridden the entire distance without even being aware of his surroundings.

With a great deal of effort he managed to put Cheyenne O'Brien and those tempting lips out of his mind and get back to the work at hand.

The female wolf, caught in unfamiliar territory without her mate, would be forced to leave her newborns for short periods to hunt enough food to keep up her strength and thus nurse her young. She would be helped by the younger males that had remained as part of the family unit. Though not as competent in the hunt as the alpha male, they could keep the pack from starvation. The more dominant of these would, in time, assume a lead position within the pack.

Quinn thought back to that female wolf of his childhood, hunting food for her young and returning to face a rancher's rifle. It was an epic contest that would never end. Ranchers had a right to protect the safety of their herds. Wolves were natural predators and would always kill whatever necessary for their survival.

Spying the remains of a fresh kill, Quinn felt a wave of

relief. This hardy pack was surviving nicely. Once the weather cleared, they would return to their old den. He had no doubt that they would be welcoming a new leader shortly afterward.

He felt a pang of heart-tugging sadness. The pack, which had been his focus for so long now, had suffered a serious loss and would be forever changed. But somehow, having found the evidence that they were moving forward, he knew that he had to do the same. It wouldn't be easy to let go. He would have to accept the fact that within a matter of weeks this female and her young would welcome a strong, new male as leader of their pack and the life cycle would begin anew, with or without Quinn there to record their history. He would have to make a decision about whether to continue to follow this pack soon, if he intended to tag the new alpha male. Since Quinn knew where their permanent den was located, it wouldn't be difficult to locate them after the snow melted.

He heard the yip of a wolf pup and saw a small face rise up, watching him from the den.

"Stay strong," he whispered.

He stood a minute longer, watching as a she-wolf lifted her head, caught sight of him, and quickly dispatched the youngster from sight.

On the trek back to Cheyenne's ranch, Quinn passed the spot where the male had been shot. There was no trace of the carcass. A fresh snowfall had completely obliterated the blood. The entire area had returned to a pristine wilderness, with no suggestion of the life-and-death drama that had occurred here.

Quinn spent hours seeing to the dozens of familiar ranch chores at Cheyenne's. Funny, he thought, that no matter the size of the ranch, or the location, the work was always the same. What with the demands of the animals, the upkeep of the buildings and equipment, and the whims of the fickle weather, ranchers never took a vacation. They worked from sunup to sundown and often all night, grabbing their rest when they could. And, he thought with a smile of satisfaction, they wouldn't trade places with the wealthiest company president in the world.

For all its demands, ranching satisfied some deep basic need in him. He loved being one with the herds that trusted him. And he liked nothing better than to pit his strength against Mother Nature.

With the chores finished, he stepped into the stall for one more check on the calf and its mother. Despite the calf's having been born in a blizzard and half-frozen immediately afterward, there was no sign of trauma now. Cow and calf stood contentedly as Quinn did a quick examination. Satisfied that mother and baby were progressing nicely, Quinn walked from the stall and stood a minute, watching the calf nurse.

When Quinn turned away, he stepped out of the barn into a blinding snowstorm.

The snow had risen at least a foot in the hours that he'd spent working in the barn. And the wind had picked up, sending a spray of snow laced with ice against his face. Winter, he thought, was not giving in to the calendar without a fight. It may be springtime in Wyoming, but the land was still layered in snow.

Turning up the collar of his parka, he made his way to the house.

Inside it was as quiet as a tomb. A check on Cheyenne found her sound asleep, lying in the same position as when he'd left.

After adding a fresh log to the fire, he stood for long minutes watching the steady rise and fall of her chest.

The whiskey had erased her inhibitions. She'd never know how much that slow, easy kiss had made all the day's chores more pleasurable. Just the thought of it had him smiling.

He returned to the kitchen. Lifting the lid of a large pot, he gave thanks for Micah's chili. Ravenous, Quinn ate the first bowl cold while he heated the rest. Then he finished another heaping bowl of chili before starting a pot of coffee. While he waited for it to brew, he rummaged through the cupboards and found a package of chocolate chip cookies. Before he could open the package he heard a sound and looked over to see Cheyenne standing in the doorway.

"Never nap, huh?"

The teasing grin on his face had her laughing. "I guess there's always a first time for everything."

"How're you feeling?" He set aside the cookies and started toward her.

"I'm fine. Great." She rotated her arm and gave a slight grimace of pain. "By tomorrow, I'll probably be good as new."

"Want some chili?"

"You going to join me?"

"I just inhaled two bowls of it. But sit and enjoy, and by the time you're done, the coffee will be ready."

"Sounds great. Smells great, too. I'm sure it was the coffee brewing that woke me. Micah's coffee always greets me first thing in the morning." She nodded toward the door. "Maybe I'll just go out to the barn first, and check on the calf."

"I already did. He's fine. So's his mama."

"I'd better take care of a couple of—"

He shook his head. "The chores are done for the day."

"I didn't want you to feel obligated—"

"Hey. We're neighbors. That's what neighbors do."

"I don't know how to thank you."

"Thanks aren't necessary. Now sit." He turned away and filled a bowl with steaming chili before setting it in front of her.

"Oh." While she ate she made little happy noises that had him grinning.

When she looked up and saw his face she stopped. "What?"

He shrugged. "I've never known anybody to eat and hum, or should I say hum while they're eating?"

"I hum?"

"Um-hmm." He imitated her until she was howling with laughter.

"Do I really sound like that?"

He nodded, and she only laughed harder.

After emptying the bowl she sat back with a sigh of pure contentment. "I feel fantastic." She glanced at the last of the daylight beginning to fade outside the windows. "I can't remember the last time I slept away an entire day."

"After that accident, I'd say you earned it."

He saw the sudden frown that clouded her features.

He filled two mugs with coffee. "How long has that mustang been trained for the saddle?"

She accepted the coffee from him and sipped. "A couple of months. I guess that's not nearly enough. We have a herd of mustangs that roam freely across our land, at least the part of our land that isn't fenced. This one kept hanging around the pasture, and I figured I'd add him to our stock. He's always been a bit high-strung, but until today he's never done anything like that."

Quinn nodded and leaned against the counter while he drank his coffee. "Something definitely spooked him. Maybe it was me. Maybe the storm. Whatever it was, I'd be cautious around him until you decide whether or he's just skittish or a real danger."

"Yeah. I was just thinking the same thing. If I'd been alone out there, I could have been killed." She cocked her head to one side. "Why do I get the feeling that I already said that?"

She fell silent, staring intently into her cup. She could almost hear the bits and pieces of her earlier conversation with him flitting through her mind as she searched her memory.

At her silence he decided to keep things light.

He set aside his empty mug. "I ought to get on my way."

Her head came up quickly. "I know you need to get back on the trail, but as long as it's so late, why not stay another night?"

At his arched brow she was quick to add, "That way, you can get a fresh start in the morning."

Was she afraid to be alone, now that she'd been injured? Was her arm more painful than she let on? He gave a negligible shrug of his shoulders. "Suits me."

She visibly relaxed. "Good. You going to pass those chocolate chip cookies over, or are you keeping them all for yourself?"

His grin was quick and potent. "I was hoping you wouldn't notice. I guess now I'll have to share." He shoved the bag across the table and watched as she helped herself to a handful before passing the bag back to him.

He refilled his mug and topped off hers before taking a seat, stretching out his long legs contentedly.

They sat together, watching the last of the day's light fade into darkness, drinking their coffee and munching on cookies.

It was, Quinn thought, such a simple thing. But after his long, solitary time on the trail, it seemed all the more satisfying. Though he was a loner by nature and by choice, he missed home and family when he was out in the wilderness. What he missed most, he thought, were simple things. Discussing ranch problems with his father and grandfather. The laughter and teasing that was always present in his relationship with his brothers. The ebb and flow of conversation that was as natural to all of them as breathing.

Though most of his friends were married, he'd never considered it an option. What woman in her right mind would want a man who spent half his life in the wilderness chasing after wolves and the other half seeing to his family ranch?

Not that he gave much thought to marriage. He figured he'd never miss what he never had. And though there had been plenty of willing women, there had never been that one special one who made him ache with need.

Now where had that come from? He glanced across the table and felt again the quick rush of heat he'd experienced when he'd kissed Cheyenne. She wasn't so much an ache as an itch that needed scratching.

Dangerous territory, he thought.

Needing to do something, he stood and began clearing the table.

Cheyenne got to her feet. "You did the dishes last night. It isn't fair that you do them again."

"Fair?" He turned her protest into a joke. "Woman, who said anything in life's fair? You need to rest that shoulder." He pressed her back into the chair. "If you want to help, sit here and keep me company."

Cheyenne watched as he quickly dispatched the dirty dishes to the dishwasher. With a few quick wipes of the table, the countertops, the sink, the job was done easily.

"Now that wasn't hard to watch, was it?"

"Not at all." It was on the tip of Cheyenne's tongue to say he was very easy to look at. Again she had the distinct impression that she'd already told him that.

Aware of where her thoughts were heading, she decided to match his light tone with her own. "You keep that up, you may have a shot at taking over Micah's job if he ever decides to retire."

"A word of warning." He chuckled. "I may have picked up a few cooking tips along the trail, but most of them are just to stave off starvation. Anything fancy, I'm not your man."

"*Fancy* doesn't exactly describe my taste in food."

"No, but having tasted Micah's flapjacks, I'd say you're already spoiled. Anything I offered would be like yesterday's oatmeal. Lumpy, and tasting like glue."

"Thanks for that warning. I guess Micah will have to stick around for another few years."

Quinn held up the coffeepot. "There's just enough left for two more cups."

When he'd filled their mugs, he said, "I wouldn't mind sitting by the fire before I go up to bed."

"Great idea." Cheyenne was oddly pleased that the evening wasn't over. Smiling, she led the way to the great room.

CHAPTER SEVEN

———◆———

Quinn tossed a fresh log on the coals, sending a shower of glowing embers dancing up the chimney. His interest was snagged by the array of framed photos on the mantel. He focused on the largest one.

"This has to be your dad. You look just like him."

Cheyenne walked up beside him. "Yeah. Funny. I'm the image of my father, except for his red hair. My brother, Buddy, looked just like our mother. She was from the Northern Cheyenne Arapaho. Buddy's given name was Daniel Eknath O'Brien, but we never called him anything except Buddy."

"Eknath? Yeah. Definitely Arapaho."

Her eyes widened. "I'm surprised that you know that."

He shrugged. "Ela has been with our family since my dad was a boy. We've all picked up words and phrases from her. She told us that her name means 'earth.' What does 'Eknath' mean?"

" 'Poet. Saint.' " She smiled dreamily. "It suited him. He loved reading and writing. He always kept a journal. When I was a kid, he let me read parts of it. Beautiful passages about this part of the country, and its changing seasons. My mother always hoped he would become the great American writer who would introduce the Arapaho culture to the world."

Her smile grew. "Buddy was four years older than me, and I was his shadow. Wherever Buddy was, my folks knew they'd find me trailing behind. I absolutely adored him. In my eyes, Buddy could do no wrong." She shook her head. "I still find it hard to believe he's gone."

"What happened?"

She stared into the flames of the fire. "An accident on the highway. His truck skidded off the road. He died before the authorities could get to the site."

"Was he alone?"

She pointed to another photo, of two young men standing beside the barn, wearing matching smiles. "That's his friend Austin Baylor. He was driving behind Buddy and saw everything. Austin was too late to save him." She took a deep breath. "They'd been drinking at the Watering Hole, a bar in town."

Quinn nodded. "Everyone in this part of the state knows the Watering Hole."

"Buddy wasn't much of a drinker, so it wouldn't have taken much for him to get drunk. Dad and I were shocked that he'd drink and drive, though. It was really out of character for Buddy."

"I'm sorry. How long ago did this happen?"

"Two years ago." She shivered despite the heat of the fire. "My dad was really devastated. Buddy had pretty much taken over the operation of the ranch. Dad had finally reached a point in his life where he was able to kick back and move at a slower pace. That suited both of them perfectly, since Dad was a slow-and-easy kind of guy and Buddy was a take-charge person who never even knew what *slow* meant. They'd been a perfect balance for one another. And then Buddy was gone. My poor dad was lost."

"You had to be just as affected by it."

She nodded. "My heart was broken. It still is. Everywhere I look, I see Buddy, and all the things he loved here. It took me the longest time to accept that he was really gone. But I had to, for my dad's sake. He was determined to move forward, despite our loss. Wes Mason, our foreman, wanted to hire a couple of wranglers to fill Buddy's position, but when Austin offered to step in, Dad insisted that Wes give him a chance to prove himself."

She sighed. "Dad knew that Austin was carrying a load of guilt after witnessing Buddy's death. Austin kept bemoaning the fact that he could have done more. Dad thought it would be a chance for Austin to put the past behind him."

"That sounds like a good arrangement. How's it working out?"

She pointed to a photo of an older man with his arm around a younger man's shoulders. "It wasn't long before Dad was calling Austin his second son. It's funny. Dad was a stickler for rules. Everything had to be done a certain way." She chuckled. "His way. But in Austin's case, he was always willing to go that extra mile. No matter how many things Austin did wrong, or how badly he messed up, Dad would have a logical explanation. I'd hear him telling the wranglers that Austin was a city boy. He'd never been on a ranch before. The crew was expected to cut him a lot of slack. Dad insisted that he'd get the hang of things when he'd had more time under his belt."

"Did he?"

She shrugged. "We can all see that he's really trying."

"So he's still here. What about his family?"

Her voice lowered. "He never talks about his past. According to Buddy, it was a really sad story. Austin had been in foster care, then living on the streets, when Buddy saved him from an attacker one night in Laramie."

"Was Buddy in college there?"

"Yes." She nodded. "After that they bonded and became friends, and when Buddy graduated he brought Austin here to work on the ranch."

"I can see why your father wanted to keep him around." Quinn paused, wondering how to ask the next logical question.

Finally, gathering his courage, he asked, "What happened to your father?"

He saw the pain in Cheyenne's eyes. "A ranch accident. Dad had taken one of the all-terrain vehicles up into the hills. When he didn't return, we went searching and found him in the snow. Apparently he'd taken a steep hill too fast, and the vehicle flipped on him, pinning him. Chief Fletcher said it looked as though he froze to death out on the trail."

She fell silent, and Quinn thought it wise not to press for more details.

With a shake of his head he muttered, "That's a heavy load of bad luck to shoulder. What about Austin? Where is he now?"

"Up in the high country with the wranglers. He keeps saying that he wants to learn everything he can about ranching, and there's no better way than by spending time with the whole crew."

"That's good. It sounds as though he's found a home here."

She looked down at the cup of coffee in her hands. "I really feel that I owe it to Dad and Buddy to give him as much time as he needs to learn the ropes of ranching."

Quinn moved closer to the framed photograph of a beautiful young Arapaho woman in flowing native dress, her dark, waist-length hair spilling over her shoulders. "Your mother?"

She nodded.

"She was beautiful."

Cheyenne dimpled. "My dad was absolutely crazy about her. And she felt the same way about him. I've never known two people more perfectly suited to be together. Her Arapaho name was Lolotea. It means 'gift from God.' Dad always called her Lola."

She settled herself on the sofa, tucking her feet underneath her as she reminisced. "When cancer took her, Buddy and I thought our dad would never get past his loss."

"How old were you?" Quinn sat beside her, on the opposite end of the sofa.

"Seventeen. A senior in high school. Buddy and I did our best to comfort our dad, but he was inconsolable. It's funny." She stared down into her cup. "I can still remember the first time I heard my dad finally laugh again. He and Micah were talking about something that had happened years earlier. It was an old story, one we'd heard many times. About an ornery mare that had tossed my dad headfirst into a creek. He came up mad as a spitting cat. Suddenly Dad and Micah were convulsed with

laughter. Buddy and I sat there drinking it in, and thinking there had never been a lovelier sound than our dad
laughing."

She looked up and found Quinn studying her. "It
taught me something special. I learned that every person has to work through grief in his own way. And when
we reach that other side, that happier, less painful side, it
seems all the sweeter because of the pain of the past."

Quinn nodded and realized that his own cup was
empty, though he couldn't recall drinking the coffee. He'd
been mesmerized by this woman and her story.

It occurred to him that he could sit and listen to that
soft, breathy voice all night. Added to the voice was that
sweet, expressive face that gave away every emotion she
was feeling. "You've told me about everybody in the family except you. Where'd you go to school?"

"Homeschooled until high school. How about you?"

He nodded. "The same."

"The town was just too far from the ranch to travel
back and forth every day. But once I was old enough to
drive, I felt a real sense of freedom. And when it was time
for college, I followed Buddy to Laramie." She gave a
self-conscious laugh. "Still his shadow." She shrugged. "I
really only went to college to please my father. He never
had any formal education, and it was a source of pride
that both his children graduated from college. In truth, all
I ever wanted to do was be a rancher like him. But once I
got caught up in college life, and got over my homesick-
ness, I found that I really liked learning so many new
things in a different setting."

Quinn laughed. "You sound just like my brother Jake.
His first thought was to get his college degree online, so

he could stay home and be with the family. Our pa was having none of that. He practically had to kick Jake out of the house to get him to go. Then, after Jake got over his rebellion, he discovered that he was a really good student, and decided that he could become an even better rancher if he took the time to study veterinary medicine."

"How did your folks feel about letting their son go?"

Quinn's smile faded. "Like you, we all had to deal with our life decisions on our own. Our mother's been gone since I was ten."

"I'm sorry. What did she die of?"

Quinn frowned. Even after all these years, he hated having to answer this puzzling question. "She went missing without a trace."

Cheyenne clapped a hand to her mouth. "What was I thinking? I've heard about your mother's disappearance. Not when it happened, of course," she added with a nervous laugh. "I was probably around five or six. But through the years I've heard bits and pieces of the story. Have you ever found out what happened?"

He shook his head and tried for a flip answer. "It's our big deep, dark family mystery. 'Where did Seraphine Conway go? And why did she leave her loving family without a word?'"

Cheyenne reached a hand to cover his. "That's just horrible. I can't even imagine losing a parent without knowing the why and where and how of it. It has to eat at your soul. I'm so sorry, Quinn."

At her touch he felt the quick sexual rush and was reminded of the kiss they'd shared.

His head came up sharply and he turned to her with a look so fierce, she was reminded of the animals he studied.

Wolf eyes. A predator's eyes, and she the prey.

At once she removed her hand and struggled to her feet. "Well, I think it's time I went up to bed."

"Yeah. Me, too." He reached out for her empty cup.

When she handed it over their fingers brushed and they both turned away quickly.

Quinn deposited the two mugs in the sink in the kitchen and followed Cheyenne up the stairs.

At the door to his room he paused. "If that shoulder gives you any trouble, let me know. I don't mind losing sleep to drive you to town. In fact, I'd feel a lot better if a doctor looked at it."

"Thanks, Quinn." She started to reach out a hand, then seemed to think better of it and clasped her hands in front of her. "For everything. 'Night."

"Good night." He waited until she reached the door of her bedroom. When it closed behind her, he stepped into his room.

Buddy's old room, he thought. Now that he knew a little more about the man who'd once lived here, Quinn could see it through new eyes.

He circled the room, seeing the framed photos of a younger Buddy on horseback, in a hay wagon, in the bull-riding ring at the fairgrounds in Paintbrush. There was a small photo atop the dresser of Buddy and Cheyenne, arms around each other, grinning like two conspirators. There was no disputing their relationship. Their dark hair and eyes and wide smiles were identical.

As he stripped and climbed into bed, Quinn thought about the tragic losses Cheyenne had suffered in the past years. It must seem as if her entire family had disappeared in the blink of an eye.

What would it be like, he wondered, *to lose everyone who mattered most?* He lay very still, staring at the crescent moon in the midnight sky outside the window. There were times, even now, when the loss of his mother was like a quick, unexpected knife to his heart, and she'd been gone for better than half his life. Plenty of time to get used to it. And yet he never had. None of his family had. Especially their father.

Quinn couldn't imagine what he'd have done if he'd been forced to deal with not only the loss of his mother but of his father and siblings as well.

Just thinking about them had Quinn eager to head home. He'd been gone way too long. He wanted, needed, to touch base with his family. To sleep in his own bed. And to get back into the routine of hard, challenging ranch chores alongside Josh and his father and Big Jim.

It had felt good to clean the stalls here and to handle the dozens of ranch chores that had piled up overnight. It would be even more satisfying to tackle the chores on his own family ranch.

Just the thought of home had him smiling as he drifted into sleep.

Favoring her shoulder, Cheyenne undressed slowly before turning out the light and climbing into bed. After sleeping away most of the day, she ought to be feeling wide awake. But the truth was, she felt sluggish. As though her brain and her body had somehow disconnected.

She thought again about the mustang's unexpected attack. It had all happened so quickly. In the blink of an eye she'd been rendered nearly unconscious from the pain. If not for Quinn's quick thinking, she wouldn't be lying here comfortably in her own bed. She shivered and drew the blanket firmly around her.

As warm as Quinn's arms.

The thought had her eyes going wide. Quinn's arms? Around her?

Had she dreamed it, or had he actually held her? In fact, kissed her?

She touched a finger to her lips. In that instant the realization dawned.

It hadn't been a dream. He had held her and kissed her, and she'd kissed him back.

The feelings that had stayed with her throughout the day hadn't been just her imagination. The wild thrill that had coursed through her veins, the hot, sexual awareness that had remained even in sleep, was real.

And then she remembered her words.

Have I told you that you're easy to look at?

Hold me, Quinn.

Kiss me, Quinn.

And he had. Sweet heaven, he had. Because she had initiated it.

On the one hand, she was mortified at her own boldness. The man had saved her life, and she'd acted like some kind of seductress. She knew it was out of character. Knew, instinctively, that it had been the effects of the tall glass of whiskey. But she couldn't deny that she'd enjoyed it.

Even while her face grew hot with the memory, she found herself smiling at the amazing feelings that lingered.

Quinn Conway wasn't only easy to look at; he was also a man to be trusted. She could have found herself in a precarious situation, if he hadn't proven to be a perfect gentleman.

A perfect gentleman. And a fantastic kisser.

She was still smiling as she drifted into sleep.

Quinn had always been a light sleeper. He'd never decided if that was a blessing or a curse. Many a night as a kid he'd lain awake for hours, hearing sounds in the house that had him absolutely certain that his mother had returned. He would creep down the stairs and peer around in the darkness, eager to hear her call his name.

He'd lost count of the number of disappointments he'd experienced through the years when the sounds turned out to be the hum of a furnace or the rattle of a window-pane in a storm.

Now he lay very still, listening to the alien sounds that told him, with every fiber of his being, that someone was moving around downstairs. He knew he could be wrong. He had no idea what hisses, creaks, and moans this old ranch house was capable of making. But he knew, too, that he wouldn't be able to go back to sleep until he inves-tigated the sounds he was hearing.

He didn't bother with a shirt or shoes. Pulling on his jeans, he slipped quietly from his room and headed for the stairs.

He was halfway down when a light was suddenly thrown on, momentarily blinding him.

He lifted a hand to shield his eyes.

And heard a deep voice say, "You take one more step, stranger, it'll be the last you ever take."

CHAPTER EIGHT

◆——◆

Quinn froze.

The man at the base of the stairs was wearing a parka and boots, his head covered by a knit cap, his pale beard frosted with snow. Though not as tall as Quinn, he was powerfully built. His stance, feet planted wide apart, eyes focused and unblinking, gave the impression of a soldier in combat.

He was holding a rifle aimed directly at Quinn's chest.

"Who are you?" Quinn asked.

"I'll do the talking here. You're trespassing, stranger. And the law says I have every right to shoot first and ask questions later and that's just what I intend—"

"I'm Quinn Conway. And I'm here at the invitation of Cheyenne O'Brien."

"Liar!" The man's voice was a snarl of fury. "If you were a friend of Cheyenne's, I'd certainly know about it."

Quinn saw the man's finger tighten on the trigger and

braced himself to prepare to hit the floor before the bullet found his heart.

"Austin." Cheyenne, wearing a sleep shirt and boxer shorts, raced down the stairs and stepped in front of Quinn. "Put down that rifle."

The man blinked and frowned but continued to take aim.

"Did you hear me? Put it down. Now. Before someone gets hurt."

Reluctantly he lowered it to his side.

Cheyenne continued to stand in front of Quinn. "What are you doing here, Austin? You're supposed to be with Wes and the wranglers up in the hills with the herd."

"I was. But with Micah gone, you were alone."

"And you rode through a blizzard just to keep me company?"

"That's my job. We're family now. I promised your dad I'd take care of you." He crossed the room in quick strides and dropped an arm around her shoulder. His smile was warm enough to light up the room. "I'm all the family you have. I have a right to worry about you."

"Oh, Austin." Her tone was edged with weariness. "What am I going to do with you? There's no need—"

"There is." He drew her close and gave her head a quick shake like a big, friendly puppy. "Now, more than ever, I need to worry about you. I heard..." He paused, as though considering his words carefully.

Her head came up. "Heard what?"

He lowered his hand and stepped away. "I heard that Deke Vance was seen nearby. One of the wranglers spotted him, and I was worried that he might learn that you were here all alone."

"He has a right to be in the area. His ranch is nearby and his cattle share pasture with ours."

"Maybe so." He looked past her to where Quinn stood watching and listening. "But now that I see you letting a stranger spend the night, it's a good thing somebody's watching out for you."

"Quinn's not exactly a stranger. His family owns the big ranch across the hills." She suddenly remembered her manners. "I'm sorry. Austin Baylor, this is Quinn Conway."

The two men nodded in silent acknowledgment.

"I never heard Buddy or Dad mention you, Conway."

Cheyenne was quick to add, "The Conway family may not be close friends, but their ranch has been our neighbor across the hills for a lifetime. And if it weren't for this good neighbor, I might not be here."

Austin's eyes narrowed. "What's that supposed to mean?"

"He saved me from a kick by that mustang out in the barn."

"A kick?" He looked her up and down. "It doesn't look like you're any the worse for it."

"A dislocated shoulder." She touched a hand to the spot. "I thought I'd pass out from the pain, but I'm fine now, thanks to Quinn. And it could have been so much worse."

She turned to Quinn, standing on the stair directly behind her, and placed a hand on his arm. "Sorry for that rude awakening."

"No harm done." He arched a brow. "Though it could have been deadly if you hadn't come down when you did. Austin had already convinced himself that I was trespassing, and no amount of explanation on my part was about to change his mind."

"It's lucky I could hear the sound of your voices through my closed door."

Austin shot her a startled look. "You were in your room and he was...?"

"In Buddy's room." Cheyenne studied Austin more closely when she realized that he'd assumed something more intimate.

"Hey, man." Austin's smile brightened as he extended a hand toward Quinn. "I hope you understand. I'm just more than a little protective of Cheyenne after everything that has happened."

"Yeah. I get it." Quinn accepted his handshake.

"It's late. I've had a long day. Now I'm going back to my room"—Cheyenne turned away—"to try to get some sleep."

As she started up the stairs she paused and turned back to Austin, still standing in the same spot. "Are you going back up to the herd tonight, or are you planning on staying the night in the bunkhouse first?"

He seemed to think about it for a moment before answering. "Guess there's no reason for me to stay here, since you've got your own private bodyguard." He sucked in a breath. "If you don't need me, I'll be heading back up to join the wranglers."

"'Night." Cheyenne continued up the stairs.

Quinn stayed where he was.

"No need to wait." Austin's smile widened. "I'll let myself out."

"Just thought I'd lock up when you leave." Quinn leaned a hip against the stair rail.

"Don't bother. Didn't Cheyenne tell you? I'm family. I've got a key." Austin shot him another smile before turning away and walking out the door.

Quinn listened to the turn of the lock before starting up the stairs to bed.

It was understandable for a wrangler to be concerned for the safety of his boss, especially a woman, and one who had been through so much in the past. Cheyenne was lucky to have someone watching her back.

Still, Quinn thought, it had been an interesting introduction to Austin Baylor.

Maybe he'd been spending too much time in the wild. He feared he was reading way too much into this encounter. If he were to describe in his journal what had just transpired, he would say that he'd had an encounter with a feral animal, laying claim to his territory while confronting an unknown predator.

Quinn's dream was disjointed. He'd been tracking a wolf. A clever, devious wolf that had abandoned its pack and had become a rogue, breaking into locked barns to feast on helpless calves.

Suddenly the animal paused at the very top of a mountain and lifted its head, sniffing after new prey. Quinn, trailing behind, did the same and was startled to smell smoke.

A forest fire. It had to be close by. Already he could hear the crackle of flames.

He sat up, suddenly awake and alert.

Not a dream. The smoke was real. As was the unmistakable sound of a fire.

He raced down the hallway and threw open the door to Cheyenne's room.

"Fire! Wake up."

Without giving her time to get her bearings, he lifted her out of bed and set her on her feet.

She jerked awake, clutching his arm for balance.

"Grab some clothes. I'm going to check it out."

He was gone in an instant, racing down the stairs. Halfway down, he stopped and ran back up.

Cheyenne had hurriedly dressed and was struggling into boots.

"Grab whatever you consider important and bring it to my room."

Inside he hastily dressed before opening a window and tossing his gear down to the snow-covered porch roof below. At least, he thought with relief, there was something there to break their fall.

When Cheyenne came rushing in, he took the bag from her hands and tossed it out the window.

"I know an open window can fan the flames, but we're going out over the roof, just in case." He took her hand and helped her out into the cold. Then he followed behind, quickly closing the window to cut off the draft.

They inched their way across the snow-and-ice-laden flat porch roof until they came to the edge. Quinn tossed his gear, then dropped into the snow and lifted his arms.

"Come on. I'll catch you."

"No need." Cheyenne followed suit, dropping down beside him. "Buddy and I used to go out this way when we didn't want our parents to hear us leaving."

From the ground they could see the dull red of flames licking along the wall of the utility room.

Growing up in the area, they both knew that there was

no one they could count on but themselves. The town of Paintbrush had a volunteer fire department, but it was made up of business owners and ranchers who could be ready at a minute's notice to fight fires in town. Ranches that were miles from their nearest neighbor often had to rely on their own resources.

"Do you have a fire extinguisher?"

Cheyenne nodded. "One in the kitchen. Another at the top of the stairs. And a third in the barn."

He pulled a handkerchief from his pocket and rolled it in snow to wet the fabric before tying it over his nose and mouth.

"Stay here."

With that muttered command he disappeared into the darkness.

Minutes later Cheyenne could make out his silhouette through the window as he located the extinguisher and began spraying foam.

She raced to the barn and grabbed a second extinguisher. With a cloth tied over her lower face she joined him in the house.

By now Quinn had managed to kill the flames in the utility room and kitchen and was spraying foam along the stairway. Cheyenne stepped up beside him, spraying one side of the stairwell while he sprayed the other.

By the time they'd extinguished the last of the flames, they could see that the fire had managed to climb halfway up the stairs.

"A few minutes longer and it would have spread to those rugs along the hallway." Quinn continued spraying foam up the stairs and along the upper floor, in order to assure that there weren't any dangerous sparks left.

At his words Cheyenne dropped down on a charred step and stared around in wonder. If the fire had been allowed to reach the upper floor, she and Quinn would have been overcome with smoke and could have possibly died without a chance to escape.

As the enormity of their situation dawned, she felt a trembling begin in her legs, and then her arms, until she was forced to drop the extinguisher.

Quinn started down the stairs. "Okay. I think it's safe to say we got the most of it. Of course, there could still be some hot spots here and there. I'll keep—"

He saw Cheyenne, her face in her hands, her body slumped on the stair, and dropped down beside her, gathering her into his arms. "Hey. You all right?"

"Yeah." Her voice was muffled against his chest. "It's just…"

"I know." He could hear the anguish in her voice. And the fear.

"Oh, Quinn, when I think what almost—"

"Let's get into the fresh air." He helped her to her feet and kept his arm around her shoulders as he led her through the kitchen and out the utility room door.

Once in the snow they both breathed deeply, filling their lungs with frigid air. That had them both coughing until their lungs cleared.

He caught Cheyenne's hand. "You're not going back in there. Too much smoke."

"Where will we go?"

"The barn."

They crossed the distance in silence, pausing with each step to breathe deeply.

Quinn paused to slide the heavy door open. Inside,

Cheyenne stepped into an empty stall and dropped down into a nest of fresh straw.

Quinn snatched a saddle blanket from the side of the stall and draped it over her shoulders. "Stay here and rest."

As he started to turn away she caught his hand. "Where are you going?"

"Just going to check on the house one more time, to make sure we got all the sparks."

She started to scramble up. "I'm going with—"

With both hands on her shoulders he gently pressed her down. "I can handle it. You rest."

She fumed as she watched him stride away. It was her house. Her responsibility. And though a part of her wanted to stay here and avoid seeing the extent of the damage, another part of her knew that she needed to step up to her responsibility, no matter how frightened she felt.

She caught up with Quinn as he walked through the charred remains of the utility room, which lay in smoldering ruins.

Seeing his look, she put her hands on her hips. "I need to see it for myself."

As they peered through the smoke and gloom he muttered, "I'm no expert, but it looks as though the fire started here." He pointed to the furnace, now bent and twisted, and the water heater, which had collapsed and was practically welded to the floor. "Either of these could have been the culprit."

They made their way to the kitchen, opening windows as they did, to clear the air of smoke and dust. The electric stove was blackened and badly damaged. As was the microwave.

"It could have just as easily begun here with either of these appliances," Cheyenne pointed out.

"You're right. Still, my instincts are with the utility room, since the damage was greatest in there."

She nodded her agreement as she followed him up the stairs.

He paused halfway up to study the area where the fire had been stopped.

"You realize that we were minutes away from disaster. Once the flames ignited the carpet and walls, there would have been no time left to react."

They each gave an involuntary shudder as they moved quickly along the upper hallway. Finding no evidence of sparks or smoke, they returned to the downstairs area, walking through each room.

After a thorough examination of the entire house, they returned to the barn.

Inside, Cheyenne picked up the discarded saddle blanket and wrapped it around her shoulders. Quinn found another hanging over the side of a stall and wrapped himself in it before dropping down into the straw beside her.

"Think you can sleep?" he asked.

Cheyenne shook her head. "I'm too keyed up."

"Me, too."

So many troubling thoughts were racing through his mind.

He was glad now that he'd agreed to stay on another night. He shuddered to think what would have happened to Cheyenne if she'd been asleep upstairs alone.

A faulty furnace or water heater had been the cause of many a household fire on ranches, and with these old wooden structures the outcome was often tragic.

From his quick examination, it certainly looked like the furnace was to blame.

And then he remembered something else Austin had said.

I need to worry about you... I heard that Deke Vance was seen nearby.

Quinn had a lot of questions to ask Cheyenne about the mysterious, and possibly dangerous, Deke Vance. But for now, with the trauma of the fire so fresh, he would bide his time and give her a chance to calm her jangled nerves.

Come morning, he vowed, they would report all of this to Chief Everett Fletcher in the little town of Paintbrush and let the lawman handle it from there.

CHAPTER NINE

———◆———

Cheyenne awoke with a start and realized that she'd been dozing. Seeing Quinn standing over her had her going very still.

"What are you doing?"

He gave her a heart-stopping grin. "Watching you sleep."

His words, and the way he said them, caused a tingling sensation along her spine.

She sat up, feeling suddenly warm and vulnerable at the thought of being watched while she slept. "I hope I wasn't humming."

That had him throwing back his head with a laugh. "You only hum when you eat."

He dropped to his knees in the straw and faced her. "I'm glad you caught some rest. It gave me some time to think. I think you should phone Chief Fletcher over in Paintbrush and ask him to send someone out to investigate this fire."

She wrapped her arms around her drawn-up knees and studied him. "Why? What have you found?"

"You saw the same things that I saw in the house. Both the furnace and water heater are in shambles. Either one could have caused the fire. But the insurance company will insist on an investigator's report before they'll pay for any damage."

He handed her his cell phone.

Minutes later she handed it back, after reporting the fire to the police chief and assuring him that it had been brought under control.

"He's on his way."

"That's good."

"Why do I get the idea that there's more than what you're saying?"

He shrugged. "Let's talk about Deke Vance."

When she arched a brow he explained. "At our first"—he shot her a rogue smile—"encounter in the barn, you suggested that I'd been sent by Deke. Last night, Austin said he was worried about you being here alone because he'd heard that Deke Vance was seen nearby."

She nodded. "Deke was Buddy's childhood pal. The two had been inseparable since they were both kids. Deke's father owns a small ranch just outside of Paintbrush, and he used to work for my father to earn extra income. Whenever he worked here, he would bring Deke along, and Deke and Buddy would spend their days working and fooling around in the barn. My family really liked Deke, and he often spent weeks here, while his father was up in the hills with the other wranglers. Deke ate with us, slept in Buddy's room, and was just like one of the family."

"Was." Quinn paused. "What happened to change things?"

She cocked her head to one side. "Shortly after coming here, Austin told Buddy and my father that he'd seen Deke helping himself to money from a drawer in the kitchen where we always kept our household accounts. Deke denied it, and Austin went out in the utility room and carried in Deke's parka. Sure enough, there were two one-hundred-dollar bills in the pocket. When Dad counted the money in the drawer, he discovered it was two hundred dollars short."

"What did Deke have to say about it?"

"At first he was speechless. Then he denied having ever done it. My dad tried to smooth things over. He told Deke that he understood that times were hard now that his dad's debts were mounting and they were struggling to hold on to the ranch. We'd heard that Deke's mother took a job at the Watering Hole in Paintbrush. When Deke continued to deny that he'd done anything wrong, Dad told him to take the two hundred and pay him back whenever he could." Her voice lowered with emotion. "I still can't believe how calmly my dad reacted to such an ugly scene. But the more reasonable Dad became, the angrier Deke got. He insisted that he would never steal from us. That we were his second family. He grabbed Buddy by both shoulders and started shaking him, demanding that he believe him." She sighed. "Buddy told him to take his hands off him. That's when Austin stepped in and shoved Deke against the wall so hard he hit his head and fell down. Deke said some really ugly things to Austin until my dad stepped between them and ordered Deke from the house." She shook her head. "That's the last time I saw

him, except at Buddy's funeral. He stood at the back of
the church, but when it looked as though he might come
forward to speak to Dad and me, Austin made it plain that
he wouldn't be welcome. He left without a word. When
Dad died, I thought I saw Deke at the cemetery, but when
I looked again, he was gone."

"And now he's been spotted hanging around."

"And for that you want me to report him to the sheriff?
Quinn, Deacon Vance lives in the area. Our herds share a
common rangeland. He has a right to hang out wherever
he pleases."

Quinn nodded. "I agree. But it just makes sense to take
precautions. If he's been spotted nearby, it ought to be in
the chief's report."

"All right. But I just don't believe that Deke would
hurt me."

"I hope you're right about that."

At the sound of a truck's engine they got to their feet
and walked from the barn to find Micah pulling up beside
the house. Behind him, a second truck slowly made its
way along a winding dirt trail.

"What in hell happened here?" Micah climbed down
from the truck and leaned heavily on his cane while staring in disbelief at the destruction.

"A fire." Cheyenne hurried up to the old man and
gave him a fierce hug, which he returned. "Quinn said it
could have been caused by the furnace or the hot-water
heater."

"You okay?" Micah released her and held her a little
away to give her a long, steady look.

"I'm fine, thanks to Quinn. He was the one who woke
and smelled the fire."

The old man turned to study Quinn. "How come you're still here?"

Cheyenne answered for him. "The mustang out in the barn kicked me so hard I dislocated my shoulder and—"

"Wait just a minute." Micah held up a hand just as Austin and a lean, lanky cowboy exited the second truck and walked up to join them.

When the cowboy shot Cheyenne a puzzled look she said, "Quinn, this is Wes Mason, my ranch foreman. Wes, this is Quinn Conway."

The foreman extended his hand. "As in the Conways from across the hills?"

"That's right." Quinn studied the silver-haired cowboy, whose loose-limbed walk and leathery skin were a trademark of every cowboy he'd ever known. With a smile he accepted his handshake.

"I've met your daddy and granddaddy through the years. Good men, both of 'em."

"Thanks. I couldn't agree more."

"Which son are you?"

"The oldest."

Micah interrupted. "Cheyenne was just telling me that she dislocated her shoulder."

"The mustang," she explained. "I've never had any trouble with him before, so I wasn't expecting him to go crazy. I stepped into his stall, and the next thing I knew I was lying in the corner and barely conscious."

She gave a shaky laugh. "My shoulder was dislocated." Seeing the sharp looks from the two men, she added quickly, "Don't worry. It's good as new now. Again, thanks to Quinn. "

"And this?" Wes pointed to the charred section of house that lay exposed.

"The fire started during the night." Cheyenne turned to Austin. "Shortly after you left."

Both Micah and Wes turned to Austin, who looked absolutely thunderstruck. "I wish now I'd have followed my hunch and stayed on at the bunkhouse. It's like I've been telling you. I don't trust Deke Vance."

Cheyenne gave a quick shake of her head. "Quinn said it could have been caused by the furnace or the water heater, since they're both really damaged. Anyway, at Quinn's insistence, I phoned Chief Fletcher in Paintbrush."

The foreman shot Quinn a piercing look. "So you agree with Austin? You think there was more here than a simple fire?"

Quinn shrugged. "I didn't say that. But I'm sure the insurance company will want an investigator to make a report before they agree to pay for the damage."

Wes nodded. "Makes sense to me. How bad's the damage?"

"Bad enough that it's going to take some time to put it all back together."

"Come on." Cheyenne led the way. "You may as well take a look for yourselves."

They moved through what was left of the utility room, then on to the kitchen, and then up the stairs. Except for a few muttered curses, the men were silent as they assessed the damage.

By the time they'd made a complete tour of the house, the police chief was driving up in his four-wheel-drive truck.

Everett Fletcher had been the football star of Paint-brush High School. At nearly six feet of pure muscle, he'd gone on to play college football until an injury ended his chances of going pro. After a career with the state police, he'd returned to his hometown, where for the past years he was content to deal with drunks and petty criminals. He knew everyone in town, and most of the outlying ranch-ers, by name. They knew Everett to be fair and honest. A good man, they would say. Competent and patient.

Chief Fletcher ambled over, his cell phone in one hand, his clipboard in the other.

"Cheyenne." He could see her lingering pallor. "You've been through some tough times lately. Sorry about this latest one."

"Thanks, Chief." She accepted his handshake. "You know Micah and Wes and Austin. And this is—"

"Quinn Conway." Everett pumped Quinn's hand before Cheyenne could finish the introduction. "I've known him and his family since we were kids." He grinned at Quinn. "What brings you to this side of the mountain?"

"Just passing through," Quinn said with a smile.

With the formalities over, the police chief got down to business. "Cheyenne, I'd like to walk through the house with you, and you can tell me as much as you know about this fire."

She drew in a deep breath before leading him back into the charred building.

An hour later Cheyenne and Everett emerged from the house and into the frigid air, where they paused, breath-ing deeply.

Cheyenne saw Quinn talking quietly with Micah and

Wes. The looks on the faces of her cook and foreman were as grim as the feelings swirling around in her mind.

With each tour of the destruction, she seemed to sink deeper into the realization of just how close she'd come to disaster.

"I've got enough pictures for now." The chief dropped his cell phone into his shirt pocket and carefully inserted a series of signed documents into a file folder before tossing it on the seat of his truck. "I'm sure the insurance company will want to do their own inspection. But I have enough information for now."

He shook hands all around before giving Cheyenne's shoulder a squeeze. "You stay safe now."

She mumbled something and watched him drive away, wondering why she suddenly felt exhausted and overwhelmed. Maybe, she thought, it was the realization of what she and Quinn had survived.

Quinn was talking in low tones with Micah and Wes. The two men listened intently, before nodding their agreement.

Quinn led the way as the three approached.

"I really need to be getting home."

Cheyenne blinked and tore her gaze from the house. "I guess I've kept you long enough."

"I'm glad I was here to lend a hand. But now that I'm leaving, I wonder if you'd like to ride along?"

"Why would I want to go to your place?"

"We've got plenty of room. You could stay until you get word that the heat and water are restored and the house is livable."

Austin was just crossing the yard from the barn. When he overheard Quinn's offer, he hurried over just as Cheyenne was shaking her head in denial.

"Hold on, Chey." Wes Mason's voice was soft, but with a note of authority, like a man who was accustomed to giving orders to a crew of headstrong cowboys and having them followed without question. "Conway is offering you the perfect solution. He already suggested it to Micah and me, to see if we'd have any objection. We both agree that you can't stay here without heat and hot water. And the bunkhouse is no place for a lady. You can ride over whenever the contractor needs to consult with you. That way, we have the satisfaction of knowing that you're safe and comfortable until the house is repaired and good as new."

Austin shot her a bright smile. "He's right. I'm sure Dad would say the same thing."

Seeing the way Micah turned to study him, he patted the old man's shoulder. "Sorry. A slip of the tongue. That's what he told me to call him."

He caught Cheyenne's hands in his and gave her a boyish smile. "It makes sense for you to find a place to stay until the house is ready. Don't think of it as abandoning your legacy, or turning your back on your responsibility. It'll only be for a little while. That's what Dad would say, and that's what I'm saying."

At his words a sad, haunted look came into Cheyenne's eyes.

She turned away quickly, to hide the tears that sprang up unexpectedly. For long moments she kept her gaze averted, arms crossed over her chest, her booted foot tapping, as she mulled her options.

She lifted her head, studying the charred wreckage of her childhood home, and the heartbreak was there for all of them to see.

When she turned back to them, the sad look remained,

but her voice was strong as she said to Quinn, "I can't bear the thought of leaving. But I know I can't stay here, at least until the furnace and hot-water heater are replaced. So I guess, for now, the best thing I can do is go with you. Thanks for the offer, Quinn. I appreciate it."

"That's my girl." Micah leaned heavily on his cane as he gathered her into his arms and pressed a kiss to the top of her head. "Cheyenne, honey, it'll only be for a couple of weeks."

She sighed. "I'll need time to pack up my things." She pointed to a second barn where the trucks and heavy equipment was stored. "The wranglers will need the stake truck, but they can spare the other pickup. The keys are on the wall, just inside the door."

Austin turned away. "I'll take care of it."

Quinn stepped around him. "You've got enough to do with the ranch chores. I'll get it."

As he strolled toward the barn, Austin continued watching him until he heard Wes Mason say to Micah, "So that's the wolf whisperer."

The older man grinned. "That's him."

"Wolf whisperer?" Austin spun around, eyes narrowed.

Micah started toward the house. "That's what I call him. I'm sure he's got some fancy title. He's some kind of expert on wildlife, especially wolves. Not surprised," he added. "That man may have grown up on one of the most successful ranches in Wyoming, but there's just something in his eyes that tells me he'd be as comfortable in the middle of nowhere, with a pack of hungry wolves as his closest neighbors."

CHAPTER TEN

◆◆◆

"Look." In an attempt to lift Cheyenne's spirits, Quinn lifted a hand from the steering wheel to point to the melting snow along the highway. "Spring is trying to make its way to Wyoming."

Cheyenne managed a smile. For much of the ride, she'd been locked in her own dark thoughts about the damage to her family home. "Somebody forgot to tell Mother Nature." She glanced toward the distant hills. "I hope you're right, though. I've had enough of winter. Before I left, Wes brought me up to date on the cattle. It was a mistake taking that first herd up to the hills. We can blame it on an early break in the weather. It fooled us into thinking it was safe to start the spring migration. But as soon as the snow is gone for good, he'll have our wranglers take the rest of the cattle to the high country for the season."

"We always do the same. Much better rangeland in the

hills." He had a thought. "I bet our herds spend their summers on the same range."

She nodded. "Could be. I've never found any strays bearing the Conway brand."

"We keep a close eye on the herds." Quinn adjusted his sunglasses. "Before we left I checked on the calf born in that snowstorm. He's doing just fine."

Her smile grew. "I can't believe you thought to check on him, after all that's happened."

"I feel responsible for him. He was almost dinner for my wolf pack."

She sobered. "I'm really sorry, Quinn. I wish there had been a way to spare your—"

He laid a hand over hers to stop her. "It's old news. Besides, I'd have never met you if it hadn't been for that wolf pack."

"I hadn't thought of it that way before." Her smile returned. She leaned back, determined to put aside her worries and enjoy the scenery. "How far to your ranch?"

"We're on it. Our land started a couple of miles back. We won't get to the ranch house for a while yet."

"It's beautiful."

"Yeah." He fell silent, drinking in the sight of the land that owned his heart. "It's funny. No matter how much time I spend in the wilderness, the thrill is always the same when I return."

"I know what you mean." Cheyenne thought about the charred remains of her home, and the work that would have to go into rebuilding it. She was torn between wanting to be there, to take charge of the cleanup and rebuilding, and knowing that she needed to step away and give the workers time to put it back into some sort of order before the actual rebuilding began. "When I left for college, I was so homesick after the first week, my dad sent Buddy to bring me home. I was only able to spend a day and a half there before we had to head back to college, but it made such a difference to sleep in my own bed and ride my horse out over the hills."

"I remember missing home, too." He looked over at her. "I guess that makes us the lucky ones."

At her quizzical look he explained. "I had a roommate who was so glad to get away from home, he never wanted to go back. He hated everything about ranching. He called it drudge work, and said he'd rather haul garbage than have to muck another stall."

"Different strokes," Cheyenne muttered.

They shared a laugh.

Cheyenne was still laughing as the truck veered off the paved highway and onto a gravel road. After several twists and turns in the road she caught sight of the open gate and the weathered sign with the big *C* that stood for *Conway*, and the words *Devil's Wilderness* burned into the wood.

Up ahead stood a lovely old three-story building of wood and stone that was as graceful and natural as the foothills of the sunlit mountain range that formed the background.

"Oh." Cheyenne caught her breath. "It looks too pretty to be a working ranch."

Quinn gave a laugh. "Trust me. I have the scars and bruises to prove it's a down and dirty ranch." He slowed the truck to give her a better view as they approached.

He found himself seeing it through her eyes. The big curving driveway that led to a wide porch that ran across the entire front of the house. A pair of weathered rockers his grandfather had made for his grandmother sat beside several comfortable modern gliders. Though the porch was still snow covered, the family would soon gather there to sit on a warm night and watch the parade of deer and elk that often wandered across the yard.

There were double front doors, and beyond them the huge foyer that led to a great room.

Quinn avoided the front driveway, choosing instead to drive around to the back, where several vehicles were parked.

"Looks like everyone's home for a change." He brought the truck to a halt and released his seat belt.

Opening the door, he walked around and held the passenger door for Cheyenne. "Come on in and meet the family."

Cheyenne trailed Quinn to the back door and stepped into a big mudroom much like the one at her own place, except that it was twice the size. The floor was concrete and sloped toward a drain, making it easy to hose off muddy boots. A hose attached to a low faucet was coiled nearby. A parade of clean boots stood in a row atop a low perforated shelf, allowing their soles to dry. Wide-brimmed hats hung on pegs along the wall.

Despite an accumulation of gear, there was order here. She found herself admiring it and made a mental note to duplicate some of this when the contractors started work on rebuilding her utility room. She especially admired the floor drain and the hose and the long, low sink where a person could wash up before stepping into the house.

Quinn opened the door to the kitchen. Cheyenne heard

the low hum of voices suddenly cease when his family spotted him.

There was a rich, deep baritone barking a welcome and then a feminine voice giving a cry of surprise. Laughter and raucous comments followed, and Cheyenne stood back watching as Quinn was caught in a series of bear hugs by his family.

After greeting them warmly he turned and caught Cheyenne by the hand. "I'd like all of you to meet Cheyenne O'Brien."

He nodded toward the white-haired man who was already starting forward with his arms outstretched. "Cheyenne, this is my grandfather, Big Jim."

"Nice to meet you." The older man gave her a long, steady look. "Are you Dan O'Brien's girl?"

She nodded.

He surprised her by taking both her hands and holding them. "You look just like your daddy. I was really sorry to hear about Dan's accident. And before that, your brother. That's quite a load of sorrow. How are you managing without them?"

"It's been a tough adjustment, but I'm okay."

"I'm glad to hear that. And very happy to meet you." Big Jim stepped aside as Quinn said, "Cheyenne, this is my father, Colby."

"Everybody calls me Cole." He offered a firm handshake.

"Nice to meet you, Cole." Cheyenne was aware of his careful scrutiny.

"My brother Josh."

"Welcome to our humble ranch, Cheyenne." He closed her hand in his big one and gave her a warm smile that immediately put her at ease.

He was as tall as Quinn, but his eyes were brown instead of gray. His smile was quick and easy.

"And my brother Jake."

"The veterinarian," Cheyenne said as they shook hands.

At Jake's arch look she added, "You brother was bragging about you, Doctor."

"Well, that's nice to hear. He usually has some disparaging remarks ready whenever we're together. As for the title, it may take me a while to get used to it. I just got my degree a few days ago." He shot a look at Quinn. "Thanks for missing my graduation."

"Did you stick around for it?"

Jake flushed. "Actually, I skipped the ceremony. But I knew I'd earned my sheepskin. I aced all the finals."

"Does that mean you delivered a calf to the good professor's satisfaction?"

The family laughed, and Jake joined in. "It means I didn't cause death or bodily harm to any of my test subjects."

"That's a relief." Quinn gave him a hard punch to the shoulder before turning to their father. "Now you can fire old Dr. Hunger and let Jake start earning back all that money it cost you to send him to school."

"You use Dr. Hunger, too?" Cheyenne turned to Cole.

He shrugged. "I think everybody in Wyoming has used him. He may be old as the hills, but he knows his stuff."

"Are you suggesting that I don't?" Jake asked.

"Not at all." Cole winked at the others. "But I don't think we ought to fire old Doc Hunger just yet."

"It's nice to have the trust of my family." Jake turned

to Cheyenne with a mock frown. "See what I have to put up with? No respect, I tell you."

That had all of them laughing aloud.

Phoebe Hogan entered carrying a tray of longnecks. When she spotted Quinn she set aside the tray and hurried over to give him a welcoming hug.

"We've missed you," she said.

"I missed all of you, too." He turned to include Cheyenne. "Cheyenne O'Brien, this is Phoebe Hogan, our housekeeper, all-around den mother, and the best cook in Wyoming."

The two women shook hands.

Cole picked up the tray and began passing around the drinks.

"So," he asked, "how did you two meet?"

"I killed Quinn's wolf," Cheyenne said simply.

That had everyone staring in surprised silence.

"There's a little more to the story than that," Quinn said with a grin. "And I intend to tell it. But first I ought to explain that I brought Cheyenne with me in the hope that she could spend some time here while her house is being repaired."

"What happened to it?" Big Jim tipped up his longneck and took a long pull.

"There was a fire. It caused a lot of destruction, and since she lost her furnace and hot-water heater, I thought she'd be more comfortable here while things get restored."

"Of course." Cole nodded. "We have plenty of room."

Phoebe gave a sigh. "How awful for you, dear. I hope nothing of value was destroyed."

Cheyenne shook her head. "It was pretty much confined to the utility room and kitchen. But when I think how close I came to losing everything…" She shivered.

Phoebe closed a hand over hers. "Don't think about that now." She turned to Quinn. "Why don't you take Cheyenne up to the spare room?"

"Sure thing." Quinn laughed as he started to lead Cheyenne to the stairs. "I'd better warn you. This is a pretty masculine place. But at least you'll get a suite of rooms, with all the bells and whistles."

Phoebe started toward the kitchen. "I'll let Ela know that we're having two more for supper. She'll be thrilled to hear that Quinn is home. According to Ela, the spirits never rest until the family is all together."

Cheyenne paused on the stairs. "Quinn mentioned that Ela is Arapaho. So was my mother, and she used to say that very thing."

"Ela will be thrilled to have a kindred spirit in the house." Phoebe hurried away while Cheyenne followed Quinn up the stairs.

The upper hallway seemed to go on forever. Cheyenne found herself thinking that the space was as big as a hotel.

To Quinn's back she called, "How many rooms are there?"

"It's hard to say, since Ela and Phoebe both have their own suites downstairs. Probably fifteen or more." Quinn stopped and held open a door.

Cheyenne preceded him into a huge bedroom with a king-size bed and long, custom cabinets on either side of a soaring fireplace made of granite.

"The bathroom is right through those doors. Since you don't have to share it with anyone, you can put all your own things in it and make yourself at home."

"Thank you." Cheyenne walked to a wide floor-to-ceiling window that looked out over the snow-covered landscape and offered a grand view of the mountains in the distance. Somewhere, just beyond those foothills, was home. The thought comforted her.

"Well." Sensing her thoughtful mood, Quinn turned away. "You can unpack and freshen up, then join us downstairs before supper."

"I will. Thanks, Quinn."

"You're welcome. I think Ela and Phoebe will enjoy having another woman around."

The door closed, and Cheyenne found herself alone.

She walked around the room, touching a hand to the pretty desk and chair set in an alcove. The perfect place to set up her computer and keep in contact with Wes and the wranglers.

She was pleased to see a television on a stand near the bed. If she began to feel too intimidated by the Conway family, she could always sneak up here and tune them out.

The Conway family. Quinn's family. Her introduction to them had been easier than she'd anticipated. Their acceptance of her had been warm and welcoming. And for that she was so grateful.

She'd seen their speculative glances and knew that they were wondering what her relationship was to Quinn. That thought had her smiling wistfully. What was their relationship?

He'd burst into her life like an avenging angel, and she'd both feared and disliked him on sight. The change in her attitude had been so gradual, so easy, she hadn't even been aware of it. But it had seemed the most natural thing in the world to invite him to spend the night. After all, he was a neighboring rancher and that's what neighbors did for one another.

Of course, his reaction after the kick from the mustang had been above and beyond neighborliness. And his quiet competence while her shoulder recovered from the trauma had cemented her trust.

She stood, shaking her head in wonder at what had transpired next. The fire had left her much more shaken than she'd wanted to admit. She'd almost lost everything, including her life. It was Quinn who'd alerted her to the danger.

What if he'd left earlier? What if he had awakened too late?

She took a deep breath and deliberately shut out the troubling thoughts. After the loss of both her brother and her father, she'd had to teach herself ways to stay positive. It hadn't been easy. In fact, there were times when she'd feared that she would never again know happiness. It would have been so easy to remain mired in misery. But through sheer effort she'd managed to turn despair into hope.

Work had always been her solution when she couldn't turn off her brain.

She opened drawers and doors in the custom cabinets until all her things were neatly filed away. Then she made her way to the bathroom, which was equally elegant, with both a large walk-in shower with glass doors and marble bench and a sunken whirlpool tub. The perfect way for a rancher to ease aching muscles, Cheyenne thought with a smile. She wished she could give it a try right now.

After washing up, she turned away with a sigh of contentment. At least, if she had to leave home for a little while, she couldn't have found a better spot to settle in.

CHAPTER ELEVEN

Cheyenne descended the stairs and followed the sound of voices to the kitchen, where the family had gathered around an enormous fireplace. Big Jim and Cole were carrying on a heated discussion about the need for a new flatbed truck to haul feed. Josh was teasing Jake about replacing old Dr. Hunger on the ranching circuit. Quinn was reaching over an old woman's head to help himself to one of the steaming biscuits she had removed from the oven. She rapped his knuckles with a wooden spoon, causing him to chuckle and press a kiss to her withered cheek before turning away.

When he did, he caught sight of Cheyenne, standing hesitantly in the doorway.

He hurried over to take her hand. "Did you get lost?"

She laughed. "Only once or twice. This place is huge."

"Really?" He feigned innocence. "I hadn't noticed. You haven't met Ela yet."

He drew her across the room to where the old house-keeper was arranging hot biscuits in a linen-lined basket.

"Ela, this is Cheyenne O'Brien."

The woman's blackbird eyes studied Cheyenne with great interest. "I knew your mother, Lolotea."

"You did?"

"All our people are connected here." Ela touched her heart.

Without thinking Cheyenne caught the old woman's hand in both of hers. "What do you remember about her?"

She was unaware of the eagerness in her tone. But it wasn't lost on the old woman.

"Young Lolotea was considered a great beauty among our people. Many of our young men hoped to win her heart. She greatly displeased her aunt and uncle when she chose to marry her rancher. Like all of our people, they wanted to keep her with her own kind. They feared that she would not be welcomed by his people. And they secretly worried that he might not respect her."

Seeing the little frown line between Cheyenne's eyes, she added quickly, "But in their old age her relatives grew satisfied that she had made a fine choice. And though she chose his way of life, she never forgot the old ways. All of us could see that there was great love between Lolotea and her rancher. Great love," she added for emphasis.

Cheyenne felt her eyes fill and blinked quickly. "Thank you." It was all she could manage over the lump in her throat as she squeezed the old woman's hand.

Before she could turn away Ela added, "You have your mother's sweet smile and spirited nature."

Cheyenne wondered at the lightness around her heart. She could have kissed this old woman. It had been years since she had spoken with anyone who had known her mother so intimately. Cheyenne felt a sudden connection to this woman with the lively eyes and parchment skin.

"I hope…" She swallowed and tried again. "I hope we can talk more another time, Ela."

"That is my hope as well."

Sensing Cheyenne's emotions, Quinn decided to deflect attention away from her for a moment, to give her time to gather herself.

"Well?" He lifted a hand to encompass the room. "What do you think of Ela's domain?"

Cheyenne recognized his intention and was grateful for it. Taking a breath, she studied the kitchen.

There was a big trestle table with cozy wooden benches along each side of it, cushioned with cheery fabric decorated with native symbols that appeared to be hand-stitched on both the seats and backs. At the head and foot of the table were sturdy armchairs, the dark wood softened with cushions of the same fabric.

In the middle of the table was an enormous lazy Susan holding an assortment of napkins, salt- and pepper shakers, sugar and creamer, and cruets of various sizes holding oil, vinegar, and spices.

The pretty, bright colors and the cozy fireplace gave the room a warm, inviting feeling. It was plain that this was the heart of their home.

Quinn pointed to a tray of glasses. "There's milk, water, and beer. Name your poison."

She laughed. "Nothing right now."

"Okay. Let's join the others." He leaned close to add in a stage whisper, "Just don't let the arguing get to you. It's the Conway equivalent of hugs and kisses."

"I heard that." Big Jim looked up with a grin. "I only argue with those who think they know more than me."

"Which is just about everyone in this room," Cole deadpanned.

The others burst into gales of laughter.

"It's the folly of the young to think they know it all." Big Jim took another drink of beer. "I just don't see how spending forty grand on a flatbed truck can be practical."

"What's impractical is having valuable cattle wintering in the hills without enough feed to see them through, and no way to bring them down through all this snow." Cole gestured with his longneck. "The way I see it, we spend the money or we sacrifice half a herd to starvation."

"I've been feeding cattle from the back of my pickup for the past fifty years."

"Because you had no choice. But it's time to move into the twenty-first century, Big Jim, and you know it."

Quinn, Josh, and Jake exchanged glances and rolled their eyes but refused to be sucked into the argument.

"Dinner is ready," Phoebe called.

Big Jim refused to concede. "You're always knocking the old ways. But they were good enough—"

"Oh boy, have I heard this one before." Cole turned away and headed for the table, leaving his father to stare after him.

"That's right," the older man called. "Walk away. That only proves that you don't have any evidence to back up your claim."

Cole took his seat at the foot of the table and watched as the others drifted over.

Quinn indicated a spot on the cushioned bench. "Sit here, Cheyenne."

When she was seated, he sat beside her while Josh and Jake sat across from them.

When Big Jim reluctantly took his place at the head of the table, Cole looked up with a sly smile. "I don't need evidence or advice, Big Jim. I've already ordered the flatbed."

"You . . ." Big Jim's eyes widened, before narrowing on his son. "Just like that? Without even a word to me?"

Cole shrugged. "I figured we could have the argument before the fact, or after. And since the snow refuses to melt fast enough, I made an executive decision and decided to order the equipment we needed, and deal with the fallout later."

Cheyenne's gaze darted from father to son and back again, and she waited for the explosion.

Instead, the older man surprised her by lowering his head, then lifting it to reveal a wide grin. "Damned if you aren't a chip off the old block."

He picked up a platter of roast beef and heaped meat and potatoes on his plate before passing it to Josh, who did the same before passing it to Jake. As the platter made its way around the table, Cheyenne listened to the conversation veer to the weather, and then to the barn roof that needed patching, and then to Josh's favorite mare favoring her left front hoof.

"I'll check her out in the morning," Jake said before helping himself to a forkful of potatoes and gravy.

"Good. Brand and I started her on a liniment, but I'd feel better if you gave your professional opinion."

"Where is Brand?" Big Jim asked.

"Heading back up to the herd." Josh glanced at his father. "He figures he'll be gone at least a week, unless the snow melts sooner."

Quinn leaned close to Cheyenne to whisper, "Brand's been with us for years. I don't think there's anything he can't do. Doctor sick cattle. Fix a broken window or a broken fuel line. He spends most of his time up in the hills with the cattle, living in the bunkhouse, but if there's anything that goes wrong here at the ranch, Brand is the one we call on."

"Sort of a combination of Micah, Wes Mason, and old Doc Hunger?"

At her words Quinn chuckled. "I never thought of him that way, but I'd say that pretty much describes Brand Hudson."

"Temperature's supposed to climb into the forties tomorrow," Big Jim muttered.

"And into the fifties by the end of the week," Phoebe remarked as she passed around the basket of biscuits.

She and Ela finished serving the last of the dishes before joining the family at the table.

"That ought to start the snow melting," Jake said with a sigh.

"Sounds like all those years spent away from Wyoming turned you into a softie," Josh teased.

"You bet. You wouldn't believe how much sooner spring and summer come in the East and Midwest. Their trees are already in bloom when we're still shoveling tons of snow."

"But they don't have that to brag about." Josh pointed to the window and the glorious view of the Tetons, their snow-covered peaks sparkling in the last rays of the daylight.

"That's true." Jake gave a long, deep sigh. "I can't believe how much I missed seeing all this."

"And now you're home for good." Cole reached over and clapped a hand on his son's shoulder.

"That's right. You're stuck with me now."

Cole flashed his son the famous Conway smile. "A burden, but I'll just have to bear it."

That had everyone around the table laughing.

Cheyenne sat back, letting the sound wash over her.

There had been a time when she and her brother and father had enjoyed just this sort of easy, joyful relationship. There'd been so much to share. Not only their love of one another but also the sheer pleasure they took in working side by side, doing the thousand and one chores required to keep the ranch operating. They'd shared a mutual love of nature, and felt a real thrill at the beauty of the countryside.

Until this moment, she hadn't realized just how much she'd been missing this easy camaraderie.

"What do you think, Cheyenne?"

Hearing her name, she looked up in confusion. "Sorry. I was distracted."

Quinn was quick to come to her aid. "That's easy to do with this noisy bunch. Big Jim asked if you could remember a spring with this much snow."

"Oh." She flushed when she realized she had everyone's attention focused on her. "We got fooled by that warm spell, and took a herd up to the hills. They're still up there with most of the wranglers forced up into the hills to tend them."

"I'm glad we're not the only ones who got fooled by this weather, even though we ought to know better by now." Big Jim sat back. "I'll be glad when spring decides to stay."

"Amen to that." Cole set aside his napkin. "That was a fine meal, Phoebe."

"Thanks. Ela made a couple of johnnycakes. Anybody ready for dessert?"

At the murmured comments that followed her question Quinn turned to Cheyenne. "Johnnycake is the Conway family's favorite dessert. Ever have it?"

She shook her head.

"Then you're in for a treat," Josh announced. "Ela's been making this since we were kids."

"She's been making it since I was a kid," Cole said with a laugh.

"She's been here that long?" Cheyenne arched a brow.

"She came here when my Clementine died." Big Jim winked at his son. "Cole here was just a baby."

"And whenever I wanted that boy to eat his supper," the old woman said with a twinkle in her eyes, "I just promised to bake him johnnycake and he cleaned his plate."

"Which is a roundabout way of saying that all this"— Cole patted his middle—"is Ela's fault. Instead of urging me to clean my plate, she should have told me to always leave a little something for tomorrow."

That had everyone laughing as Phoebe began passing around slices of a moist yellow cake, the consistency of coffee cake, drizzled with a white frosting glaze and sprinkled with crushed peanuts.

Cheyenne took a taste and glanced over at Ela. "Oh, this is wonderful. I remember my mother making this every Christmas. But she never left the recipe."

The old woman was beaming. "I'll see that you get it."

"Thank you." As she continued eating the cake, she was humming to herself.

The sound had Quinn grinning from ear to ear.

"What's that?" Big Jim glanced around the table.

"The sound of a happy guest," Quinn said with a grin.

Cheyenne glanced over and felt her cheeks grow hot.

When the others moved on to other topics of conversation she turned to Quinn. "Was I humming loudly?"

He shook his head. "You were very discreet. But obviously happy. Would you care for another slice?"

"No, thanks." She stared at the tabletop. "Next time I hum, give me a nudge."

"And stop the music? Not a chance."

She looked over, intending to argue. Then, seeing his smile, she stopped herself. It was amazing how everything, even anger and embarrassment, dissolved beneath that infectious grin of his.

Phoebe filled a tray with cups. "Anyone for coffee or beer in the great room?"

The men were already pushing away from the table.

Ela yawned behind her hand. "I'm going to my room."

As she walked away Quinn leaned close to whisper to Cheyenne, "She does this every night. But nobody's fooled by it. She's not going to sleep. She's going to curl up with her handwork and sip a tall glass of whiskey or two. She's done that for as long as I've known her."

"Your family doesn't mind?"

"It's her life. Her ritual. Why should we mind?"

Cheyenne watched the old woman leave. "I thought the artwork on these cushions looked familiar. My mother had a blanket that had belonged to her grandmother, and some of the symbols are the same. Is all of this Ela's work?"

Quinn nodded. "According to Phoebe, it's practically

a lost art. And though I've never been in her rooms, I've heard that the place is filled with her handwork. She gives it all away to her Arapaho women friends."

Cheyenne smiled. "That's sweet."

Quinn shrugged. "Whatever makes her happy. Come on. Let's join the family."

Family.

The word sent a tiny shiver along Cheyenne's spine. It was, she realized, something she'd been missing for such a long time.

CHAPTER TWELVE

———◆◆◆———

The family room reminded Cheyenne of a ski resort owned by a friend of her family. Floor-to-ceiling windows on three sides of the room, offering views of the magnificent snow-covered mountains. A soaring fireplace made of natural stone dominated the other wall. On the raised hearth a log blazed. Comfortable sofas were arranged around the fire for easy conversation.

On a huge coffee table rested a tray of longnecks, while on a side table there was a coffee server and mugs.

Cheyenne helped herself to coffee, and Quinn did the same.

As they settled themselves on a sofa, Josh and Jake were having a heated discussion.

"So, what happened to that big, mysterious job you'd been offered?"

At that Cole and Big Jim stopped talking and turned to listen.

"I decided that I'd been away from home too long. Though it was tempting, I just couldn't accept."

Cole set aside his beer. "How come I never heard about this job offer?"

Jake winked at Josh. "I guess it slipped my mind."

"What was the offer?" Big Jim, like his son, set aside his beer and crossed his arms over his chest.

"I was approached by a Kentucky racehorse breeder, on the recommendation of one of my professors. He was looking for someone to join his staff and work with his longtime vet, who was thinking about retiring. He came up to Michigan to meet with me, and offered to pay all my expenses if I'd spend some time at his Kentucky farm to see if I'd be interested in the job."

"Were you?" Cole's voice was more a challenge than a question.

"His persistence certainly caught my attention." Jake's smile grew at the recollection. "The first time I refused, he fattened the offer by fifty thousand."

That had Quinn and Josh whistling in appreciation.

"The second time I refused his offer, he said he would make me a partner in his entire operation."

Big Jim snorted. "That's fine if his farm is showing a profit. Of course, he could be inviting you to share a big, fat loss."

Jake's smile remained in place. He was, Cheyenne thought as she watched and listened, enjoying this give-and-take with his family.

Jake's grandfather, father, and brothers were watching and listening like hawks watching a tasty rabbit. Except, Cheyenne thought, this rabbit was merely leading them on a merry chase, and enjoying every minute of it.

Jake chuckled. "I checked out his ranch. It's one of the most successful in Kentucky. He breeds nothing but winners. And, he told me, he's accustomed to getting what he wants, no matter the cost."

"And he wanted you." Cole studied his youngest son with new respect. "So, what did he finally offer you?"

Jake took a long swig of beer. "The moon."

"So." Cole casually picked up his longneck. "What're you doing here, Son?"

"Living the life I want. I'm not interested in doctoring Thoroughbreds, Pa. I'm a sucker for cattle. My job of choice is ranching. My life is here."

Cole took a long drink before setting aside his bottle and crossing to his son.

"I'm glad you came to your senses." His voice was cool enough, but the look in his eyes spoke volumes.

"That's the Kentucky farmer's loss," Big Jim said with a grin. "And our gain."

Phoebe had watched this exchange in silence, but the smile on her face revealed how happy she was at the outcome.

After pouring herself a cup of coffee, she retreated to a big, comfortable chair by the fire and propped her feet on a footstool.

"That was a fine meal," Cole remarked.

"Thanks." She turned to Cheyenne, gently drawing her into the conversation. "Do you have help at your ranch?"

"Do you mean with the ranch chores or in the house?"

"Both," Phoebe said softly. "Quinn told us that you lost both a brother and a father within the past two years. I can't imagine that you can handle that spread by yourself."

"I couldn't do it without good people to help. Wes

Mason is my foreman, and he's been with us since I was a kid."

"I know Wes," Cole said. "He's worked for us a time or two. A good man."

Cheyenne nodded. "And Micah Horn. He started out as a wrangler with my dad when I was little, and now he's my chief cook and bottle-washer. I don't know what I'd do without Micah."

Big Jim gave a nod of recognition. "Another good man. Micah used to give us a hand at roundup."

"That's what he told me," Quinn put in.

"There was some kind of accident one winter that left him lame." Big Jim glanced at Cheyenne for confirmation.

"A truck got stuck up in the hills. The rancher he was working for asked Micah and another wrangler to push, while he stayed behind the wheel. The truck swerved, Micah lost his footing, and the truck ended up crushing one of his legs. By the time they airlifted him to the hospital, the damage was pretty severe. He walks with a cane, and can drive some, but every year it gets harder for him to do much else. He even had to give up riding his favorite horse a couple of years ago."

"He makes a damn fine chili," Quinn muttered. Seeing Phoebe's arch look, he added, "Not as good as yours, mind you. But it runs a close second."

"You just want to make sure I don't put arsenic in your soup tomorrow," Phoebe said with a laugh.

"You bet. I'm no fool," Quinn added.

That brought a round of laughter from all of them.

"That reminds me"—Cole was still laughing—"of the time you three decided you weren't going to eat your sandwiches unless Phoebe cut off the crusts of your bread."

Big Jim was quick to add, "That was right after a visit to town and lunch in that fancy restaurant."

"A restaurant," Cole said, "that lasted about a month before going broke. Whoever heard of cowboys wanting quiche for breakfast when they can have steak and potatoes for half the price at Flora's Diner?"

Cheyenne, caught up in the laughter, turned to Phoebe. "So, did you cut off the crusts?"

"Are you kidding?" Phoebe shook her head. "Can you imagine spending the rest of my life throwing away all that bread?"

Quinn looked at his brothers for confirmation. "She conned us, as usual."

"Yeah," Josh joined in. "Phoebe told us that eating bread crusts made us smarter and stronger."

"Well? Did I lie?" Phoebe swept a hand to indicate the three handsome men. "Those bread crusts produced giants. Though I'm not so sure about the brainpower," she added with a straight face.

That had everyone laughing louder.

Phoebe turned to Cheyenne. "I bet your mother told you to eat your crusts so your hair would be curly."

"And it would be if you didn't use all that stuff to make it straight," Quinn remarked.

Though the others laughed, Cheyenne was aware that they'd paused for a moment after his remark, as if to wonder just how he would know such a personal thing about her.

To make matters worse, he tugged on a strand of her hair and winked.

She felt the quick, sexual jolt all the way to her toes and hoped the others wouldn't notice her face flaming.

As the conversation continued swirling around, Cheyenne studied the Conway family, teasing, scolding, arguing, and laughing together.

She'd better be careful. It would be very easy to let herself get so caught up by Quinn Conway and his big, noisy family that she might never want to go back to her own ranch.

Just when she'd begun to accept the emptiness, the loneliness, of life without her father and brother as her new reality, they had to come along to remind her of all that had been taken from her.

Beside her, Quinn glanced at her before asking, "Getting tired?"

"I…Yes." She quickly covered her lapse. "I think I should probably go up to bed now."

"I'll walk with you."

"That isn't necessary."

When she stood, he reached for her empty cup and placed it on the side table.

To everyone in the room she called, "I'll say good night, now. Thank you again for your kind hospitality."

As they said their good nights, Cheyenne climbed the stairs, aware of Quinn trailing behind her.

At her door she paused. "I didn't want you to feel that you had to leave your family. You've only just returned. I'm sure you have a lot to catch up on."

"And a lifetime to do it." His smile eased her worries. "But this is your first night in my home, and I'd like it to be a comfortable one."

"I love your family. They've made me feel so welcome."

"It's a gift they have. All my life my friends have felt comfortable here."

She couldn't help teasing. "I'm sure you've brought a lot of women home unannounced through the years."

He chuckled. "Good try." He shot her that look that always reminded her of his wolves. Direct. Piercing. "Actually, you're the first."

"Well." Her throat was suddenly dry as dust and she was forced to swallow. "Thank you. And good night."

"Good night, Cheyenne."

Without warning he dipped his head and brushed her lips with his. It was the merest touch of mouth to mouth, and yet she felt the heat shiver along her spine.

She drew back to stare up into his eyes, only to find him studying her carefully.

"This is a first. I've never kissed a woman good night in my own home before."

"I seem to be all sorts of firsts for you."

"Yeah." His smile was quick and disarming. "Maybe I just wanted to show you that I could be a good kisser even without the effects of whiskey." Seeing the color that rushed to her cheeks, he said, "Sorry. Is that subject taboo?"

Her chin came up defiantly. "The fact that I got drunk? Or the fact that I called you a good kisser?"

"You only got drunk because I forced it on you to deaden the pain of that shoulder."

"As I recall, you only kissed me because I forced myself on you."

"Is that what you think?" Again that smile, and this time it took deadly aim at her heart.

Without warning his arms were around her, drawing her close. His mouth covered hers in a kiss that had her fingers curling into the front of his shirt and holding on as though her life depended on it.

She hadn't seen this coming.

Caught by surprise, she could only hold on as he kissed her with a thoroughness that had her fully engaged.

Without her giving thought to what she was doing, her fingers uncurled, the palms flattening against his chest before sliding slowly upward to encircle his neck.

His hands were in her hair, drawing her head back as he continued kissing her.

"Now we're even," he murmured against her lips. "You didn't initiate this one. It was all my choice."

Before she could respond his mouth was claiming hers again, taking the kiss deeper, until all she could taste was him.

The kiss spun on and on, filling her, then draining her. She felt as light as air, her bones as soft as melted wax. The thought flitted through her mind that if he chose to take her here and now, she wouldn't have the will to resist.

When at last he lifted his head, she continued holding on to him, afraid that if she let go she would surely slide boneless to the floor.

"That's how I wanted to kiss you that first time. But I wanted you awake, alert, and able to give your full consent."

As she sucked air into her starving lungs, he lifted a hand to her cheek.

He opened the door and waited until she'd walked past him. "Welcome to my home."

He paused, with his hand on the doorknob. "If you need anything in the night, my room is next door."

"I'm sure I won't come calling."

His smile widened. "I can always hope."

He stepped back and pulled the door closed.

She stood very still, listening to his footsteps recede.

She crossed the room and dropped down on the edge of the mattress, her mind in turmoil.

What had just happened here? That unexpected kiss changed everything.

She'd come here to be comfortable while her house was repaired.

Comfortable? The word had her laughing aloud. That wasn't a word she would use to describe Quinn Conway. The man made her extremely uncomfortable.

On the one hand, she loved being with him. In these few days that they'd been together, she'd laughed more than she had in a year. She really liked his family. They were warm and funny and loud and informal, and she felt an almost instant acceptance by all of them.

On the other hand, things were moving way too quickly. Too much had happened in her life that had been beyond her control. The loss of her mother, brother, and then father would be enough to have any sane person reeling. Added to that, within days she'd had to deal with a dislocated shoulder and a nearly deadly fire.

She wanted, needed, the world to slow down. She wasn't ready for any more complications in her life.

And Quinn Conway was definitely proving to be a complication. An interesting, challenging, and thoroughly head-spinning complication.

CHAPTER THIRTEEN

———◆———

Quinn walked into the kitchen and poured a mug of coffee.

Ela was baking corn bread. Phoebe was busy pouring orange juice into glasses she'd arranged on a tray atop the counter.

"'Morning," he called to both of them.

Ela merely nodded a greeting as she opened the oven to check her corn bread.

"Good morning, Quinn." Phoebe set aside the empty pitcher and began removing eggs from a carton. "You're up earlier than usual."

"Am I?" He leaned a hip against the counter and watched as she deftly cracked one egg after another until she had more than a dozen in the bowl. "I didn't look at a clock. Just figured if I was awake, it was time to get moving."

Phoebe smiled. "That's what I tell myself every morning."

"Have you ever overslept?"

She shrugged. "Not that I recall. It's just not in my nature to be lazy."

An understatement, he thought, since he'd never seen her when she wasn't busy. Not only did she manage dozens of chores each day, but she had always made time for all of them through the years, listening to their troubles, easing them through the various stages of their lives. And all without a hint of impatience.

"Yeah. I know what you mean." He glanced at the sky outside the window. "Looks like the sun might shine."

"About time." She added milk to the egg mixture. "I'm so ready for spring."

He lingered, enjoying the coffee and the wonderful scents of morning, and the company of these two women, who were so different in looks and temperament. Phoebe the eternal optimist and Ela terse and brutally frank.

"I like your Cheyenne."

Though Phoebe said it simply, he looked over and found her staring at him.

He shot her a grin. "I knew you would."

"Hearing about her personal losses, and the accidents that have befallen her, I expected a wounded bird. Instead, she strikes me as very strong."

"Yeah."

"Like her mother." Ela began cutting squares of corn bread and placing them in a linen-lined basket.

Quinn looked over. "You made Cheyenne really happy by talking about things you remembered about her mother."

The old woman smiled. "Those who lose their parents at a young age have a need to keep them alive in their minds."

Quinn digested this as he drained his coffee and placed the mug in the dishwasher. Though her words were always simply spoken, there was a depth of soul to them. This time, he had the feeling that she was directing them at him as much as at Cheyenne.

"Got some chores to see to before breakfast," he muttered. "Guess I'll get to them."

As he ambled out of the room the two women watched him go.

When the door closed behind him, Phoebe looked over. "Was that necessary?"

At Phoebe's questioning look Ela said softly, "If they had been allowed to speak of her, her spirit could have found some solace in their words. Instead, I sense her restlessness."

"Her restlessness? What about theirs? Don't you think all these years of uncertainty have taken a toll on Cole and his children?"

Ela smiled at the vehemence in Phoebe's words. Through the years Phoebe Hogan had become their fierce protector. Not only of the three sons but of their father as well. "A great toll. It eats at them like a beast."

Neither woman mentioned her by name. They didn't have to. It was clear that Seraphine Conway remained just as powerful a presence in her family years after her disappearance as she did when she was with them.

Cheyenne came fully awake and lay a moment, trying to recapture her dream. Like wisps of fog it was gone from her mind. She thought Quinn had been part of it, but she couldn't be certain. She knew only that it had been pleasant and she hadn't wanted it to end.

It seemed strange to wake and have no agenda. She'd always thought it would be a pleasant experience to have the opportunity to escape ranch chores, if only for a few days, and do nothing more than pamper herself. But now that she was here at the Conway ranch, she was feeling oddly dejected. The truth was, she liked to work hard. Relished the satisfaction of mentally crossing off chores on her list of things to do.

If she couldn't find anything to do here, she could always drive back to her ranch and help direct the cleanup. She imagined it would take several days, perhaps as long as a week, to haul all the debris from the rooms affected by the fire.

As she slipped from bed and made her way to the shower she began thinking about all the things she would have to do in the next few days.

Satisfied that she would have more than enough work to keep her busy, she stepped under the warm spray.

"'Morning, Cheyenne." Quinn was the first to greet her as she walked into the kitchen.

"Good morning." She brightened at the sight of him fresh from morning chores, sleeves rolled to his elbows, hair messed and curling slightly over the collar of his flannel shirt.

"Coffee and juice over there." He pointed to the tray on the kitchen counter.

While she helped herself to a glass of juice she greeted Big Jim and Cole, Phoebe and Ela.

Phoebe turned from the stove, where she was draining sausages before transferring them to a platter. "We'll be eating as soon as Josh and Jake return from the barn."

Just then the two could be heard in the mudroom, removing their parkas and boots before stepping into the kitchen.

"Well, Doctor," Quinn said with a mock-serious look, "will the patient live?"

Jake feigned an equally serious look. "I may have to perform a lobotomy on the cranium mandible..." He looked around dramatically. "Oh. Sorry. Not on Josh's horse, but on Josh."

When they were through laughing he said, "Actually, the liniment he used is doing the trick. I think that hoof will be good as new in a day or so."

"Does this mean you won't charge me, Dr. Conway?"

At Josh's question Jake shot him a dark look. "I believe I ought to charge you double, for insisting that I do the examination before I had even one bite of Ela's corn bread."

Big Jim was shaking his head from side to side. "I think Jake's going to charge you double for all those big words he just used to impress us."

Jake turned to his grandfather. "I hope you were suitably impressed. I want Pa to know he got his money's worth after all those years of study."

"Son." Cole dropped an arm around his shoulders. "I knew I got my money's worth the minute you came home."

"With a degree."

"With or without it. I'm just happy you chose to come here instead of some"—his tone lowered—"fancy, la-di-da Kentucky horse farm."

"I do believe that impressed you the most," Jake said with a laugh.

"Damned right." Cole winked at Big Jim, who had taken a seat across the table. "It means we're doing something right here."

"Well," Jake remarked. "The pay's not what I'd hoped for, but there's always Ela's corn bread." He reached for a piece and was rewarded with a rap on his knuckles by the old woman.

"Wait for the others," Ela said.

"So much for my importance," Jake grumbled. "I still get no respect."

That had the rest of the family in stitches as they took their places around the table.

Cheyenne, seated beside Quinn, joined in the laughter. As they passed around platters of scrambled eggs, sausage, fried potatoes, and corn bread, the easy banter continued.

It was, she thought, a most pleasant way to begin a new day.

"I'm phoning an order to Paintbrush this morning," Phoebe announced as she circled the table filling their cups. "If there's anything you'd like me to add to the grocery list, speak now."

"Chocolate chips," Quinn said as she paused beside his chair.

She arched a brow. "Now that's something you've never asked for before."

"I have a sudden craving for chocolate chip cookies." He winked at Cheyenne and she felt her face grow hot.

"I'll add them." She topped off Cheyenne's cup. "Anything you'd particularly like while you're here? I phone in a grocery order every couple of weeks to the Paintbrush grocery, and they send it along with our ranch supplies."

Across the table Josh chuckled. "Good thing you're one of us, Cheyenne. I'm sure a visitor from a big city would think they'd landed on another planet if they saw a delivery of saddle soap, motor oil, animal antibiotic, and chocolate chips."

That had everyone roaring.

When she'd stopped laughing, Cheyenne shook her head. "I can't think of a thing, Phoebe. But," she added to Josh, "I did wake up this morning and wonder where I'd landed. If not another planet, at least a spa. The guest bedroom is really luxurious."

"I'm so glad you're comfortable here." Big Jim lifted his cup in both hands and regarded Cheyenne over the rim.

"Very comfortable, thanks to all of you."

"We're happy to have you." Cole looked around the table before saying to his father, "It's nice having all the family home, isn't it, Big Jim?"

"You're only saying that because now you've got free laborers." Jake helped himself to another piece of corn bread.

"Well, of course that's what I mean." He eyed his son's corn bread. "But when you consider just how much all of you eat, it cuts into the profits considerably."

"Especially our new doctor, who could always outeat the rest of us," Josh added.

Jake stuffed the last bite into his mouth and turned to him with an exaggerated grin. "Don't forget my superior brain, big brother."

"To match your superior ego." He managed to evade Jake's fist directed at his shoulder while the others laughed.

"I can see that we're going to have to go back to the old days of assigning chores to anyone who can't behave at the table." Their grandfather managed to keep a straight face, though the hint of Irish brogue deepened. "Maybe it's true what they say, boyo. Kids grow older, but never grow up."

Jake smiled at his brothers. "I think the saying really goes like this. Our parents and grandparents only grow older, not better."

After another round of laughter, Cole conceded. "Okay. So we're all going to have to pull together. Right now, Big Jim and I are planning on driving up to the hills to see what the wranglers need. That leaves the barn chores for the three of you to divide up."

"We've got it covered," Quinn assured him.

"I can help," Cheyenne said. "I can drive back to my place later to see how the cleanup is progressing."

Quinn drained his cup and set aside his napkin. "If I'm caught up with my chores, I'll join you."

By mutual consent they began pushing away from the table and depositing their dirty dishes in the sink before heading toward the mudroom to prepare for the day.

"We have plenty of spare boots and work gloves," Jake called.

Cheyenne eyed the neat shelves. "Thanks. I'm sure I can find what I need."

She slipped into a pair of boots and chose a pair of work gloves before trailing the others toward the first barn.

Picking up a shovel, she worked alongside Quinn mucking stalls and loading the straw and dung into a cart.

It was, she thought, good to be able to work again.

There was something solid and right about tending to daily chores. And best of all, after they had shared a fine meal and a lot of laughter, the jokes and conversation continued between Quinn and his brothers. Though they often spoke about their experiences growing up, they took the time to explain, and she never felt like an outsider.

What she liked best about their reminiscences was the glimpse she was given into their early years. She could see the esteem in which Quinn was held by his younger siblings. Despite all the teasing, they absolutely trusted his judgment and really enjoyed his company.

As for Josh and Jake, she began to see, through their childish antics, just how independent they'd been forced to become, after the sudden, wrenching disappearance of their mother. Though they never mentioned her, their loss colored all their lives.

From their stories she began to see three tough little boys who learned, earlier than most, that nothing in this world was certain. And because life was so fleeting, they began taking risks that would have caused most boys their age to run home and hide behind their mothers' skirts.

For the next several hours the four of them fell into an easy rhythm as they tackled the routine chores with equal parts of energy and good humor.

And all the while, they continued regaling Cheyenne with hilarious, and sometimes poignant, tales from their childhood.

CHAPTER FOURTEEN

———◆———

Cheyenne and Jake were spreading fresh straw in each stall. Josh was busy filling troughs with water. Quinn was emptying a sack of oats while regaling all of them with yet another wolf tale.

His stories were all fascinating. Cheyenne could have listened for hours. She loved the image conjured in her mind of Quinn alone in the wilderness, charting the path of wild creatures.

She paused in her work to fold her arms atop the pitchfork. "How did your fascination with wolves get started?"

"Who knows?" Quinn gave an expressive shrug.

Seeing it, Jake looked up. "Maybe he won't tell you, but I remember it as if it were yesterday. It was an incident from our childhood." He described the den, the litter of wolf pups, and the absolute delight he and his brothers felt at being allowed to play with them without restraint.

Caught up in the story, Cheyenne smiled dreamily. "What an amazing gift, to have beautiful, wild creatures all to yourselves, without any threat."

She saw Quinn's quick frown.

Jake shook his head. "No threat from the adult wolves. Mama wolf wasn't there at first. But we could see her returning with a fresh kill just as we were leaving."

"Good timing," Cheyenne said.

"Yeah. We thought so, too." In vivid detail Jake continued the story, recounting the sound of rifle shots and the scene of carnage they encountered when they raced back to the den.

Cheyenne covered her mouth with a hand. "Oh, that's just awful. And all of you so young and unable to express your outrage to that rancher."

"That was the worst part, I think," Jake said. "It was so soon after our mother's ... disappearance, and we were all hurting for that mother wolf and her babies."

Cheyenne heard the slight hesitation in Jake's voice. It didn't seem that he, like Quinn, had ever fully come to terms with that painful episode regarding the loss of their mother.

Josh chimed in. "For me the worst part was knowing that we couldn't say a thing to Porter Stanford. Big Jim had warned us to stay away from his property. He was a hothead and a loner, and Pa and Big Jim always feared that the smallest thing might set him off and he'd fly into a rampage. So when he finally rode away, we were all relieved. That's when Quinn took charge and started burying the wolf and her pups in their den. The two of us followed his lead and gave him a hand before hightailing it for home."

Cheyenne watched Quinn. Throughout the narrative, his face had gone from cheerful to grim. It was obvious that the memory still had the ability to strike a nerve.

"And so you decided to become a voice for the wolves," she said softly.

He turned to look at her and she could see the gradual change in his features as he relaxed once again. "Yeah. It had a huge impact on my life. As a rancher, I perfectly understand the need to protect my herd from predators. But this land belongs to more than just people. Those wild creatures were here before us. They have to have some rights. Who speaks for them?"

"You do," Cheyenne said simply.

Quinn's gaze flew to Cheyenne's mouth with a raw, impassioned look that had her face growing hot. She had the distinct impression that if they were alone, he'd have dragged her into his arms and kissed her soundly.

"Yes, you do, big bro. And very eloquently, I might add." Jake slapped his arm.

Quinn and Cheyenne continued staring at each other with a look that wasn't lost on his siblings.

With knowing smiles they returned to their chores while Quinn and Cheyenne seemed to fumble about uncomfortably before resuming their work.

"What's that up there?" Cheyenne stood in the doorway of the barn and pointed toward a windswept hillside.

"Come on. Let's take a break from work and I'll show you." Quinn caught her hand and together they set out to climb.

Behind them, Josh and Jake set aside their pitchforks and followed along.

When they arrived at the spot, Cheyenne caught sight of the marble headstone. "It's a cemetery."

"Not just a cemetery." Quinn shared a smile with his brothers. "According to Big Jim, this is hallowed ground. This is where his wife, Clementine, and their five sons are buried."

Cheyenne moved closer to read the inscriptions on the tombstone and then on the five smaller stones, set in a circle around their mother's grave. "Your father was the only one to survive?"

"Yeah." Jake grinned. "He'd tell you only the good die young. But the truth is our pa's one tough survivor."

She noted the fresh slice of corn bread on Clementine's headstone. "What's this?"

"Looks like Big Jim dropped by before heading up in the hills. He does that a lot. Stops by to have a talk with his wife about how things are going and leaves her little tokens of his love."

Cheyenne felt tears sting her eyes. "That's…just so sweet."

Josh nodded. "Big Jim acts like this big, tough cowboy. And he is. But when it comes to his Clementine, he's all mush. He comes up here all the time just to talk, or complain, or brag. He said he wasn't going to allow death to stop him from sharing his life with his best girl."

Cheyenne looked around at the circle of graves and the rustic wooden bench set to one side, where Big Jim could sit and talk with his wife. "I can see why he calls it hallowed ground. You can feel the love here. There's a sense of peace in this place."

The three brothers nodded.

Quinn spoke for all of them. "We all feel it. Every time we come here."

As they made their way down the hill, there was a spring to their steps, as though they'd been somehow invigorated by their visit to their grandmother's grave.

It occurred to Cheyenne that, though Clementine and her five sons had all died before any of them had been born, Big Jim had kept them all alive for other generations by the sheer love in his heart.

It was just one more thing she couldn't help admiring about this amazing family.

"Time for a lunch break," Josh announced.

Cheyenne looked up. "Did your stomach tell you that?"

"Not my stomach. This." He lifted his cell phone from his pocket, letting the others hear the vibration.

"You actually get an alert when lunch is ready?" Cheyenne started laughing while shaking her head in wonder.

"Phoebe and I set it up. It's a lot easier than the old dinner bell." He hooked his shovel on a peg along the wall and headed out of the barn, with the others following suit.

In the mudroom they hosed down their rubber boots before stashing them on the low shelf rigged with drain holes to allow the water to escape.

"I've been meaning to say how clever this is." Cheyenne turned to study the design. "Since I have to rebuild my room anyway, I want to incorporate some of these ideas."

Quinn smiled. "Then you need to talk to Big Jim. After a lifetime of ranching, he has more ideas than a dozen men combined. He and Brand Hudson get their heads together and talk over a need, then figure out how to design something to fit the need. They make a great team. Big Jim sees a problem, the two of them figure out the solution, and Brand comes up with the design. Sometimes it's as grand as a spillway to carry the spring runoff from the mountains into our ponds. And sometimes it's as simple as a shelf with drain holes."

"I hope Brand won't mind if I copy this one."

Quinn shook his head. "If anything, he'll be flattered. And he'll probably want to help you improve on his design."

"I'd welcome his help." She stashed her parka and the borrowed work gloves before washing her hands and then stepping into the kitchen.

She paused in the doorway behind the others. "Oh, something smells wonderful."

As Cheyenne took her place beside Quinn, Ela ladled steaming homemade beef-and-barley soup into bowls while Phoebe passed around a tray of submarine sandwiches brimming with steak, grilled onions, and green pepper.

"Oh." Cheyenne managed a sigh of pure pleasure as she took her first taste. "And I thought breakfast was grand."

Phoebe's smile brightened. "I'm glad you approve."

"Approve?" Cheyenne took another big bite of her sandwich before giving a hum.

Beside her, Quinn chuckled before leaning close enough to whisper, "Music to my ears."

Though her cheeks went pink with embarrassment, within minutes she was humming again as she emptied the bowl of soup and devoured the huge sandwich on her plate.

. . .

"A great lunch, as always." Josh kissed Ela's withered cheek, causing the old woman to blush like a schoolgirl. "Now Dr. Jake and I have an appointment with a patient in the barn."

"See all the money I'm saving you?" his brother teased.

Josh punched his arm hard enough to stagger him. "Considering what it cost Pa for all those years of schooling, it'll probably take him until the age of ninety to earn it back in fees you won't be charging him."

"You're right." Jake returned the punch. "I think I'd better double your fee just to earn my keep."

"Double nothing is still nothing." Josh glanced toward Quinn and Cheyenne. "You two want to come along and watch the genius at work?"

Cheyenne shook her head. "I'm planning on driving back to my ranch to see how the cleanup is going."

Quinn pushed away from the table. "I'll go with Cheyenne."

Phoebe turned from the stove. "Will you be back in time for dinner?"

"I wouldn't miss it." Cheyenne glanced at Quinn for confirmation.

He nodded in agreement.

Outside they climbed into Cheyenne's ranch truck.

With Cheyenne driving, they headed along the curving gravel road that led to the highway.

The storm clouds had been replaced with sunny skies and a temperature that had climbed steadily all morning. Snow melted from fence posts and ran in little rivers along the side of the road.

"I love springtime in Wyoming." Cheyenne gave a deep sigh of satisfaction.

Quinn adjusted his sunglasses before turning to her. "Me, too. And after a winter like ours, we deserve some sunshine."

They drove in silence until she looked over. "I can't tell you how much I like your family. I thought I'd feel awkward. But they've all made me feel so welcome."

"They like you, too."

"How can you tell?"

"I just know." He opened the window, letting the fresh air fill the cab of the truck. It took the ends of her hair and lifted them in a dance about her shoulders. Without thinking he caught a handful and watched as it sifted through his fingers. He'd thought it was black, but it was, in the sunlight, a rainbow of colors, from deepest mahogany to strands of russet and dark brown.

Cheyenne felt the tingle of his touch all the way to her toes.

When she glanced over he was smiling and studying her with a kind of fierce concentration.

"What're you thinking?"

He arched a brow before saying, "That I'd like you to pull over so I could kiss you."

"Quinn…"

He grinned. "You asked. I thought I'd be honest."

"Well, next time try to be a little less honest," she said with a laugh.

"Okay. I'll lie. I really don't want to kiss you. Like any guy looking at a gorgeous woman, I'm thinking about how many ranch chores I ought to be doing right now instead of being here with you."

"You think I'm gorgeous?"

"Did I say that? I meant to say 'average looking.' In fact, very average looking. Doesn't every woman have long, dark hair, a peaches-and-cream complexion, and the most kissable lips in the world?"

"Kissable lips? Really?" She batted her lashes. "I believe I like your lies, Mr. Conway. Tell me more."

He gave her a long, steady look. "Don't let all that flattery go to your head. By today's standards that long, curly hair ought to be straightened with lots of hair goop and that peaches-and-cream complexion really should be plastered over with heavy makeup like those models on magazine covers and those entirely too kissable lips should be painted with candy-apple-red lipstick, so they can sell a million tubes of the stuff."

"You like candy-apple red?"

"I didn't say that. I just said the so-called experts would tell you the whole package could probably use some help." His gaze slowly swept her. "They'd be lying. And then there's that body. It probably took you years of ranch chores to have what Hollywood stars are able to achieve with only a few thousand dollars and a couple of hundred hours with a personal trainer." He shot her a dangerous smile. "How'm I doing?"

"I'm not sure. I'm feeling very conflicted at the moment. Truth or lies? If truth, I'm in trouble. If you're lying, you're very good at it."

"I gave it my best." He put a hand on her arm. "Wow. Wait a minute. Pull over here."

She brought the truck to a halt and looked around in consternation. "What is it? What's wrong?"

"Too much talking. And way too much time spent

looking at you." He unclicked her seat belt and drew her across the seat and into his arms. Against her mouth he growled, "Like I said, the only thing I really want to do is to kiss you. Now."

Before she could utter a word of protest he lowered his lips to hers. Caught by surprise, she could only give a quick little gasp before his mouth captured hers.

The kiss was as hot and hungry as the look she'd seen in his eyes just moments before. A kiss that was all fire and flash and sizzle. The mere touch of his lips on hers had sparks igniting between them.

Oh, his clever lips. So warm and firm as they moved slowly, deliberately, on hers, engaging her fully before she was even aware of what she was doing.

The arms that held her were so strong she couldn't have resisted if she'd tried. Not that she wanted to resist. Not when there was so much pleasure here in his embrace, where she could feel his wild, unsteady heartbeat inside her own chest.

He kissed her with a measured, steady patience that had her blood heating and her bones melting like wax to flame.

"Thanks. I needed that." He spoke the words against her lips, nibbling and teasing the corner of her mouth as he did.

She made a sound that could have been a gasp or a laugh. "My pleasure." She could feel her head swimming. It had all been so sudden. He'd caught her completely by surprise.

"No, ma'am. The pleasure was all mine." He lifted his head and the smile he gave her had her heart melting like the snow outside their window.

She pressed her palm to his cheek. "I have to admit, that was . . . very satisfying."

"Speaking of satisfying . . ." His smile grew. "I know what could make us feel even better."

"I think I'm afraid to ask."

"We could pull the truck behind those trees up ahead and take this a whole lot further."

"I just bet we could." She gave a small laugh and wondered if he could hear how breathless she felt. "Nice try, Conway."

With an effort she pushed away and settled herself behind the wheel before fastening her seat belt.

"I take it that's a no." He reached over to play with the ends of her hair.

A series of shivers raced along her spine. The man definitely knew what he was doing. "A really big, fat no."

"Can't blame a guy for trying."

As she put the truck in gear she was forced to take several very deep breaths before her poor heart returned to its normal rhythm.

She glanced at her hands on the wheel and was relieved to note that they appeared steady.

A very good sign that she appeared to be in control.

There was no sense in letting him know just how tempting his offer had been, and how hard it had been for her to refuse.

As for control, she was hanging on to hers by a thread.

CHAPTER FIFTEEN

—◆◆◆—

As Cheyenne turned the truck onto the lane leading to her ranch, she fell silent. The closer she got, the more quiet she became.

Even though she thought she was prepared, the first sight of her fire-damaged home was a terrible blow to her heart.

Debris was strewn about the yard. The misshapen remains of the hot-water heater and furnace had been piled into one of the hay wagons. Several wranglers, apparently brought down from the high country to assist in the cleanup, were busy tearing out charred walls and flooring. The back door had been removed, and in the unheated utility room icicles hung from the charred beams.

Cheyenne brought the truck to a stop but made no move to step out.

Seeing the stricken look on her face, Quinn was out in a flash, circling the truck and opening the driver's side door. Taking her hand, he kept hold of it as they walked side by side toward the house.

"Remember that this is only the first step. Before things can get better, they'll probably get much worse."

She shook her head in denial. "I can't imagine anything worse than this, Quinn."

"It's superficial." He pointed. "The structure is still sound. With new floors, new walls, new windows, and new appliances—"

He heard her deep sigh of impatience.

"I know. It sounds like a lot, but think of this: As you move forward, you get to incorporate any changes or improvements that you've ever wanted and wished you had."

"Like the conveniences I saw in your mudroom."

"Exactly. In the words of Big Jim, turn this disaster into the deal of a lifetime. Make it a winning proposition."

She squeezed his hand. "Okay. I get it. Think like a Conway."

"That's it."

She took a deep breath. "Now to see what progress has been made."

They stepped inside, walking gingerly over floors littered with pieces of drywall and charred wood. The walls were being stripped down to the studs.

In the midst of the chaos stood Wes Mason, directing a crew of wranglers.

He looked over. "Hey, Cheyenne. Quinn. The insurance appraiser is inside with Austin."

Cheyenne and Quinn moved past the workers and, finding the kitchen empty, climbed the stairs to find the inspector, along with Austin, in the upper hallway.

"Hey, Cheyenne." Austin turned to the man beside him. "Lyle, this is the ranch owner, Cheyenne O'Brien."

Cheyenne offered a handshake.

"Lyle Worthy, Miss O'Brien." The man wore a heavy parka and work boots. Thick, round glasses gave him an owlish appearance as he stared around at the destruction. In his hands was a clipboard on which he had already made several notations.

"Lyle, this is Quinn—"

"Conway." The inspector stuck out his hand while explaining to the others, "I've known Quinn and his family for years. I guess there isn't anyone in these parts that hasn't met one or more of the Conways."

The two men greeted each other before the inspector returned his attention to his clipboard. "Austin was just answering my questions, Miss O'Brien. Now that you're here, you can help me fill in some blanks."

"I'd be happy to."

As they descended the stairs the inspector said, "I'd hoped to have a look before the debris was removed, but your men got an early start and I was delayed. Because the furnace and hot-water heater were removed before I got here, I can't be certain just how or why the fire started, but I can tell you that it started in your utility room. For the record, Wes Mason told me that there were what appeared to be charred rags near the furnace, but they'd been removed along with the rest of the debris and nobody can seem to find them. Without them, I'm unable to conduct tests to see if an accelerant may have been used."

"You think this was deliberately set?"

He shook his head. "I'm not saying that at all. This is a working ranch. Rags are frequently left after a cleanup.

But a test could have told me if there was a foreign substance on them."

When they reached the kitchen Lyle Worthy paused to look at his clipboard. "My report will state that a person of interest was spotted nearby shortly before the fire started."

"A person of interest?"

He peered at Cheyenne over his glasses. "Deacon Vance."

She gave a quick shake of her head. "Deke's family ranch isn't far from here. Several of us share open rangeland. He has every right to be seen nearby."

"My job is to report everything of interest. If there is even a hint of arson, I would be remiss if I left anything out of my report."

Cheyenne nodded. "Of course. I understand. But I know Deke and his family. He would have no reason to want me harmed."

Lyle dipped his head and gave her another long look over the rim of his glasses. "Austin tells me that Deacon Vance was caught stealing from your family, and that he was ordered to stay away."

"That was several years ago. Since then there's been no contact between us. Besides, arson is quite a leap from petty theft."

"Two hundred dollars isn't petty. And most criminal acts progress from something small to something much bigger. His name will remain in the report I send to my home office."

In silence, he walked around the kitchen area before returning to the utility room.

Satisfied, he offered his hand to each of them before

turning to Cheyenne. "I understand that you're forced to live away from home until heat and hot water can be restored. I'll authorize a payment as soon as I return to town so that you can begin rebuilding immediately."

"Thank you. I'm grateful for the help."

"That's my job, Miss O'Brien. Good luck." He nodded toward the pile of debris in the hay wagon. "If you happen to find those rags, bag them and send them along to me for lab tests. That would certainly help me get a report back to you."

When he was gone, Cheyenne turned to Wes. "Thanks for getting on this cleanup so quickly."

"It was Austin's idea. He was the driving force behind getting everything started. But we all wanted to help in any way we could." He closed a hand over her arm. "How're you holding up?"

"I'm fine." She managed a smile. "I'm glad you and Micah persuaded me to go to Quinn's ranch. I can't imagine trying to live here while it's like this."

"Yeah. It's pretty much a total mess. Have you contacted a builder?"

She shook her head. "Big Jim gave me the name of a friend of his in Paintbrush who'll give me a fair price. I plan on stopping in there today on our way back to Quinn's place."

"That's good. If the builder is a friend of Big Jim Conway, you can be assured that he'll take good care of you."

He nodded toward the stairs. "If there's anything you want to retrieve from your room, you'd better do it now. We're going to have to tear out those stairs before the day is through. After that, except for a ladder, the upper floor will be cut off until a builder replaces the staircase."

"Thanks, Wes." Cheyenne disappeared up the stairs.

A short time later she descended the stairs carrying a bulging suitcase.

Seeing it, the foreman said, "If you find that you need anything more, just give a holler. I can have one of the wranglers drive it over to the Conway ranch."

"Thanks, Wes. I'll be staying at Quinn's ranch, but I plan on spending most days here. Between the ranch chores and the renovation, I can't afford to be gone too long or things will start to pile up and bury me."

Wes patted her arm. "You can count on us to pick up the slack."

"I know. And that means the world to me." As she turned toward the door Quinn took the suitcase from her hands.

Wes walked outside with them.

While Quinn was stowing her suitcase in the back of the truck, Micah drove out of the barn in the ranch's stake truck.

Spotting Cheyenne, he sped toward them and parked behind her vehicle before climbing down from the driver's side.

Leaning heavily on his cane, the old man rested a hand on her shoulder and studied her a moment. "You're looking much better today. How're you feeling?"

"Better than the last time you saw me," she said with a laugh.

That had Micah smiling. "Nothing like a good night's sleep to put everything right."

"I don't know about making everything right, but at least it seems less shocking than it did when it first happened."

"And every day it will get a little better." He turned to Quinn. "How's your family, wolf whisperer?"

Quinn grinned at the nickname. "They're all fine. My father and grandfather remember you, and they send their good wishes."

"That's nice to hear. They were good men to work for." His eyes twinkled as he turned back to Cheyenne. "Getting spoiled over at that fine, big ranch?"

"You bet."

He quirked one bushy brow. "And the food?"

"Not nearly as good as your cooking, Micah, but I'll just have to make do until I move back home."

Beside her, Quinn swallowed back his smile. It was easy to see that she was treading carefully around the old man's feelings.

Austin glanced from Cheyenne to Quinn. "So how does it feel to be staying on the biggest ranch in Wyoming?"

Cheyenne laughed off his remark. "I don't know if it's the biggest, but I can admit that my first day there I could have easily lost my way. There are an awful lot of rooms in that big house." She turned to Quinn with a smile and laid a hand on his. "I think you said there are sixteen or more."

He shrugged. "I'm not sure. I'll leave it to you to count them."

Austin stared pointedly at her suitcase in the back of the truck. "That tells me you're not planning on coming home any time soon."

Cheyenne shrugged. "Just some personal stuff. I haven't set a timetable on my return. But I figure, if I have to be away from home, I'll take my home with me."

That had Micah nodding in agreement. "No matter how comfortable you get over at the Conway place, I'm betting you won't be able to stay away for even one day."

"You'd win that bet." She brushed a kiss on his cheek.

"Come on," Micah called to Austin. "If we're going to head to town, we'd better get moving." He tossed the keys to the younger man before they settled themselves in the stake truck and drove off.

Cheyenne postponed her departure to pay a visit to the barn to check out the cow and her calf. Satisfied that the calf was thriving, Cheyenne looked around and noted that the chores had already been tended to.

"I guess there's nothing for me to do here."

Quinn grinned. "You don't sound too happy about that."

She flushed. It was difficult to explain how she felt. She was proud of the way Wes and Micah and the crew had stepped up to the added chores, but it left her feeling oddly deflated. As though she weren't really needed here. "I'm glad everyone's pulling their weight. I guess we'd better head out." She turned toward her truck.

After calling their good-byes to Wes and the wranglers, she and Quinn drove slowly away.

Until they reached the main road, Cheyenne kept glancing in the rearview mirror.

Beside her, Quinn arched a brow. "Afraid it will disappear unless you keep it in sight?"

She gave an embarrassed laugh. "Mind reader. How did you know that's what I was thinking?"

"There's nothing quite like our own home. Whether it's . . . the biggest ranch in Wyoming, or charred ruins, it tugs on the heartstrings."

She noted the slight note of sarcasm that crept into his tone and realized that Austin's remark had rankled more than Quinn had let on. "Yeah. Home is...for better or worse, our safe refuge."

At her words Quinn frowned as a familiar thought, which had been a constant in his life, flashed unbidden into his mind.

Why would a mother, with a loving husband and children waiting anxiously for her, leave a grand home, with every comfort imaginable, and never return?

Had Seraphine Conway been so desperately unhappy that she had fled without so much as a good-bye to those who loved and needed her?

Or had she been taken against her will? Had she raged helplessly against the forces that had abducted her?

Was she raging still?

He blinked, struggling to banish the negative thoughts from his mind. He'd waged these arguments countless times through the years. And always, the questions had no answers. There was no logical explanation for what had happened.

"You're awfully quiet."

He looked over to find Cheyenne watching him.

He carefully composed his features. "Just thinking about home, and how it calls to us."

Cheyenne averted her gaze, keeping her focus on the road ahead.

She'd been right when she'd said that he wasn't a very good liar.

Wherever Quinn had gone in his mind, the little frown line between his eyes told her that it hadn't been a pleasant place.

"I guess that means you wouldn't like to take a...
detour on the ride home?"

At her words his smile was back, as dangerous as ever.
"If you're offering what I think you're offering, I'd be
more than happy to take that detour, ma'am."

"Just checking to see if you were alive."

He pretended to take his pulse. "Heart's beating. Trust
me. I'm alive. And more than capable of handling a...
detour or two."

At his chuckle she relaxed, grateful that she'd been
able to bring a smile to his lips.

She found herself hoping that the dark thoughts that
had plagued him were gone for good. Just as suddenly,
she found herself wondering why it should matter to her.

Though she didn't want to probe her feelings too
deeply, it occurred to her that she was beginning to care
about this man's many moods.

That knowledge was troubling. It wasn't at all like her
to want to get up close and personal with a man she hardly
knew.

And yet there were times, when Quinn Conway looked
at her in a certain way, that she felt as though she'd known
him for a lifetime.

Chapter Sixteen

———◆◆◆———

Cheyenne was smiling. "Remind me about that... detour, after we make a stop in Paintbrush."

"You're going to see the builder my father recommended?"

She nodded and veered off the road onto the highway leading to Paintbrush.

She'd always loved this little town, with its collection of stores and shops along a sleepy little main street. The older ones, many of them weathered wood buildings, proclaimed the services of Thibalt Baxter's Paint and Hardware, Dr. April Walton's Family Practice and Clinic, and Flora's Diner, serving the hottest chili fries in the state. A small, square building with big glass windows overlooking the street bore a peeling sign that said: ODDS N ENDS.

Both Cheyenne and Quinn read aloud the faded words on the sign, "If we don't have it, you don't need it," and burst into laughter.

Beyond that were small frame houses, and on a hill

overlooking the town stood the Paintbrush Church, an old brick building that had served the town for over a hundred years.

The Paintbrush High School sported a new football field and track, compliments of a fund drive that had spurred the citizens and surrounding ranchers into sprucing up the tired old building, as well. The bricks had been tuck-pointed, the windows replaced with newer, more efficient ones, and the newly shingled roof glistened in the sunlight.

At the very end of town was a fairground that boasted several wooden warehouses, pens, and a track with a viewing stand where an annual rodeo was held. Ranchers for hundreds of miles took precious time away from ranch chores to pit their skills against one another and the few celebrities who traveled the rodeo circuit to earn awards and enhance their chances for the big time.

The builder's office shared space with an insurance office and a barber/beauty shop.

Cheyenne pulled the truck into a parking lot across the street, and she and Quinn made their way to the office.

The front room was empty. They followed the sound of hammering to the back room.

A man paused in his work and peered from his perch on a ladder. "Can I help you?"

"Rusty Perry?" Cheyenne asked.

"You got him."

"I was given your name by Cole Conway."

He climbed down from the ladder and spotted Quinn standing behind her. "Hey, Quinn."

"Rusty."

The two shook hands.

Quinn handled the introductions. "This is Cheyenne O'Brien."

"Miss O'Brien." The builder's skin was freckled, and though his hair was threaded with gray, it still bore traces of red. He wore a faded shirt with the sleeves rolled above his elbows. At his waist was a tool belt. "Cole phoned me this morning and told me about the fire at your ranch. He said to expect you in the next day or two."

Cheyenne smiled. "Well, that was good timing. My crew is already cleaning up the mess. I was hoping you could take a drive out to my place and give me an esti-mate for rebuilding."

"Sure thing." He led the way up front to his desk. "Give me directions to your place and I'll be there tomorrow."

After a few more details and handshakes all around, she and Quinn walked from the building.

As they were making their way to her truck a figure stepped out of the barbershop and stood blocking their way.

For a stunned moment Cheyenne and the man merely stared at each other in silence.

It was Cheyenne who found her voice first. "Hello, Deke."

"Cheyenne."

"Deacon Vance, this is Quinn Conway."

The two men gave a nod of acknowledgment, but nei-ther of them offered a handshake.

Deacon Vance was tall, well over six feet, his dark hair freshly cropped close to his head. He held a wide-brimmed hat in one hand. The other was fisted at his side.

"I just left the barbershop, where Austin Baylor was busy telling everyone in the place that Chief Ever-ett Fletcher would be paying me a call. It seems some-one reported seeing me near your place just before a fire ripped through your house and I'm now the prime suspect in arson."

"Deke..."

He held up a hand to stop her. "Just a yes or no." His eyes narrowed on her. "Is that true?"

Cheyenne swallowed. "If it's arson..."

"Yes or no, Cheyenne."

She looked away, hating the mixture of pain and anger in his eyes. "Yes."

His furious gaze swung to Quinn, then back to her. "He said you're now staying at the Conway ranch until your house can be restored, and that he and your crew are running things while you're away. Austin even bragged that he's family now. He referred to your father as his dad."

She nodded. "Deke, I want you to know—"

He raised his hand, still clenched into a fist, stopping short of her face. His voice was tight with barely contained fury. "I guess I know all I need to."

He started away, then turned back to add, "Cheyenne, the day will come when you'll be sorry."

Quinn took a menacing step toward him, his eyes narrowed. "Is that a threat?"

Before Quinn could reach out a hand to him, Cheyenne caught it between both of hers and held tight.

Deke barely glanced in Quinn's direction, keeping his gaze fixed on Cheyenne. "Just stating a fact. You're making a big mistake."

He crossed the street and climbed into a battered red truck.

Quinn looked down at their clasped hands, his frustration evident in his tone. "Why did you stop me? That guy was making threatening noises."

"The last thing I wanted was an ugly scene right here in the middle of Main Street. Deke's hurt and angry. It can't be easy to learn about something like this in front of half the town." Her voice lowered to a whisper. "I wish Austin hadn't gone public with this. If Micah had been there"—she nodded toward the barbershop—"instead of ordering supplies, he wouldn't have allowed Austin to broadcast the news."

"I agree that this should be Chief Fletcher's job, not Austin's." Quinn followed the direction of her gaze and could see the object of their discussion seated in the barber chair, laughing with the customers. "It's too late now. He's let the genie out of the bottle. There's no way to put it back." He touched a hand to her shoulder. "You want a coffee or something before we head home?"

She shook her head, unwilling to glance right or left at the people who passed by. She felt sick at heart, and more than a little dazed by this unexpected public confrontation.

"I'll drive," Quinn said.

Numbly she handed him the keys. He held the passenger door and she climbed in.

As their truck moved along the main street, she stared at the shops and buildings without really seeing them. All she could see was the pain and anger etched in the face of a man who had once been her brother's best friend.

When had it all gone so terribly wrong?

"Want to talk about it?" Quinn asked quietly.

She spoke haltingly, as she struggled to sort out her feelings. "Even after all that's happened, I've been trying to defend Deke. It isn't easy believing that a lifelong friend of my family could betray us. But there's no denying his anger. Deke really wanted to lash out at something."

"Or someone," Quinn muttered.

Her head came up sharply. "Are you suggesting that he might have hurt me if I'd been alone?"

Quinn shook his head. "I'm just saying that I saw a man ready to explode."

They drove in silence as they left the town behind and found themselves once more on the open road.

The melting snow was now a river, running along the edges of the highway, flooding across the pavement in spots.

Cheyenne slipped on her sunglasses, telling herself that the moisture in her eyes was the result of too much sunlight.

Quinn fiddled with the radio until he found some soothing oldies. With the windows down and the fresh air blowing about the cab of the truck, Cheyenne couldn't help keeping time with Neil Diamond singing about sweet Caroline.

Quinn changed the words, replacing them with *sweet Cheyenne* until she could no longer hold on to her sad thoughts.

"Feeling better?" He tugged on a lock of her hair.

She gave a nod of her head. "Life is crazy, isn't it?"

"Yeah." He carefully avoided any mention of their encounter with Deke Vance. "What did you think of Rusty Perry?"

"A really nice guy. I don't know why, but I'd been expecting to have to answer a hundred questions before getting started on rebuilding."

"Don't worry," Quinn said with a laugh. "I'm sure you'll be sick of all the questions before it's over."

As they started along the highway he said, "Now, about that...detour we were talking about earlier."

She made a great show of checking her watch before saying, "Darn. It's too close to dinnertime. If we don't speed things up, we'll risk Phoebe's wrath."

"I'm willing to make the supreme sacrifice."

She laughed. "You may be willing, but I'm a house-guest. I don't dare break any rules or I could find myself out in the cold."

They were still laughing easily together an hour later as they drove under the arch that proclaimed to all who entered that they'd arrived at the Conway ranch.

After parking the truck in the vehicle barn, Quinn retrieved Cheyenne's suitcase and they walked side by side toward the back door and up the steps.

Phoebe and Ela were busy at the stove while the family had gathered around the fireplace at the other end of the kitchen, sipping beer and talking about ranch chores.

"Here you are." Phoebe shot them both a smile when they stepped into the kitchen. When she spotted the suit-case, her smile grew. "I guess that means you're not ready to leave us yet. I was afraid that once you got home you'd change your mind and decide to tough it out. I hope this means that you're planning on a much longer stay."

"I'll probably be here so long you'll be sick of me."

Phoebe laughed. "Weren't you listening? Ela and I are thrilled to have another female in this house." She glanced pointedly at the oversize suitcase. "That looks really heavy."

Cheyenne returned her smile. "I tried to stuff as many things as I could manage in a single trip."

She turned to Quinn. "I'll take that upstairs."

He shook his head and set it aside in a corner of the room. "I'll haul it up for you later."

Cole turned from the fireplace. "Have your men started cleaning up from the fire, Cheyenne?"

"They have. And it's a mess."

"Fires are never tidy," Big Jim remarked.

Quinn picked up a tray of drinks and held it toward Cheyenne.

She snagged an iced tea. "The inspector was there. Lyle Worthy. Very nice and very thorough. On the way back we stopped in Paintbrush and I met with the builder you recommended."

"Rusty? A good man. He'll give you a fair price, and ride herd on his crew to see that the job's done right, and on time."

Quinn helped himself to a longneck. "Rusty's crew did a great job on our last barn."

Big Jim nodded. "He brought the job in ahead of schedule, and under budget. It doesn't get any better'n that."

Cheyenne relaxed. "That gives me some peace of mind." She hesitated slightly before addressing Quinn's grandfather. "I mentioned to Quinn that there are some changes I'd like to make, as long as I'm forced to remodel anyway. And he suggested that I talk to you."

"About what?"

At Phoebe's signal they began settling themselves around the table.

"For one thing, I really like the way the floor slopes in the mudroom, toward that built-in drain."

"And don't forget the drains in the shelves," Quinn added.

"Yes." She nodded. "Those are really clever."

"Thanks." The older man looked pleased. "Feel free to use whatever ideas you want."

"Thanks, Big Jim. But I feel as though I'm stealing from you."

He looked around the table at his family. "Now I'm beginning to feel like a genius inventor. Maybe I should have patented all my clever ideas."

"Oh no." Cole groaned. "After all this flattery, just don't let your head get so big it won't fit through the barn door."

That had the others laughing as they passed platters of roast beef smothered in mushrooms, a bowl of tiny red-skin potatoes, and rolls fresh from the oven.

While the others enjoyed the easy banter, Quinn sat back, aware of something else.

In such a short time Cheyenne had become so comfortable with his family she was able to not only laugh and joke with them but also call his grandfather by name. *Big Jim* had rolled off her tongue as easily as if she'd been calling him that for a lifetime.

As Quinn watched, he saw the softness that came into Big Jim's eyes whenever he looked at Cheyenne.

The comfortable feeling, apparently, was mutual.

For some strange reason that Quinn didn't want to probe too deeply yet, he found that oddly satisfying. It suddenly seemed important that his family like Cheyenne and accept her as one of their own.

Over dinner Cole glanced at the water dripping down the windowpanes. The sunlight reflecting through it created little rainbows across the tile floor.

"If the temperature keeps climbing, the last of the snow could be gone in a week."

"Wishful thinking," Big Jim remarked. "I think the

only way we'll ever see the ground again is if we have a huge rainstorm."

"Careful what you wish for," Josh teased. "Too much rain before the ice melts and we'll have flooding everywhere."

"Wouldn't be springtime without floods," Jake muttered. "And as I recall, big bro, we're always stuck with the ditchdigging, while the old-timers sit high and dry on their machines."

Big Jim bristled. "Who're you calling an old-timer?"

"I think he meant you," Cole said with a wink at Cheyenne. "He certainly didn't mean me. My hair is barely gray."

Big Jim touched a hand to his own white hair. "I may have snow on this roof, but that doesn't mean there isn't still heat in this furnace."

That had everybody laughing.

"Good one, Big Jim." Phoebe handed him a platter.

He turned to his youngest grandson. "I'm going to need you up in the hills for a few days, Doctor."

"Sure thing. Calving?"

He nodded. "Brand and his wranglers were able to keep up with it until now. The birthing's in full season, and they could use an extra pair of hands. I'd like to leave as early as possible."

"I can be ready at dawn."

"Good." The old man's eyes widened as Phoebe began cutting slices from a pie mounded with whipped cream. "Is that banana cream?"

She laughed. "Your favorite. I had some ripe bananas, and knew just how I could use them."

When she handed Cole a skinny slice, he started to

frown. Seeing the others watching him, he forced a smile. "I guess a taste is better than nothing."

"And I have a bowl of sliced bananas to go along with it, instead of ice cream," Phoebe explained.

He waited until the others were busy eating their dessert before dipping his fork in his son's whipped cream.

At a sidelong look from Josh he shrugged. "Just reminding myself what it is I'm doing without for the rest of my life."

"Stop being a martyr, Pa." Jake's cheerful voice caused him to wince. "Just think of all the good you're doing for your heart."

"I will." He stared pointedly at the forkful of confection Jake popped into his mouth. "And I'll remind you of what you're doing to yours."

"Your heart has thirty years over mine."

Cole sat back and smiled. "I'm a patient man. I'll wait until you catch up with me. Then, when you're forced to watch your children eating ice cream, I'll remind you how tasty those carrot sticks are, and how good they are for your tired old heart."

That had everyone howling.

"On that note," Phoebe said with her quiet manner, "why don't we retire to the great room for coffee and other 'healthy' beverages."

They were still laughing as they pushed away from the table and walked to the other room.

Two hours later Jake stifled a yawn. "If I'm going to be up at dawn to help with the calving, I need to grab some sleep."

"I'd better do the same." Big Jim set aside his empty coffee mug and got to his feet.

The others followed suit.

Cheyenne started to get to her feet.

Seeing her cup half-full, Quinn put a hand on hers. "There's no rush. We can stay and finish our coffee."

"All right." While the others called their good nights, she and Quinn lingered by the fire, watching the flames burn low as they sipped their drinks and talked in low tones.

When the household became silent Cheyenne set aside her empty cup. "I'd better get my suitcase."

"I'll get it." Quinn turned away.

She waited until Quinn returned with her luggage. The two of them climbed the stairs and followed along the hallway to her room.

Once there she opened the door and stood aside to allow Quinn to carry her luggage inside.

He paused in the middle of the room. "Where would you like this?"

"How about here?" She indicated a low bench beside the closet.

He set it aside and turned, nearly bumping into her.

When she took a step back his hand automatically shot out, catching her by the elbow.

"Sorry."

"No harm done." She smiled up into his face.

He was smiling when she saw the way his gaze fastened on her mouth. His smile faded, replaced by that fierce look she'd come to recognize.

"Alone at last."

"Quinn..."

"Shhh." He touched a finger to her lips. Just a touch, but she felt the heat curl along her spine, sending tiny ripples of pleasure all through her system.

Without a word he lowered his face to hers and kissed her long and slow and deep. On a sigh she wrapped her arms around his waist and gave herself up to the pure pleasure.

His big hands moved along her back, igniting tiny fires wherever they touched. At once the blood in her veins began to heat and flow like molten lava. She could actually feel herself sinking into all that heat, until she wondered that she didn't just burn to ash.

Quinn lifted his head and framed her face with his hands while he sucked in a breath. "I've been wanting to do that for hours."

She managed a dry laugh. "And here I thought you were having such a good time talking with your family."

"I don't remember a single thing we talked about. Every time I looked at you all I could think about was getting you alone." He ran his hands up and down her arms, his eyes narrowed on her with a look of concentration. "Do you know how good you feel here in my arms?"

"You feel pretty good to me, too."

He glanced over her head. "That bed looks big enough for two."

"Or two dozen."

"I have only two in mind." He dipped his head and claimed her mouth again.

This time the kiss wasn't slow and easy. It was hot and hungry, and full of dark promise as his arms gathered her so close she could feel his erratic heartbeat inside her own chest.

Fully engaged, she wrapped her arms around his neck and poured herself into the kiss.

She knew this was all happening too soon. She'd always been a careful, cautious person who examined things from every angle before making a decision. But there was something about Quinn that kept putting her off her stride.

It wasn't just his charming smile, though he certainly knew how to use it to his advantage. And it wasn't just his dedication to his work, which matched her own and added a layer of attraction.

As the kiss spun on and on she sighed and tried to concentrate on being sensible. But how was that possible when he was holding her like she was some sort of fragile doll and feasting on her like a starving man?

Her poor heart had taken so many somersaults, she was dizzy with need. All thought flew from her mind except one. She wanted what he was offering. And didn't have the will to resist.

For the space of a heartbeat they lifted their heads, as though to clear their thoughts.

In that instant they caught a brilliant flash of strange red light outside the window.

"What was that?" Cheyenne strained for another glimpse, but the night sky was dark. "The moon? A shooting star?"

"More like a flashlight." Quinn stared out the window. "Or..." He swore savagely. "God in heaven. A torch."

And it had just been tossed in the direction of the barn.

CHAPTER SEVENTEEN

───────◆◆◆───────

Fire!"

Quinn raced across the room and tore open her door before cupping his hands to his mouth. "Fire! The main barn!"

Up and down the hallway doors began opening and the family, groggy from having just fallen asleep, became suddenly alert and wide-eyed as they raced toward the mudroom, stepping into boots, snatching up parkas. Cheyenne joined them, her boots untied, jacket unbuttoned, as she ran into the cold night.

At first there was no sign of fire, and Cheyenne found herself hoping that it had all been a mistake. Maybe all this talk of her fire, and the confrontation with Deke in town earlier today, had their imaginations working overtime.

As they rounded the barn, they could see a thin red line gleaming in the darkness.

Amid shouts, the Conway family leaped into action. While Jake and Big Jim began leading the horses from their stalls and outside to a nearby corral, Josh and Quinn began uncoiling a hose and attaching it to a water pump, leaving Cole and Cheyenne to haul the other end of the hose outside.

Once Quinn and Josh managed to crank the pump handle, the force of the spray was tremendous, nearly knocking Cole off his feet, which had been firmly planted in a wide stance.

"Over here," he shouted, and Cheyenne hurried to stand behind him and feed him the length of hose while he aimed the spray on the flame that had appeared to have begun on the roof and was slowly working its way down the back wall of the barn.

Quinn and Josh hurried over to replace Cole and Cheyenne, using their combined strength to move the spray slowly and carefully over the roof and entire back wall of the barn until it had been thoroughly saturated.

When they were satisfied that the fire had been completely extinguished, they moved inside the barn to check for hot spots.

"With the last of the winter hay, this place is a tinderbox," Quinn muttered as he and the others climbed a ladder to the hayloft.

Armed with flashlights and fire extinguishers, they went over every inch of the interior, spraying foam along the wall, wherever they found it warm or smoking, until they were satisfied that there was no chance of the fire springing up again.

When they descended the ladder, Jake stood holding the charred remains of what appeared to be a pitchfork.

The others gathered around.

"This has all the makings of a torch." He pointed to the grooves burned into the wood. "Looks like there was something here, maybe plastic strips that would have melted in the fire, used to hold some rags in place. If the fire hadn't been extinguished so quickly, this would have been consumed by it, and no one would have been the wiser."

"We'll save this for Everett Fletcher," Big Jim muttered. "Whoever tossed this had given it some careful thought. By torching the back of the barn, the fire should have been full-blown before it would even be spotted by anyone in the house. If things had gone according to his plan, the fire would have been too consuming to be stopped and we would have lost the entire barn and our stock before we even knew there was a fire."

He turned to Quinn. "It's a good thing you were still awake."

Quinn's face was grim. "Whoever did this wasn't counting on anyone being left awake."

Jake turned to his grandfather. "What about the horses? Should I bring them back to their stalls?"

He shook his head. "I'd rather they stay in the holding pen. It's only for a night, and I'll feel safer with them out there." He paused meaningfully. "Just in case."

Jake nodded.

Cheyenne stared around at the serenity of the night. A half-moon glowed bright orange in the midnight sky. Snowflakes drifted down, frosting their hair and parkas. A snowy owl hooted in a nearby tree, and overhead a hawk glided soundlessly. Except for the acrid odor of smoke that hung on the air, there was no sign of the tragedy that had almost occurred this night.

Cole's tone was weary. "Let's get inside out of the cold."

They followed his lead, removing boots and gloves and parkas in the mudroom and washing the grime of the fire from their hands, arms, and faces before stepping into the kitchen.

Phoebe and Ela turned from the stove. The wonderful fragrance of freshly brewed coffee filled the room with warmth and cheer.

The table had been set for a meal. Plates heaped with cinnamon toast had been placed on either end of the table, along with a platter of scrambled eggs and thick slices of ham.

It was obvious that the two women had hurried from their beds at the first sign of trouble and had set to work immediately in the kitchen.

The family took their places around the table.

As she circled around, filling mugs with steaming coffee, Phoebe laid a hand on Cole's shoulder. "Are you all right?"

Instead of a reply, he merely patted her hand and lifted his cup to drink.

Quinn glanced toward Cheyenne, who stood alone in the doorway, looking close to tears. From the look in her eyes it was obvious that the enormity of what had just happened was descending upon her like a dark cloud of doom.

"Hey, Cheyenne, what's wrong?" He started to scrape back from the table when her words stopped him in his tracks.

"I'm so sorry. I never intended this to happen."

"What...?" He glanced around the table, where their food lay forgotten as his family stared at her in silence.

"You're such good people. You don't deserve this. And it's all my fault."

"You're not making any sense, girl." Big Jim started toward her, but she held out an arm.

"Don't you see? It's just like before. I can understand him wanting to hurt me, but I had no right to bring this to your doorstep."

"Him?" Big Jim looked toward Quinn. "What's this about?"

"Deke Vance." Quinn's tone was flat as he fought to keep the anger from his voice. "When Cheyenne and I stopped in Paintbrush today, there was an ugly confrontation. Deke found out from Austin Baylor that he was a suspect in the fire at Cheyenne's ranch. He was furious that it was made public knowledge, and told her she'd be sorry."

Cheyenne stood very straight and still, fighting to keep her tenuous emotions in check in front of these people. "And now I've made all of you a target of his anger, as well."

"You haven't done anything. This isn't your fault." Big Jim crossed to her in quick strides. He took both her hands in his and held them tightly when she tried to pull away. His voice lowered with feeling. "We'll turn this over to Everett Fletcher and let him take it from there."

She shook her head. "You're a hundred miles from town. Chief Fletcher can't be here to see that it doesn't happen again."

"No, he can't. That's our job. The chief's job is to find out where this Deke Vance was tonight. If he doesn't have a clear alibi, the chief can let him know his little game is over."

Quinn's voice was low with fury. "This was no game, Big Jim."

"It is to the guy who tried it. Whoever decided to play this sort of deadly game has to be out-of-control crazy. Crazy enough to think he can win."

The old man led Cheyenne to her place at the table. Beside her, Quinn caught her hand, holding it firmly while the others began passing the platters of food.

She felt the warmth of his touch and was oddly comforted by it.

As the others ate she sipped strong, hot coffee and willed herself to relax and let go of the ripples of tension that still throbbed at her temples.

"You haven't eaten a thing, Cheyenne."

At Phoebe's words she gave a shake of her head. "Sorry. I'm not hungry."

Quinn spooned a small helping of scrambled egg and ham on her plate. "A little food will settle the nerves."

"You think so?" She managed a weak smile.

"Yeah. Now eat."

"Yes, sir." In silence she managed a few bites.

Though she was reluctant to admit it, the food helped. Her energy was restored, and with it a renewed sense of purpose.

It would be, she realized, a relief to report this to the police chief and let him deal with it.

While she ate, the others talked in low tones about their plans for the coming day. It seemed to ease tensions around the table to consider it as just another workday.

Cole glanced at his family. "I think it's time we all try to get some sleep. We've got a full day ahead of us." He pushed away from the table and the others followed suit.

Quinn, Josh, and Jake held back for a moment. After a whispered conversation, Quinn caught Cheyenne's hand and walked with her up the stairs.

At the door to her room he opened it, then paused. "Are you going to be able to sleep?"

"I'll try. What about you?"

"I'll be fine." He brushed a quick kiss over her mouth.

For a moment he seemed about to gather her close and draw out the kiss. Just as quickly he took a step back.

When she walked past him, he pulled the door shut.

She listened to his receding footsteps and told herself that she wasn't disappointed. What they'd shared earlier had been spontaneous and wonderful. And though she was greedy enough to wish he would have wanted to stay long enough to offer her the warmth and comfort of his embrace, she knew it was best this way. They both needed time to clear their minds.

Though the Conway family had been vehement in their argument that she wasn't responsible, a lingering trace of guilt remained.

She shivered and hugged her arms about herself as she paced the length of the room and back.

The fire at her ranch could have been an accident. But a second fire was no coincidence.

She thought about the things her father had said after Deke was caught with the money in his pocket. There was a fine line between love and hate, and the ones we trusted the most were also the ones who could cut us deeply by betraying that trust.

Today in Paintbrush, Deke's anger had been palpable. He'd been humiliated publicly in front of friends and neighbors. That would cause anyone to want to lash out.

But to burn a neighbor's barn? A neighbor whose only offense was to offer her shelter? That was much more than simple betrayal. This seemed more an obsession. A deep and abiding hatred.

Was Deke capable of such searing, hateful emotions?

He had been Buddy's friend and had been welcomed into their home like a member of the family. He had also, when they had been much younger, let her know that he'd wanted more than her friendship. When she'd gently told him that she didn't feel the same way about him, he had accepted her rejection like a gentleman.

At least she'd believed so at the time.

Had this all been building inside him? Was that why he had betrayed her family by stealing from them?

And now this.

She paused, staring into space, before coming to a decision. First thing in the morning she would have to tell Chief Fletcher about her latest suspicions. It didn't seem possible that a long-ago teenage crush could escalate into something so hideous, but until this was resolved the police had the right to know everything.

Because the thought of lying quietly in bed wasn't possible, she continued pacing while her mind worked through the various knots and tangles tormenting her.

Quinn descended the stairs in the dark and made his way unerringly to his father's office at the far end of the house.

Inside, Josh and Jake were waiting. Without a word the three brothers headed toward a locked cabinet, where they removed rifles and ammunition. In the mudroom they dressed for warmth before heading out to the barn.

Once inside the barn Quinn withdrew a coin from his pocket. "Call it."

"Heads," Josh said.

Quinn flipped the coin and the three of them stared.

Josh climbed to the hayloft and took up a position beside the tiny window that overlooked the snow-covered range. From there he had a clear view of anything that dared to move across the far side of the ranch.

"Again," Quinn said tersely.

"Tails."

Quinn flipped the coin a second time, and Jake climbed to the rafters, settling himself beside the window overlooking the foothills of the Tetons.

Quinn closed the big barn door, leaving it open just enough to give him a view of anyone approaching from the front.

With their rifles cocked and ready, the three brothers were prepared to watch and wait throughout the long, dark hours until morning light.

As the silence of the night stretched on and on, Josh's voice drifted down from the hayloft.

""Okay, Bro. So what's with you and Cheyenne?"

"Yeah." Jake's voice sounded even more distant. "The two of you are looking really cozy."

Quinn sucked in a breath. "I don't know how to answer that."

"You want me to make this simple?" Josh's voice was warm with laughter. "Do you like the way she looks?"

"What's not to like?"

"I'll take that for a yes. Your turn, Jake."

Their younger brother's voice drifted down. "Do you like her personality?"

"She's funny. She says what's on her mind. She knows her way around a ranch. And she's sexy as hell."

"Another yes." Josh paused. "Okay, we know you like her. The question is, do you more than like her?"

"I think so."

"You think so?" Jake's voice sounded incredulous. "We're talking the *l* word, Bro."

That had Quinn snorting with laughter.

"Don't laugh. I'm serious. Do you love this woman?"

Quinn went perfectly still. "I hadn't planned on it. But now..." He shrugged, determined to deny what he was feeling. "We all know I'm a loner. My lifestyle doesn't exactly lend itself to being half of a couple. I'd say it's way too soon."

"Too soon for what?"

"Hell. We haven't known each other long enough to even learn our favorite colors, foods, hobbies. I don't think it's supposed to happen this way."

"Maybe it runs in the family."

"What's that supposed to mean?"

Josh's voice drifted down from the loft. "Jake's right. We've all heard the story about Pa and his Seraphine. He took one look at this exotic dancer, and said it was all over. He'd never be able to look at another woman. And he never has."

"Yeah." Quinn gave a snort of disgust. "Well, if it runs in the family, we'd better run the other way."

Josh shifted in the hay. "Okay, so they didn't get their happy ending. But I'm just saying, it was love at first sight, and I doubt that either of them would have it any other way."

Quinn stared out at the darkness and thought about

how Cheyenne felt in his arms. With one touch she could set him on fire in a way no other woman ever had before. They'd been a heartbeat away from falling into her bed.

Just thinking about it had him aching with need. Given the choice, he'd be up in her room right now, doing exactly what they both wanted.

He liked being with her. Loved the sound of her voice. Even enjoyed the fact that she hummed while she ate. It was one of those small, endearing traits that really got to him.

"Quinn…"

At Jake's voice he shouted, "Shut up and keep watching."

"I was just going to say that I like her. I think having a sexy hot babe in the family wouldn't be hard to take."

"Do you want me to come up there and shut your mouth for you?"

Jake and Josh fell silent. But they both knew from Quinn's tone that there was no fire in that threat.

A sure sign that their big brother had his mind on something other than temper.

CHAPTER EIGHTEEN

Cole and his sons were holding a morning meeting in his office.

This room was as oversize as the rest of the rooms in the house. Located on the far end of the main floor, it had once been used as a playroom. After Seraphine went missing, Cole noticed that his children avoided going near the room. Not that he could blame them. Everything about it exuded the essence of the woman who had poured her heart and soul into it. From the hand-painted stars on a sky-blue ceiling, to the makeshift stage where she'd taught her children to dance and put on little plays, to the trunks of costumes, many of them worn by their mother when she'd been a professional dancer, it was a fantasy-land for a woman-child and her students.

All the world was Seraphine's stage. But this room, more than any other in the sprawling house, bore the stamp of the woman determined to remain active in the arts that owned her heart, even though she was hundreds of miles from civilization.

Now the playroom had been converted into Cole's retreat. It hadn't been an easy decision but, rather, a necessity.

The walls were lined with floor-to-ceiling oak shelves and cabinets. A massive stone fireplace with an oak mantel dominated one wall. In the center of the room were a desk and a leather chair. On the desktop was a framed photograph of Seraphine and her three children in younger, happier days. It was the first thing Cole looked at whenever he sat down. The last thing he looked at before turning off the light and leaving.

Facing the desk were four wing chairs upholstered in muted brown and gray tweed. Deep, manly chairs, suitable for discussions about ranch business.

This was where Big Jim and Cole and his sons spent endless hours each month discussing the operation of the ranch, as well as the coal mines and the oil wells that dotted the western range of their land. Those businesses were operated by companies that leased the land from them for huge sums of money. Though ranching was their great love, they were well aware that the bounty extracted from the earth paid the bills and made it possible for them to have one of the most successful ranches in the country. But no amount of money would persuade them to abuse the land they loved. That was why they insisted on carefully monitoring the mining and oil companies, to assure that the environment was treated with respect.

Cole sat behind his desk, facing Quinn and Josh. "After Big Jim and Jake left this morning for the high country, I had a nice long talk with Everett Fletcher."

"And?" Quinn, freshly shaved, his hair still damp from the shower, studied his father with interest.

Cole's words were clipped. "He intends to get to the bottom of this."

Josh gave a nod of his head. "The sooner the better."

Quinn nodded before saying with a laugh, "I'm not sure how many nights I can go without sleep and still carry my weight around here doing my chores."

Cole studied his sons. Despite their all-night vigil, they showed no sign of sleep deprivation.

"I appreciate what you did. I had half a mind to guard the barn myself." He gave a wry laugh. "But this old body just won't do the things it did twenty or thirty years ago."

"You shouldn't have to." Quinn's smile faded. "If Chief Fletcher doesn't come up with an arrest of the guilty party, we'll just have to rotate some of the wranglers to keep watch during the night."

"Not an efficient way to run a ranch," Cole muttered.

"It might not be cost-efficient, but it's better than the alternative. After seeing what might have happened, we can't afford to be careless." Quinn stood and began to prowl the room. "You realize that Cheyenne was right last night."

They stared at him.

He jammed his hands into the pockets of his faded jeans. "This was no coincidence. A blaze nearly destroyed her house. Now someone tries to burn our barn." He looked from his father to his brother. "How many fires have we heard about in the past year in this area?"

Josh shrugged. "I can't think of one."

"Exactly. Now, within days, we have two."

"That's exactly what Chief Fletcher said." Cole steepled his fingers atop his desk. "So, the next question is why?"

"It's what I've been asking myself all night long." Quinn gave a slow shake of his head. "Like I said, no answers yet."

Cole lifted a hand. "The chief had an interesting theory. What if the target is you, Quinn?"

Quinn looked up with a frown. "What's that supposed to mean? Why would I be targeted?"

"As Everett pointed out, there are ranchers in Wyoming who resent the fact that you've become something of a champion for wolves that are considered dangerous predators."

Quinn nodded. "All right. That makes sense. But how would a rancher know that I was spending the night at Cheyenne's ranch? Don't forget, I was there by accident."

"You could have been followed." Cole stared pointedly at his son. "Can you think of any rancher you may have offended recently?"

Quinn shook his head. "Probably a few dozen."

Cole sighed. "Everett wants you to be careful until he gets this resolved."

"I will. And if I'm not the target, we're back to Cheyenne. But if somebody is after Cheyenne, it may just be—"

Cole cleared his throat and Quinn looked over just in time to see Cheyenne standing hesitantly in the doorway.

"Sorry to intrude." She looked embarrassed, as though she'd heard more than she cared to. "Phoebe told me where to find all of you. And the door was open."

"Come on in, honey." Cole gave her his best smile. "We were just having a little talk—"

"About me." She paused on the threshold, much as she had the night before, after they'd battled the fire.

Quinn's heart went out to her. She looked like a deer run to ground by a hungry wolf.

"As a matter of fact, we were." He crossed the room and caught her hand. In one smooth gesture he led her across the room and to one of the chairs. "We're tossing around a few theories, and we'd like your take on them."

"Theories?" She sank into the chair beside Josh.

Cole smoothly took up the thread of their conversation. "You said last night that you believe you're the target of these fires."

She nodded.

Cole studied her across his desk. "So the question really should be, if you're the target of these fires, why?"

"Because..." She licked her lips. "Last night, after the fire, I started thinking about Deke. I think I should tell Chief Fletcher that Deke had a crush on me when we were younger and I didn't return his feelings." She flushed and looked down when she realized they were all staring. "I hadn't thought about it before, and it seems like a really foolish reason for revenge, but,"—she shrugged—"it's all I can think of."

Quinn turned to his father. "I hope you'll pass this along to Everett."

"I will." Cole nodded. "When I spoke with the chief earlier, he said the first thing on his list today will be to check out Deke's alibi for last night."

Cheyenne sighed.

Cole looked over. "What else is troubling you, honey?"

She gave a slow shake of her head. "Just thinking about all the things that have gone wrong in my life. My brother. My father. The fire..."

Cole shoved away from his desk and walked over to

lay a hand on her shoulder. "You've had more than your share, Cheyenne. But you have to hold on to the thought that better days are coming."

She looked up, eyes shiny. "You mean, if you ruled the universe?"

"Yeah." He chuckled. "If I ruled. In the meantime..." He glanced at his sons. "I figure by now Phoebe and Ela should have something amazing ready for breakfast."

"Oh." Cheyenne jumped up. "That's what I was supposed to tell you. Breakfast is ready."

"Come on, then." Cole put a hand under her elbow, and together they strode from the office, with Josh following.

Quinn trailed at a slower pace, his mind clearly not on the menu.

As always, the kitchen smelled heavenly.

Ela removed a pan of cinnamon biscuits from the oven while Phoebe set platters of scrambled eggs and crisp bacon on the table before lifting a skillet of potatoes fried with onions and peppers from the stove.

"A breakfast fit for a king," Cole remarked as he took his place at the table.

"Or at least a rancher," Phoebe said with a laugh. "Big Jim and Jake won't be joining you. They left hours ago."

"I heard them." Cole shot her a quick smile of thanks as she handed him a steaming mug of coffee. "My father never learned how to tiptoe. I guess Big Jim figures when he's up, everyone should get up."

That had the others laughing and sharing stories of Big Jim's morning rituals, which included, when they were younger, ringing a school bell to alert them that it was time to rise and shine and begin their daily chores.

Cole shook his head. "From what I could see, they had enough supplies in the back of that wagon to feed an army."

"Just filling requests from the wranglers," Phoebe said with a laugh. "Besides the antibiotics Jake packed for the calves, Big Jim asked for a couple of cases of longnecks, some homemade cinnamon rolls, all the fixings for pot roast, and a big pot of chili."

Quinn winked at Cheyenne. "No matter whose ranch they're working on, the wranglers always want the same thing. Beer and eye-watering, gut-burning chili. The spicier the better."

"And the smart cook always gives them what they want," Phoebe said as she circled the table filling their cups.

Cheyenne nodded. "That's exactly what Micah always says."

"Micah?" Ela's head came up sharply.

"Micah Horn. He's my cook and all-around handyman. I don't think there's anything Micah can't do."

Seeing Ela's sharp-eyed interest, Quinn said, "Do you know him, Ela?"

She ducked her head. "Used to. A long time ago."

"Really?" Cheyenne turned to say something more, but Ela was already walking out the back door to the bunkhouse.

When Quinn passed Cheyenne a platter of eggs, she helped herself to some and was soon caught up in a lively conversation about the rapidly disappearing snow.

Like all ranchers, they had the weather uppermost in their minds. The sooner the snow was gone, the better chance newborn calves would have of surviving. With spring rains they could get on with the business of driving their herds toward the lush rangelands in the higher elevations.

It wasn't that the work would be easier. The chores on any ranch were never ending. But the heart of every rancher beat a little faster when the days grew longer, the air warmer, and the nights softer.

Cole glanced over at Josh. "You going to give me a hand today with that tractor?"

"Sure thing." Josh pushed away from the table.

"Afterward, I'm hoping to take the plane up, if the weather cooperates."

Josh grinned at his father. "I figured, with the weather getting gentler, you'd be itching to fly. Where're you headed?"

"Just over the ranch. I'd like a bird's-eye view of the pockets of snow, and how far the herd has wandered. You want to tag along?"

"Yeah. I'd like to see for myself."

Cole turned to Quinn. "What're you up to today?"

"After morning chores, I'll be heading over with Cheyenne to her ranch to see how the cleanup's going."

Cheyenne was quick to protest. "If you're needed here, I can take myself."

Cole lifted a hand to halt her objection. "I've seen you working alongside my family. If you can muck stalls here, Quinn can lend a hand at your place."

Quinn winked at her before turning to his father. "I couldn't have said it better myself, Pa."

It had been on the tip of her tongue to resist, but the Conway charm worked its magic.

She couldn't help laughing. "Thanks. I appreciate it."

And she did. Despite the lingering guilt about their barn fire, she recognized that they were all going out of their way to make her feel completely welcome here.

Just having their respect and friendship lightened her burden considerably.

Of course, it didn't hurt to have Quinn dazzle her with that rogue smile of his. How could she feel anything except lighthearted around this amazing man?

As they were driving away from the ranch, Cheyenne nodded toward a large barn some distance from the others.

"What's that used for?"

"Pa's plane. He had a runway built just beyond the barn for easy liftoff."

She turned to him. "Do you fly?"

He nodded. "We all do. Big Jim insisted. Not that we needed any coaxing. As soon as we were old enough to get our driver's licenses, we qualified for our pilot's licenses."

"With a spread this big, I guess you'd need a plane to keep track of everything."

He adjusted his sunglasses. "How about you? Ever fly?"

She kept her attention on the road. "My dad talked about it, but he never followed through. He used to say that we were so far from civilization, a plane was as necessary as a truck. Maybe, if he and Buddy were still around..." Her voice trailed off.

When they came to a fork in the road, she read the sign and arched a brow. "International Chem?"

"One of our tenants. They lease a portion of our land to mine trona." He chuckled. "When Big Jim first discovered it here on his land, he had never even heard of it."

Cheyenne colored. "I've heard of it, but I'm not sure what good it is."

"Soda ash. If you've ever used bicarbonate of soda, it probably came from the trona mined on our land. This mine alone produces several million tons a year, with no end in sight."

"That's fascinating. How did Big Jim discover what he had inside the earth, and how valuable it was?"

"It started with a couple of oil prospectors, who asked if they could lease a small section of land for drilling." He chuckled. "Their grandkids are very glad they did. One of those old oil prospectors told Big Jim about what else they'd found, and how valuable it was. So he leased another section of land to a company hoping to extract it." Quinn looked over as a thought struck. "You think you might have trona on your land?"

She shrugged. "It's worth a look. It would certainly help pay a few bills."

He nodded. "We'll have a talk with Big Jim tonight. See if International Chem or one of their subsidiaries would be interested in doing a test drill."

As they followed the highway toward her ranch, Cheyenne's mind was mulling the possibilities.

Finding additional value in her land would be like winning the lottery. Of course, finding the Conway family, and especially Quinn, had already made her feel like a winner. Sometimes, when Quinn looked at her as though he meant to devour her, as he was doing now, she got all warm and tingly inside.

He touched a finger to her cheek. "A penny for them."

"Sorry." She hated the blush that rushed to her cheeks. "Too personal to share."

"Well then." There was that smile, sending her heart on a wild ride. "I hope I'm part of your thoughts."

She evaded answering. "Am I part of yours?"

"A big part." He studied her profile as she drove. "You've even managed to slip into my dreams."

"Sorry about that."

"I'm not." Still smiling, he turned to stare at the passing landscape, pleased to see more signs of spring greenery poking up along the roadside.

It wasn't the scenery he was thinking about. The thought of making his dream woman a reality, and of keeping her safe, was uppermost in his mind.

CHAPTER NINETEEN

———◆———

As they drove up the long gravel drive toward Cheyenne's ranch, Quinn pointed to a truck parked outside the house. "Now that ought to make your day a whole lot brighter."

A group of wranglers was busy unloading building supplies, under the watchful eye of contractor Rusty Perry.

"Your father was right on the money about Rusty. I never expected him to move this quickly." She parked behind the line of trucks, and she and Quinn hurried toward the house.

Rusty looked up as they approached and tipped his hat to Cheyenne. "'Morning, ma'am. Thought I'd get an early start, so you won't have to be inconvenienced any longer than necessary."

"Thank you, Rusty. I really appreciate it." She looked around with a smile, noting that the debris had been hauled away.

Rusty led the way inside the now-empty structure.

"Let's start here." He paused in the utility room. "I'd like you to take a look at the blueprints I drew up after we talked. We'll walk through all the changes you suggested, and I'll get your final input before I take this to the county for approval. Once they give me the green light, I can have this roughed in within weeks. If you order your new furnace and water heater, they could be ready for installation at the same time."

While they took another tour of the house, Quinn paused to talk to Micah and Wes Mason.

"'Morning, wolf whisperer," the older man said with a grin.

"Micah. Wes." Quinn shook each man's hand.

"How's our girl holding up?" Wes asked.

"Just fine. She's a strong woman."

Micah shook his head from side to side. "Tell me about it. Her daddy used to say she was the most stubborn female ever born."

"I'd say that's a good thing, considering all she's been through."

Quinn saw the two men exchange a look.

"Okay," Quinn said quietly. "What's wrong?"

It was Wes who broke the silence. "We don't want to hit Cheyenne with more bad news, but…"

"But?" Quinn prodded.

"We've suddenly lost an awful lot of newborn calves."

"It comes with the territory." Quinn nodded toward the snow-covered hills. "Considering how rotten the weather has been."

"This isn't the usual spring loss of a dozen or so, or even a couple of dozen. By my count, nearly fifty newborns have been found dead."

Quinn's tone roughened. "Then the wranglers haven't been doing their job. With snow this deep up in the hills, they ought to be singling out the weakest and keeping them isolated in a holding pen with their mothers until they're past any crisis."

"My wranglers know what they're doing." It was plain that Wes was keeping a tight rein on his anger and frustration. "Most of the dead ones didn't give any sign of being sick or weak. Yesterday they were fine; this morning they were just gone."

"Predators?" Quinn's tone sharpened.

Wes shook his head. "Wolves would haul the carcass back to their den. A few have gone missing, but even more were just left dead and frozen in the snow."

"That doesn't make any sense. The only predator who kills without eating its victim is man."

Wes exchanged a look with Micah.

Quinn looked from one man to the other. "So you both believe this is deliberate."

Wes said between clenched teeth, "I know it for a fact. Those calves had their throats slit."

Quinn muttered a savage oath. "You think Deke Vance is behind it?"

Wes studied the toe of his worn boot. "It's hard for me to wrap my mind around that. Deke grew up on his daddy's ranch just miles from here. He has to know how much the rancher depends on new calves to double his herd."

"Exactly." Quinn's voice lowered with anger. "What better way to ruin an enemy than to destroy his chance to earn a living? I guess if a fire won't drive Cheyenne away, losing her ranch to debt would do it."

Micah's free hand curled into a fist at his side. "I've been around cattle all my life. I can't imagine what kind of man could go around killing healthy calves."

Quinn thought about the angry confrontation in town. "A man filled with rage." He paused, tamping down his own anger. "Have you reported this to Chief Fletcher?"

"I figure I have to run it past Cheyenne first. I wouldn't want her to hear it from the police chief before she hears it from me." Wes stuffed his hands in the pockets of his worn denims. "I hate like hell to have to give her this news on top of everything else."

"It can't be helped. She has a right to know." Quinn glanced toward Cheyenne, descending the stairs behind Rusty Perry. There was an eagerness in her voice, a spring in her step, at the thought of getting her house in order.

Like Wes and Micah, Quinn resented the fact that this latest news would steal even this meager joy from her day.

"Thanks again, Rusty." Cheyenne shook hands with the contractor. "I can't wait to see what you'll do with the plans."

"My pleasure, ma'am. I guarantee that you'll be happy with the outcome."

He called out his good-bye to the others before climbing into his truck and trailing behind the now-empty delivery truck.

Austin ambled out of the barn and joined Cheyenne and the men, who were listening in silence as she described all the changes she and Rusty were planning.

"Rusty said it's an easy matter to slope the cement floor toward a drain, and add a bigger sink and hose attachment. That way we can clean our boots right in the utility room, and then let them dry on custom-built slotted shelves." She added with a laugh, "And before any of you think I'm a genius for dreaming up this plan, I can't take any of the credit. I saw this at the Conway ranch, and learned it was Big Jim's idea."

"Big Jim?' Austin rolled his eyes and grinned at the others. "Sounds pretty cozy to me. What're you calling Quinn's father these days? Big Daddy?"

Cheyenne joined in the laughter. "You can tease me all you want, Austin. I'm not going to take the bait. The day is too perfect to let anything spoil it."

Wes glanced at Micah and cleared his throat before laying a hand on Cheyenne's arm. "Chey, honey, we need to talk."

"Okay. What's up?"

"Not here." He nodded toward the corral beyond the barn. "Why don't we take a walk?"

As he turned away, he couldn't hide the misery that clouded his eyes.

Cheyenne returned from the corral, her movements stiff, her eyes as dark as storm clouds. "Quinn, I won't be going home with you. If you'd like to take my truck back to your place, I'll have one of the wranglers pick it up later."

"I'm not going anywhere." He studied her face, eyes and mouth taut with barely controlled anger. "Have you contacted Everett Fletcher?"

Her head came up sharply. "You know?"

Before he could say a word she turned on Wes. "You told him before telling me?"

Wes nodded. "Sorry, Chey. I needed to vent. I told him while you were talking to Rusty Perry."

She let out a long, deep sigh and touched a hand to her cell phone in her shirt pocket. "I contacted the chief. As soon as he gets here, we'll head up to the hills. I need to see for myself. And he'll want to examine the calves before filing his report."

Wes touched a hand to her arm. "You could go back to the Conway ranch and let me take care of the chief."

"It's my ranch. My herd."

"I know." Wes gave a reluctant nod of his head. "But it's pretty grisly. Some of the wranglers were so upset they had to walk away."

"I'll deal with it." She turned away and walked to the house, moving from room to room in silence.

Quinn remained outside with the others, giving her time to process all that she'd learned. He understood her need to be alone with her thoughts.

When the police chief arrived, Cheyenne, Quinn, and Wes climbed into Everett Fletcher's truck and began the drive into the hills.

As he drove, he said to Wes, "Give me all you've got so far."

While the others listened in silence, Wes filled in the details as the police chief maneuvered the sturdy, four-wheel-drive vehicle along the twists and turns of the snow-and-mud-covered trail.

When they arrived at the site, they stepped out and walked among the lowing cattle.

It was a familiar scene that always tugged at Quinn's heart. The soil soggy underfoot as the snow melted in the afternoon sunlight and was trampled by hundreds of animals. The plume of warm breath in the frosty air. The smell of earth and dung. The sight of calves standing on wobbly legs and cows seeking their errant young as the herd milled about.

Above the din could be heard the more urgent lowing of cows, heavy with milk, searching for their newborns, who were nowhere to be found.

Wes led the chief, Cheyenne, and Quinn to an area of the range ringed by mounds of earth high enough to keep the cattle at bay. As they climbed atop a mound they peered down to see that it was a burial ground, freshly dug, holding the bloody carcasses of calves.

Cheyenne wasn't the only one to gasp. Even the police chief, who had witnessed his share of the seamier side of life, couldn't hide his horror at the scene of carnage.

While the others remained above, Chief Fletcher strode down into the pit and began examining the bodies. When he rejoined them, his lips were a thin, tight line of fury.

"It's just as you said, Wes. Their throats were slashed. This was a deliberate act. And whoever did it wanted that fact to be known."

He strode toward his vehicle, with the others trailing.

Quinn kept his arm around Cheyenne's shoulders and could feel how tightly she held herself, as though afraid that if she should relax the tight grip she had over her emotions for even one moment she would fall apart.

The chief drove almost the entire distance back to her ranch in silence, his eyes narrowed in thought.

When they came to a halt he waited until they'd exited the vehicle before lowering the window.

"My first stop will be at the Vance ranch. Young Deke claimed he was home the night of your fire, Cheyenne, and his father confirmed it. But since then I haven't been able to reach him or his father. There's been no answer at their ranch. Something like this would have taken a man several hours to inflict so much damage, so young Deacon had better have witnesses who'll swear under oath exactly where he's been spending his time, or he'll be answering a whole lot of questions from behind bars."

Quinn's voice was low. "Do you think he's capable of this kind of violence, Everett?"

The chief shrugged. "Hard to believe that any man who's grown up on a ranch could do something like that to helpless animals. But right now he's my prime suspect, and he'd better have an airtight alibi."

As the chief drove away, Quinn turned to find Micah and Austin standing alongside Wes and Cheyenne.

She looked so defeated, Quinn couldn't help wrapping his arms around her and holding her close. At his obvious sign of affection the men stared at the two of them in stunned silence. At the moment, Quinn didn't care if the whole world was watching. He just wanted to offer her a measure of comfort.

Against her temple he muttered, "You okay?"

She stood very still, grateful for the strength of his arms. "I feel...numb."

"Yeah." He looked over her head to where the others were standing and watching them with rapt interest. "I'm going to take her home now."

Austin shot him a look. "Hey, man. This is her home."

Quinn ignored him to speak directly to Cheyenne. "You're in no shape to drive. Give me your keys."

Without a word she dug into her pocket and handed them over.

Quinn helped her up to the passenger side before rounding the truck and climbing up to the driver's side.

With a salute to the others, he put the truck in gear and drove away.

As they started along the highway he shot a look at Cheyenne, her head turned away, the backs of her hands covering her eyes, as if to blot out all thought.

They drove in complete silence.

A short time later he muttered an oath and veered off the highway onto a narrow dirt road.

Cheyenne pulled herself back from her dark thoughts and turned to him with a look of alarm. "What're you doing?"

He didn't reply as the truck began climbing through a heavily forested area.

She leaned back and closed her eyes, trying to get the scene of carnage out of her mind. It was impossible. "Oh, Quinn. All I can see is that burial pit and the mutilated corpses of newborn calves. What sort of madman could do such a cruel, savage thing?"

"I wish I knew."

"I'm feeling overwhelmed. The way I did when Buddy..." Her lips trembled and she couldn't say the word.

She took in a deep breath. "And then, just a year later, my father. It was too much. I felt as though my entire life was spiraling out of control, and there wasn't a thing I could do but hang on."

She reached out a hand and Quinn curled his fingers around hers.

"There were so many days after that when it seemed too much to bear. The pain. The sadness. The emptiness of my life without them. It was all too much. And now, I'm feeling that way again. Like I'm drowning, and there's nobody there to throw me a lifeline."

"I'm here, Cheyenne."

"I know. And I'm so grateful." She clung to his hand.

The truck jolted to a halt, causing her to look up in surprise.

They were high in the hills, parked alongside a small log cabin.

"What ... ?"

"I'll tell you in a minute." Quinn unfastened his seat belt, stepped down, and rounded the truck to open her door.

Taking her hand, he led her inside. "I'll start a fire."

He left her to stare around with interest as he crossed to the fireplace and knelt, holding a match to kindling.

There was a fully equipped kitchen, with a stove and microwave and a rough-hewn table and two chairs. Across the room was an enormous four-poster bed made of logs and covered with a blanket that bore intricate Arapaho designs. A stone fireplace dominated one wall. Beside it, on handmade wooden shelves, stood a number of leather-bound books, binoculars, camera equipment.

When a fire blazed on the hearth, Quinn stood to wipe his hands on his pants, before turning to her. "Welcome to my place."

"Yours?"

He nodded. "I built it years ago. I'd originally intended it as a simple shack. A place to watch wildlife from the safety and comfort of a small, natural building in the forest and record in my journal. Then I decided to enlarge it and make it my home away from home. Whenever I need a refuge, a spot to get away from the world, I come here. It's my thinking place. My private place." He stepped close and caught her hand. "My healing place."

He looked down at their linked hands. "I've never brought anyone here before, but I thought maybe you could use a little healing of your own."

She felt her heart swell with emotion. "Thank you, Quinn. I'm...honored."

He lifted his palm to her cheek. "You're welcome. You can stay here as long as you'd like."

When he started to turn away, she tugged on his hand. "Where are you going?"

"I thought I'd give you some privacy. I understand your need to be alone. Consider this your own private retreat."

She looked into his eyes, narrowed on her with such fierce concentration her heart actually skipped a beat before starting to race.

Without a word she stood on tiptoe to press her mouth to his.

Against his mouth she whispered, "I don't want you to go. I want you to stay here with me."

"I don't think that would be wise." He took a half step back, as though unsure just what she was implying.

"I don't know about wise, but I'm tired of trying to be strong and smart and cautious, Quinn. Right now, all I want is for you to hold me."

His eyes narrowed on her. "I'm not sure I can do that."

Seeing her look of surprise, he added, "I doubt I can hold you and not want to do more."

"Ah." She suddenly smiled. "Well, then, I suggest you start with holding me, and we'll see what that leads to."

It was his turn to look surprised. "I don't think you under—"

She touched a finger to his lips. Just a touch, but the heat generated by it was enough to ignite a forest fire.

When he saw the half smile in her eyes, his lips curved into a sexy, dangerous grin. "Well, now, I guess a gentleman should always accommodate a lady."

And then there was no need for words as he dragged her close. His mouth closed over hers with such heat they both felt seared by it.

At long last all pretence fell away as they gave themselves over to an all-consuming need.

CHAPTER TWENTY

◆◆◆

Dear God, Cheyenne."

His mouth crushed hers with a fierceness that left her gasping. If she'd expected tenderness, she was mistaken. Instead she discovered a desperate passion that ignited her own, until she returned his kisses with a fever that matched his.

"Wait." He shrugged out of his parka and tore hers aside like a man possessed.

Too impatient to bother with the buttons of her shirt, he caught the lapels and tore it from her, shredding the fabric. Laughing, she kicked aside her boots and jeans, while he did the same.

Before he could finish unbuttoning his plaid shirt she had her hands on him, sliding them up and under the fabric to run her fingertips over the flat planes of his stomach and the taut muscles of his torso. She sighed from the sheer pleasure of it.

The touch of her hands on his naked flesh sent his heart into overdrive. The more she touched him, the more impossible it became to slow the madness.

Beneath her rough shirt she wore lace. Pale, nude lace.

At any other time he might have paused to enjoy the contrast of the lace beneath rough denim. Now all he could think of was tearing even that last thin barrier aside. He was frantic to see her. All of her.

He ripped aside the lace, and for the space of a heartbeat all he could do was stare.

"God, you're so beautiful. So perfect."

On a sigh his fingers dug into the tender skin of her upper arms as he dragged her close. He nearly lifted her off her feet while he savaged her mouth like a man starved for the taste of her.

He was a glutton, wanting to devour her in one quick bite. He knew he ought to slow down, but he'd waited so long. So long. And now what had started out to be a simple gesture of comfort had become so much more.

Hadn't he known that once he had her alone, this would happen?

Since he'd first seen her, she'd been this burning fever in his blood. Like the wolves he'd studied through the years, the need for her had taken on a life of its own. A driving force that was out of control. Nothing could satisfy the hunger for her except this. Only this.

She added to the fever by giving a low moan of pleasure before digging her fingers into his hair and cupping his head, driving him closer for an eager, avid kiss.

With a savage oath he drove her back against the rough wall and lifted her until her legs were wrapped around him. And all the while he was kissing her, touching her at will, driving them both so high, so fast, needs exploded through them, tearing the last threads of control, threatening to burn them to ash.

Instead of the soft words of love and whispered promises that he'd planned, he was in the grip of a deep, dark passion that had spun completely out of control. More than mere passion, this thing that had him in its grasp was a firestorm of such turbulence, all he could do was ride it to its conclusion.

His lips left hers to nuzzle her throat. She threw back her head, giving him easier access. The feel of all that soft flesh, his for the tasting, brought the most amazing pleasure.

When his mouth closed over her breast she gasped and clutched his head. He gave her no time to breathe as he moved from one erect nipple to the other until she moaned and writhed and cried out in a fever of need.

"Quinn. Please—"

He cut off her words with a kiss that spoke of hunger, of loneliness, of desperation. And thrilled when she returned his kisses with the same fervor.

He continued kissing her until they were both gasping for air.

His fingers found her, hot and wet, and he brought her to the first sudden, shattering peak. Before she could get her bearings, he took her up and over again.

With their breathing harsh and ragged, the heat rose up between them, leaving their bodies slick with sheen.

Quinn was desperate to end this madness. But not just yet. One more honeyed taste. One more touch of the perfect body that was his to explore now at will.

The world beyond the cabin slipped away. The cares

of the world, the endless ranch chores, the danger lying in wait for them, all were forgotten.

Here there was only the sweetest of pleasures. Here, caught in a storm of their own making, they embraced it.

The wind sighed in the trees, but the two people locked in one hot, hungry kiss heard only the sound of their own ragged breathing and the thundering of their two hearts. Birds sang outside the window, but they were unaware of anything except each seductive touch, each heady taste, and the dark, musky scent of passion. It clouded their vision. Clogged their throats. Drove them to the brink of insanity. And still they clung together, seeking relief yet keeping it just out of reach.

Quinn knew he'd slipped over the edge. He wanted desperately to slow down and savor. To stop the madness. But the need for her had become a wildfire that was out of control, scorching everything in its path, and he was being consumed by it.

"Cheyenne, look at me." He gripped her by the shoulders, his eyes fierce, his voice little more than a whisper.

She looked into his eyes, seeing herself reflected there.

"I've wanted you for so long. So long," he managed as he entered her and thrust deeply.

"Quinn, I . . ." The feelings were too intense to put into words.

Instead, as he drove her to the very edge of sanity, she showed him the only way she could, moving with him, climbing with him.

He whispered her name, over and over like a litany, as they stepped into the very eye of the storm until, together, they were swept into the maelstrom.

. . .

"You all right?" Quinn leaned against Cheyenne, his forehead pressed to hers.

She was grateful for his strength. She was feeling weightless, boneless. Without his support, she would surely drop to the floor like a dishrag.

"Fine." It was the only word she could manage over the lump in her throat.

Because she wanted to weep, she blinked rapidly and swallowed down the tears that threatened to choke her.

He lifted a hand to her face and stared into her eyes. He pressed his lips to the corner of her eye, kissing away the tiny drop of moisture. "You're so beautiful."

"So are you."

That had him smiling. "I've been called a lot of things in my life, but never beautiful."

She wrapped her arms around his neck, anchoring herself to him. "Then you haven't looked in a mirror. I think you're beautiful, Quinn."

"And I think you're amazing." He leaned in to run hot, wet kisses from the corner of her eye to her cheek, and then to the corner of her mouth. "You absolutely take my breath away."

"I guess we're just a mutual admiration society."

He threw back his head and laughed. "Yeah. That's us." He shifted and drew her a little away. "Sorry about being so rough."

"That's all right." She laughed, a clear, musical sound. "I'll let you pick the splinters out of my backside later."

"It would be my pleasure." He scooped her up into his arms and headed across the room, where he laid her gently on the big rustic bed.

The mattress, she realized, was unbelievably soft.

As he stretched out beside her he drew her close. Against her temple he whispered, "Let me make it up to you."

"How?"

"By spending the rest of the day making slow, lazy love with you."

"Why, Mr. Conway, despite your single-mindedness, you do have a way about you."

"You don't mind, Ms. O'Brien?"

"As long as we have this big old bed, I think we ought to make use of it. But this time, I hope you'll take the time to whisper sweet nothings in my ear."

With a laugh he leaned close to whisper, "I'll do better than nothings. How about sweet somethings?"

"I can deal with that."

"All right. Let me start with this." He traced a finger along the slope of her shoulder. "That night we first met..."

"The night you wanted to skin me alive?"

He chuckled. "I guess I did come off like an old Western gunslinger."

"Or an avenging angel."

"Whatever." He continued tracing the line of her arm. "Even in the middle of all that anger, I remember being so surprised by you."

"You were expecting an irate, tobacco-chewing rancher who hated the reintroduction of wolves into Wyoming territory? And instead you got a very tired rancher who just wanted to get in out of the snowstorm."

He nodded. "But you proved to be so much more. The more I could see, the more I realized that you're able to do the work of half a dozen men all on your own, and doing a damned fine job of it, I might add."

Flushed with pleasure, she decided to keep things light. "Ah, shucks, you're just saying that to keep me in this bed."

He threw back his head and roared, "You got that right." He bent low and brushed a quick kiss over her lips. "I've been wanting you in my bed since that first night."

"Really?" She fluttered her lashes. "Because I'm such a raving beauty while mucking stalls?"

"There is that." He grinned. "And there's the way you fill out a pair of jeans. I do admire a woman who can wear faded denims and an old work shirt and still manage to look sexy."

Her eyes danced with amusement. "You think I'm sexy?"

"Sexy as hell." He dragged her close and growled against her lips, "As if you don't know it."

She placed a hand on his chest and could feel the wild thundering of his heart. "Are you just coming back down to earth? Or are you already planning the next flying lesson?"

"Baby, you just say the word and I'll be happy to take you flying."

She wrapped her arms around his neck and drew his head down. "Quinn Conway, I believe I'm just going to lay back now and allow you to have your way with me."

They were both laughing as he levered himself above her and pressed hot, wet kisses down her throat and across her shoulder.

Minutes later their laughter turned to sighs of pleasure as they took each other on a slow, easy ride to paradise.

. . .

"You comfortable?" Quinn drew the blanket around Cheyenne's shoulder.

"Mmmm."

"I'll take that for a yes." He slid into bed beside her. He'd added another log to the fire, and the flames hissed and snapped, filling the cabin with the fragrance of evergreen and woodsmoke.

She plumped the pillows and snuggled closer to him. "I like your place."

"I'm glad."

"Does the land belong to your family?"

"To me. Big Jim gave it to me on my twenty-first birthday. He wanted each of us to have our own, so that we'd have a sense of pride in ownership."

"That's really generous of him."

"He's a generous guy. But he also let me know that I'd earned it. I've been working this land since I was old enough to hold a pitchfork. I was driving a tractor before I was old enough to drive a car. Big Jim admires anyone willing to work hard to get what they want." Quinn brushed his mouth over hers. "That's why he thinks so highly of you."

"He does? How would you know that?"

"He said so."

"He did? Because I work hard?"

"Because you enjoy your work."

Cheyenne felt a warm glow at his words. "I really do. I can't imagine doing anything else with my life except ranching." She glanced around. "Did you do all the work here yourself?"

"Yeah. At first I just wanted something simple where I

could store my gear while I was out on the trail. But then I decided that I wanted more. My own private retreat, where I could be comfortable spending as much time as I wanted." He looked around with pride. "It took me years to finish, but it was worth it."

"I can see you living here. It suits you." She traced one of the designs on the blanket. "Is this Ela's work?"

He nodded. "Isn't it amazing?"

"Really beautiful. I can't even imagine how many hours this must have taken her."

"Ela spends every night on her handwork. It's her relaxation and her passion. Her rooms are filled with it."

"She ought to open a store. Or offer it for sale on the Internet. I bet there'd be a market for something this authentic and unique."

He shrugged. "I guess you could run the idea by her."

"You don't sound very enthusiastic."

There was that grin, quick and deadly. "Frankly, I'm more interested in"—he lowered his face to hers and brushed her lips with his—"another flying lesson. This time you can be the teacher."

"Careful." She tossed her head. "I'm very demanding with my pupils."

"Yes, ma'am. I'll do whatever you say, ma'am."

"Anything?" Her eyes gleamed.

He dragged her so close she could feel his heartbeat inside her own chest. "I aim to please, Ms. O'Brien."

And then, with long, slow kisses and those big, clever hands, he proceeded to do just that.

CHAPTER TWENTY-ONE

Cheyenne's lids flickered, then opened. She found Quinn beside her, his arms pillowing his head, watching her with a look of interest.

"I can't believe I fell asleep. In the middle of the day."

"My fault. I didn't give you much time to catch your breath."

"As I recall, we had other things on our minds."

"Yeah." His gaze swept her, from her tousled hair to her eyes, heavy lidded from sleep. "The same things are still on my mind."

"Not until you feed me." She sat up, unmindful of her nakedness.

He gave her a wolfish grin. "Sorry, but when I see a naked goddess in my bed the last thing I'm thinking about is food."

"In order to fulfill those fantasies of yours, Mr. Conway, I need fuel." She placed her hands on his shoulders, urging

him out of bed. "Do you keep any supplies here? Cereal?
Soup?"

"Soup." He stood and pulled on his jeans before
ambling barefoot across the room to the kitchen area,
where he began opening cabinet doors. "I have tomato,
chicken noodle, vegetable..."

"Tomato soup sounds perfect. Any bread and cheese?"

He opened a refrigerator and nodded. "Yes to both."

"Excellent." She climbed out of bed and slipped into
his plaid shirt, which fell to her knees.

She nearly stepped on her cell phone, which was lying
forgotten on the floor amid a pile of her clothes. She
picked it up, turned it on, and dropped it on the night table
before crossing the room. "I'll make grilled cheese sandwiches while you heat the soup."

They worked side by side. When all was ready, they
sat at the wooden table eating their meal while watching
a steady parade of wildlife outside the windows. Squirrels
chased one another up and down trees. A hawk landed on
the very top of a dead tree and stared around, watching for
a careless field mouse. Deer, which only minutes earlier
had been completely invisible in the woods, now stepped
into the open to graze on the large patches of land where
the snow had melted. A profusion of birds visited the ears
of corn that had been hung from various tree branches.

Cheyenne gave a deep sigh of pleasure. "Oh, Quinn,
the more I see of your private refuge, the more I like it.
This is like a little slice of paradise."

"Yeah. It grows on you, doesn't it?"

She touched a hand to his. "It's been such a long time
since I've had the luxury of just stopping the world long
enough to enjoy what's right outside my window."

"That's the trouble with most of us. We get so busy with all the details that fill our days, we forget about the simple pleasures." He closed both hands around hers. "Like sharing a grilled cheese sandwich with a beautiful woman who hums while she eats."

"Or waking up in the middle of the day with a sexy cowboy."

He arched a brow. "You think I'm sexy?"

"Did I say that? I really meant"—She leaned close to trace a finger across his furrowed brow and down his face to the curve of his lower lip—"some poor helpless slob who—"

"—is going to carry said beautiful woman across the room and, now that he's fortified with food, intends to keep her in his bed for the entire day and night."

"Promise?"

"Count on it." He scooped her up and started toward the bed.

The ringing of a cell phone had him pausing in midstride.

"Sorry. It's mine." She couldn't hide the regret in her tone. "I'd better answer it. It could be important."

Quinn set her on her feet and she crossed to the nightstand, picking the phone up on the third ring.

"Yes?" Hearing the voice of the police chief, she said, "Quinn is right here with me, Chief Fletcher. Let me put you on speaker."

She touched the speaker button and held the phone between them as Everett Fletcher's voice pierced the silence.

"When I found no one home at Deacon Vance's ranch, I started calling around. I finally located him and his dad, where they took a job on the Melrose ranch assisting with the calving. That's about a hundred miles north of Paintbrush. They've been bunking in the hills with a handful of other wranglers, who confirmed their story. I talked with the owners to verify the date and time they were hired. And I've checked out the logistics. Even if Deke wanted to hide his activities from the others, and decided to give up sleeping to head to your ranch under cover of darkness, it would have been impossible for him to traverse the snow-covered roads there and back in time."

Cheyenne shot a look at Quinn before saying, "You're telling me that Deke has an airtight alibi?"

"That's what I'm saying."

Quinn chimed in. "Where do we go from here, Chief?"

Everett Fletcher's voice boomed over the speaker. "Cheyenne, I'm assuming that, like most ranchers, you've probably taken on extra wranglers during calving season?"

"That's right."

"I want the name and Social Security number of everyone who works at your place. Both longtime and current hires. I'll turn the information over to the state police for a background check. Maybe they'll spot something that sends up a red flag."

"I'm not at my ranch at the moment, but I'll head back there now. Once I pick up my records I'll bring them to town."

She rang off and turned in time to see Quinn give a reluctant sideways glance at the bed.

"Sorry."

"Not nearly as sorry as I am." He brushed a quick kiss to her mouth.

Then before she could turn away he dragged her close and kissed her again, lingering over her lips until they were both sighing.

He released her and reached for his clothes. "Next time, remind me to leave our phones in the truck."

As their vehicle rolled up the long gravel road toward her ranch, Cheyenne's smile turned to a thoughtful frown.

Seeing it, Quinn closed a hand over hers. "You're thinking about the calves."

She nodded. "I'm grateful for that...little break from my troubles. But now it's time I faced them."

"Chief Fletcher will get to the bottom of all this."

She turned. "What if he doesn't? What if these things just keep on happening?"

"They won't."

She heard the thread of steel in his words and tried to take comfort in his strength. But the closer she got to home, the more real and threatening the situation became. The peace she'd felt in his cabin was now shattered, and the reality of her situation seemed all the more painful after that brief reprieve.

"In the past couple of years, so many terrible things have happened in my life. My brother. My father. The fire. The calves." She hated the way her voice trembled and nearly broke. "I'm almost beginning to think I'm living under some kind of dark cloud."

He gave her hand a last squeeze before parking the truck alongside her house. "Just keep this in mind: No matter how dark the storm, sooner or later the sun has to come out."

She shot him a look. "Who have you turned into? Little Suzie Sunshine?"

He grinned. "That's me. Just a guy named Sue. How could I be anything but upbeat after what we've just shared?"

She shook her head from side to side and couldn't help laughing. "Okay. I'll admit that your little surprise visit to the cabin has made this day a whole lot brighter. But I was so hoping that Chief Fletcher would call to tell me the culprit was in jail and my worries were finally over."

Quinn turned off the engine and walked around to the passenger side, catching her hand in his. "It's only a matter of time until the police get their man. In the meantime, the sooner we get your records to town"—he leaned close to whisper in her ear—"the sooner we can think about slipping away to our favorite retreat."

She couldn't keep the laughter from her voice. "Is that all you can think about?"

He gave her a look of mock surprise. "You mean there are other things? Tell me what I've been missing."

She nudged him with her elbow. "I'd say you don't miss much, Conway."

They were both laughing as they walked into the burned-out shell of her house to find Wes, Micah, and Austin in the kitchen. All three men looked up with surprise.

"Hey, Cheyenne." Micah gave her a long look, from her radiant smile to her hand, firmly tucked into Quinn's. "I've been calling you. You never picked up."

"Oh. Sorry." Her voice said otherwise. "Quinn wanted to show me his cabin in the hills."

Though Micah held his silence, the old man's look sharpened. The new intimacy between Cheyenne and Quinn was obvious to anyone with eyes to see them.

"Why were you trying to phone me, Micah?"

He pulled himself from his thoughts. "Chief Fletcher was trying to reach you. I told him you were heading over to the Conway ranch. I didn't know you'd taken a… detour."

"That's all right. No harm done. I just spoke to him." She drew Quinn with her as she started toward the parlor. "You can give me a hand." To the others she called, "We'll be right back."

Minutes later they returned, with Quinn carrying a thick file folder.

Wes arched a brow. "Are those the employee records?"

She nodded. "The chief wants to send them to the state police for a background check."

Austin frowned. "What about Deke? I thought the chief was heading over to the Vance place, all fired up about checking out his alibi, when he left here."

Cheyenne looked from Austin to the others. "Apparently, unknown to any of us, Deke took a job at the Melrose ranch. It's too far away for him to be considered a suspect, so the chief wants to look at anyone else who might have had access to the herd."

"I'm glad he's staying on top of it." Wes nodded toward the file folder in Quinn's hands. "But I'm not keen on the idea that he thinks the culprit might be one of our wranglers."

Cheyenne touched a hand to his arm. "It's not something we like to think about. But it's a start, and as soon as everyone's name is cleared, we'll be able to breathe a little easier. I'm just so grateful that the chief is bringing the state police into it. Sooner or later they'll get to the bottom of this."

"I guess you're right." Wes turned toward Austin. "We need to get back up to the hills. We promised to bring more supplies." He turned to Micah. "You staying in the bunkhouse tonight, or do you want to head on up with us?"

The old man rubbed his thigh. "Maybe I'll stay here tonight. These bones are telling me there's a change coming in the weather."

Wes nodded toward the window. "Rain clouds up in the mountains. You can see them from here."

"At my age, I don't need clouds to tell me what my aching body has already said."

They all joined in his good-natured laughter as Cheyenne and Quinn said their good-byes and walked out to the truck. They waved before driving away.

As the truck moved away Micah continued watching before he turned to Wes and Austin, who were getting ready to load up their truck for the drive to the hills. "Now that's something I never expected to see."

"What's that?" Wes turned, one hand on the door of the truck.

"Our little Cheyenne in love." The old man chuckled. "And I'm betting she doesn't even know it yet."

"Love?" Austin shot him an incredulous look. "How can somebody be in love and not know it?"

Micah shared a knowing grin with Wes. "I guess if you have to ask, you've never been there, son. Believe me, when it happens, the ones involved are often the last to know."

"True enough." Wes shook his head from side to side. "I wonder what the hell will happen to us if she marries a Conway?"

"Yeah. It could get complicated."

"Complicated?" Austin looked from one man to the other.

"Well, let's see," Micah mused aloud. "The Conways already own more land in Wyoming than they know what to do with. One more ranch wouldn't make much difference to them. So, if Cheyenne marries into the family, and decides that she's had enough trouble with this place, and it's nothing more than a headache, she could simply sell it and live the good life as a rich rancher's wife over in that big house."

Austin's eyes went wide. "Cheyenne would never sell the family ranch."

"Like I said"—Micah idly rubbed his aching thigh—"you've obviously never been in love. When two people fall hard, stranger things have happened."

Austin said through gritted teeth, "Dad would roll over in his grave."

At Austin's vehement words Micah said patiently, "The only thing Cheyenne's daddy wanted was his daughter's happiness. And if marrying a Conway would make her happy, he'd be the first one in favor of the merger."

"And you're not going to say a word?" Austin's tone was low, with a mixture of sarcasm and disbelief. "Can't you let her know that you don't approve of what she's doing?"

"It's not up to me to approve or disapprove." The old man turned away and, with the aid of his cane, began limping slowly toward the bunkhouse.

Over his shoulder he called, "All I'm saying is what's good enough for Cheyenne's daddy is good enough for me. Whatever makes that girl happy is just fine with me."

CHAPTER TWENTY-TWO

Daylight was fading as Quinn and Cheyenne drove into town. Quinn steered the truck to the end of Main Street, where the police chief's office sat in front of the tiny two-cell jail.

A short time later, after finding the office empty, they left Cheyenne's employee records on Everett Fletcher's desk before walking outside.

Quinn caught her hand. "We're already too late to make it back to the ranch in time for dinner. Why don't we eat here in town before heading out?" He nodded toward Flora's Diner. "The sign in the window says tonight's special is meat loaf. Want to give it a try?"

Cheyenne shrugged. "I'm willing if you are."

They strolled across the street and walked into the small wooden building painted a garish pink and blue, with FLORA'S DINER spelled out in bright purple letters over the door.

Inside were a couple of tables and chairs, also in pastel shades, and a long, laminated counter lined with half a dozen metal stools that had been new more than fifty years earlier.

Flora, who was over eighty, looked up from the kitchen, where she was busy flipping burgers and draining baskets of French fries and passing them through to her sixty-year-old daughter, Dora, who served the customers.

"Why, Quinn Conway," old Flora called out. "What's the matter? Phoebe Hogan finally quit and leave you boys to cook for yourselves?"

"Last time I looked she was still there, but you never know, Flora."

"Seeing as how your daddy hasn't married that woman, I wouldn't blame her one bit for leaving. If I've told her once, I've told her a hundred times she's wasting her life out there when she could have accepted half a dozen proposals from all those handsome cowboys lusting after her. By now she could have had herself a houseful of kids of her own, instead of raising Cole's."

"You're probably not the only one who's told her that, Flora." Quinn grinned good-naturedly. Everyone in Paintbrush knew everyone else's business, and Flora more than most. "Of course, my brothers and I are grateful that she didn't take your advice. But I think it's safe to say she's done raising us."

"Don't be so sure of that. I always say men are just boys in bigger clothes. No matter their age, they still need a woman to steer them through life." She squinted. "Is that Cheyenne O'Brien?"

"It is."

He and Cheyenne sat down on two of the round metal

stools at the counter when they saw that the tables and chairs were already taken.

Flora actually came out of the kitchen to get a closer look at Cheyenne. "Why, honey, I hardly recognized you. I haven't seen you in here in a month of Sundays."

"I got pretty busy out at the ranch."

"I just guess you did." She laid her hand over Cheyenne's. "I was sorry to hear about your daddy, so soon after losing Buddy. Good men. Both of 'em."

Pain, quick and sharp, flared in Cheyenne's eyes. "Thank you, Flora."

"And now a fire out at your place. It's the talk of the town. You hang in there, honey. Your luck's got to turn."

Everyone in the diner had fallen silent, listening raptly to every word.

The old woman leaned close. "Don't bother looking at the menu. You both want the meat loaf." She turned to her daughter. "Dora, they'll have the special."

With that Flora walked back to the kitchen while Dora handed them each a small salad and roll. "Your meat loaf will be right up. What're you drinking?"

"Coffee for me, thanks."

Quinn exchanged a smile with Cheyenne, who nodded. "I'll have the same."

Cheyenne and Quinn dug into their salads.

The others in the diner returned their attention to their own food while keeping an eye on the two of them.

When the door opened, Everett Fletcher strolled in and looked around.

Spying Quinn and Cheyenne, he ambled over to the counter. "Hey, you two."

They looked up.

Quinn stuck out his hand. "Everett. We just stopped by your office."

"That so?" He glanced at Cheyenne.

"I left the employee files on your desk, Chief."

"Good. I'll fax them over to the state boys first thing tomorrow."

Spotting Thibalt Baxter at one of the tables, he waved before adding, "I'll get back to you as soon as I hear anything."

"Thanks, Chief."

They watched him join his friend.

Half an hour later, after devouring thick slabs of meat loaf and a mound of potatoes smothered in Flora's famous mushroom gravy, Quinn dug some money out of his jeans and set it on the counter.

"You're not leaving until you have a piece of my coconut cream pie," Flora declared from the kitchen.

Quinn merely grinned. "Yes, ma'am. If you insist."

"I do." She slid two slices across the pass-through and watched as Dora added forks before serving them.

"That's your daddy's favorite," Flora announced. "Whenever he's in town he always stops by to ask for it."

Quinn thought about how carefully Phoebe monitored his father's diet these days, and realized she was fighting a losing battle as long as old Flora was here in town to feed that famous sweet tooth.

When Quinn and Cheyenne finally got up to leave, Flora called, "Tell Big Jim and Cole I said hello."

"I will, Flora. And thanks. Your meat loaf and coconut cream pie could win awards at the county fair."

"Ha. I won all the ribbons I care to. I'll leave that to the young girls now." She stared pointedly at Cheyenne. "Too many of 'em have forgotten how to please their men."

When he saw the blush on Cheyenne's cheeks, Quinn couldn't help saying, "Oh, I don't know about that, Flora. There's a lot to be said for canned soup and grilled cheese sandwiches."

"That depends on where they're served, and who's doing the serving." The old woman's eyes twinkled, and he realized that nothing got by her sharp wit.

He winked at her. "Yeah. There's something to be said for that."

As he and Cheyenne walked from the diner and heads turned to watch, they could hear the old woman's cackling laughter following them.

Once in the truck, Quinn turned to Cheyenne. "We can be home in an hour. Or, if you don't mind an extra half hour or so, we could head back to my cabin."

Her smile was quick and potent. "Did I mention that I just love long drives in the woods?"

They drove away laughing like carefree children.

The night was dark and quiet. *And peaceful*, Cheyenne thought as she snuggled beside Quinn in the big, soft bed. She'd never known such complete silence. On the ranch there were so many sounds. The lowing of cattle. The laughter of the wranglers in the bunkhouse late into the night. The sounds of vehicles coming and going at all hours. Stalls opening and closing. Horses stomping. Rusty gates swinging in the breeze.

Here there were only the hoot of an owl, and the occasional call of a wolf or coyote. And the steady beat of Quinn's heart as she rested her head on his chest.

Here, she thought, was heaven. And it had arrived in the form of a dark avenging angel who had come unbidden into her barn during a blizzard and had changed her life forever.

"You're quiet." Quinn touched a finger to her cheek.

"Thinking."

"Want to share?"

She tilted her face to his. "I'm thinking how strange life is. One minute I was a rancher, feeling lost, barely holding my life together. In the blink of an eye, you came along and made me feel safe. What's more, you make me feel like a woman."

"A very beautiful woman." He brushed his mouth over hers. "And you make me feel like the luckiest man in the world."

He took the kiss deeper and Cheyenne could feel her mind emptying, her heart swelling.

With love?

She tried to deny it.

She'd always thought that love needed time to grow between two people who'd known each other for ages. She and Quinn had spent barely any time together. And what time they had was filled with ranch chores and her problems. So many problems.

Yet here she was feeling something very new and fragile. Love?

She listened to the quiet, steady breathing of the man lying beside her and slipped out of bed to pace to the window.

This wasn't the shouting, fireworks-in-the-sky kind of feeling she'd always expected to find with love. This was the whispering, wonder-filled kind of feeling that wrapped itself around her heart and squeezed ever so gently.

Maybe it was just wishful thinking.

Ever since meeting his family, she couldn't stop thinking about the Conway warmth, their closeness, their shared chores and shared lives. Though they lived in close quarters, none of them appeared to feel stifled. Instead, they fed one another's joy and laughter. Time spent with them made her realize even more how much she'd lost. There'd been a time when she'd shared such things with her mother and father and her brother, Buddy.

Was her affection for Quinn's family muddling her mind? She turned. Paced.

Despite what she felt for the Conway family, she knew that it was nothing compared to what she felt for Quinn. Being with him made her feel wildly joyful and quietly peaceful all at the same time. As though her poor, battered heart had found a safe haven, a solitary refuge from life's storms.

She crossed her arms over her chest and paced back to the bed.

If this was love, then she simply loved him and hoped desperately that he shared those feelings, though she knew it could be very different for a man. Making love didn't always mean love or commitment. For a man, loving was a pleasurable release. She didn't see why Quinn should have to be any different. But she wanted him to be different from other men. Needed him to be different. Better. Smarter. Kinder.

Or was she simply trying to make him into something he could never be?

She knew she could be setting herself up for heartbreak. He'd admitted to being a loner. He'd said nothing about love or commitment. She ought to be steeling herself against reading more into this than he intended, or her poor heart could be broken into millions of pieces.

She suddenly froze. She had the feeling that someone

was watching her through the window. Turning, she crossed the room and peered into the darkness.

She heard movement in the brush and tried to see what caused it. An animal making a nocturnal visit, perhaps? Though she strained, she could see nothing out of the ordinary.

She had a flash of memory. Of her fourth birthday, and waking Buddy to ask him to help her look under her bed for any monsters lurking there. He'd been so sweet about it, turning on his flashlight and proving, beyond a doubt, that there was nothing to fear.

It was time to stop looking for monsters in the dark.

She took one final peek into the darkness before returning to bed.

"Where were you?"

At Quinn's whispered words she snuggled close and stared into those fathomless eyes. Eyes that, in the glow of firelight, had the power to dissolve all her fears.

"Checking on a noise outside. And thinking about life's strange twists and turns."

Against her temple he murmured, "One of those strange twists brought you into my life, and I'm grateful."

As his hands and mouth began moving over her, lifting her higher and higher, she gave up the last attempt to think. It was too much effort to rationalize her feelings or his. Instead, she would simply enjoy this special time.

Steeped in pure pleasure, she showed him, the only way she could, all the wonderful new feelings that were blooming in her heart.

The sun was already climbing above the peaks of the Tetons when Cheyenne woke.

She remembered having awakened earlier, to pace, to think, to check on strange nighttime sounds. She'd been certain there had been something moving alongside the wall of the cabin. For the longest time she'd had the sense that someone was peering in the window. But she'd found nothing. And then Quinn had gathered her close and all her fears had evaporated.

She turned toward the warmth beside her, only to find that the bed was empty.

She sat up, shoving hair from her eyes, as Quinn turned from the stove.

"'Morning, lazybones. Coffee?"

"Um. I'd love some."

He crossed the room and the mattress sagged as he sat beside her and handed her a steaming cup.

"Oh, this is the best possible way to wake up in the morning."

He bent over to kiss her lips. "I agree. Tomorrow I'll let you make the coffee. Hungry?"

"You're going to feed me?"

"I am. You have a choice. Frozen waffles, or toast and peanut butter."

"I've had waffles. I haven't had toast with peanut butter before."

His brows shot up. "Woman, you've been missing one of life's great pleasures. There's nothing better than peanut butter melting into warm toast."

"All right. You've sold me on it. Do you want some help?"

"Not with the toast. But I wouldn't mind having you beside me in the kitchen." He caught her hand and she set aside the coffee before slipping out of bed.

He glanced at her clothes, still lying in a heap where she'd dropped them in haste the night before. Then he turned to look her up and down, from her tousled hair to her bare toes, and all that glorious, naked flesh in between.

With a wicked grin he muttered, "On second thought, why don't I join you in bed and we'll think about food later?"

She started to laugh, until she saw the dark look in his eyes.

Together they tumbled into bed and lost themselves in the wonder of their newly discovered passion.

"As promised more than an hour ago, toast with peanut butter." Quinn sat on the edge of the bed and handed Cheyenne a plate. "Better late than never, ma'am."

She nibbled the toast and made little humming sounds of pleasure. "Mmm. Good." She looked up. "Is this a reward for good behavior?"

He wiggled his brows like a mock villain. "I'd call what you did very bad behavior. And I'm so very grateful," he growled against her throat.

That had her laughing aloud. "Aren't you having any?"

He nodded. "Right after I pour two cups of coffee. Want to eat in bed?"

"I'll get up." She tossed aside the blanket and reached for the pile of clothes until she'd located her jeans and shirt. When she was dressed she crossed the room and joined him at the table.

Again she was reminded just how clever he'd been in building his cabin on this site. The view of the Tetons was spectacular, no matter what hour of the day. The woods surrounding them offered a sanctuary from civilization. The birds and other animals were free to go about their lives without interruption.

She looked over at Quinn. "Being here is like being in a zoo. Except we're the ones behind glass walls and the wild creatures can walk by and ignore us or stop and watch us whenever they please."

He lifted his cup in a salute. "That was the plan. I take it you approve?"

"I do. I love it. Except that last night I had the strangest feeling that one of our furry friends was watching us."

"You, too?" He paused. "Something woke me through the night. I listened, but couldn't hear a thing. But I couldn't shake the feeling that I was being watched."

"Exactly." She nodded.

He grinned. "Probably some jealous wolf that figures I got the prettiest female of the pack."

They shared a laugh.

Cheyenne sighed. "I wish we could hide away here forever, and never—" She looked up at the ringing of her cell phone.

Catching Quinn's dark frown, she muttered, "I know. We agreed to leave these in the truck. I forgot."

He glanced over. "You could ignore it."

"I could. Of course, it could be Chief Fletcher."

He shrugged and she reached for her phone.

The masculine voice on the other end sounded frazzled. "Cheyenne, this is Rusty Perry. You'd better meet me in town. I'm on the way there now, heading to Dr. Walton's clinic with Micah Horn."

"Micah? What's happened?" Fear had her voice hitching in her throat.

Quinn hurried to stand beside her and they both listened as Rusty's voice went on. "I swung by your place
to post the building permit and found Micah lying in the
snow outside the bunkhouse, which was still smoldering."

"Smoldering?"

At Cheyenne's sudden gasp Quinn spoke for both of
them. "Another fire?"

"A big one. The bunkhouse is burned to the ground. I
don't know how the old man made it out, but he's in bad
shape."

"How bad?" Cheyenne was already scooping up her
boots with one hand while holding the phone up with the
other.

"He's conscious, but just barely. Besides being half-
frozen, he's almost incoherent. He keeps babbling, but I
can't make heads or tails of what he's trying to say. I'll leave
that to the doc. You'd better get to town as soon as possible."

"Yes. Thank you, Rusty. And tell Micah—" Cheyenne's voice broke, and she had to stop and swallow the
lump in her throat several times before she managed to
say, "Tell Micah I need him. He can't leave me. He has to
hang on."

"Will do."

By the time the line went dead both Quinn and Cheyenne were frantically pulling on the last of their clothes
and snatching up whatever they needed to take with them
for the long drive to town.

As they climbed into the truck, Quinn looked over and
squeezed her hand, feeling the tremors she couldn't hide.

"He has to be all right. He's all the family I have left in
the world," she said through her tears. "Oh, Quinn, I can't
lose Micah, too."

CHAPTER TWENTY-THREE

The drive to town was the longest of Cheyenne's life. She sat as still as death, her mind playing through images of her childhood, with Micah encouraging her to ride her first pony and, later, showing her how to saddle her first mare. Micah teaching her how to bake corn bread. Micah driving the big hay wagon on her first high school date, when she and her friends from town planned a hayride.

Micah was as much a part of her life as her father and brother had been. Micah Horn was her teacher, her uncle, the grandfather she'd never had. The thought of him lying alone and injured in the freezing night, with no one around to comfort him, tormented her.

When at last she and Quinn drove through town, she kept her hands clenched so tightly the knuckles were white from the effort.

Quinn parked the truck in front of Dr. April Walton's walk-in clinic. Parked beside them was Rusty Perry's truck.

Quinn hurried around to hold the door and take Cheyenne's hand in his. She was so cold he closed her hand between both of his, hoping to lend her his warmth, as they walked into the clinic.

Rusty got to his feet and hurried over. "The doc's with Micah now." He gave a shake of his head. "I couldn't believe what I was seeing. There it was, the bunkhouse burned to the ground, and that tough old man lying there. His clothes had been burned so badly, I thought I was seeing a pile of rags, until he started moaning. Even while I was getting him into my truck, he was mumbling and muttering and waving his hands. He was like a wild man, grabbing my arm, trying to make me understand his ravings. But all I could make out was some gibberish." He laid a hand over Cheyenne's. "I'm just glad I stopped by your place when I did."

Her tone was low with emotion. "You saved his life, Rusty."

"I'll leave that to the doc."

Hearing voices, the doctor stepped from one of the examining rooms and hurried toward them.

The doctor indicated the room she'd just vacated. "Cheyenne, Micah Horn is in here."

"How bad is he?"

The doctor's voice lowered. "It's too soon to speculate. He's an old man, suffering not only from hypothermia but from a nasty blow to his head. He was probably hit by falling debris, and he's lucky to have escaped before the building collapsed."

"I want to see him."

As Cheyenne started to turn away, the doctor put a hand on her arm.

"I must caution you. He seems extremely agitated. I've just given him something to sedate him."

Cheyenne barely heard her words as she forged ahead and hurried into the room, with Quinn and the doctor trailing behind.

When she paused beside Micah's bed, Cheyenne looked over at the doctor with alarm. "Why is he wearing this mask?"

"It's oxygen. I'm hoping to clear his lungs of the smoke he inhaled during his flight from the burning building."

Cheyenne laid a hand over his and leaned close to whisper, "Micah. It's Cheyenne. Can you hear me?"

He stirred, and she saw his eyes trying to focus.

"Thank heaven you're alive." She could feel tears welling up and she blinked hard, trying to cover the rush of emotions that swamped her at the sight of him lying so battered and helpless.

When he recognized her, his hand clawed at the mask and he tore it aside.

His voice was as raspy as a rusted old gate. "Chey... honey... listen. You need to know..."

Though his lips were moving, the words were little more than a jumble of guttural sounds.

The doctor hurried over to return the oxygen mask to his nose and mouth.

She turned to Cheyenne. "Until the sedative takes effect, I think you ought to step outside. I'm concerned about this extreme agitation."

"But he's trying to tell me something."

"No doubt. Maybe it's about the fire and how it started. It could have been a spark from a fireplace, or a forgotten cigarette."

"Micah didn't smoke cigarettes. Only a pipe."

"Ah. A pipe then." The doctor paused. "He may have dropped it in his sleep and he's carrying guilt."

"I don't care how the fire started." Cheyenne could feel herself close to tears. "I just want him to live."

"I'm doing the best I can, Ms. O'Brien." The doctor efficiently steered Cheyenne toward the door. "If you'll wait in the outer office, I'll call you in when I have my patient properly sedated and I've completed my examination."

Cheyenne dug in her heels. "But I want to help."

"Right now, your presence is a hindrance. He's becoming too agitated."

"All right. I understand." With a last look at the old man in the bed Cheyenne turned away and reluctantly walked from the room.

As she did, Micah snatched aside the mask yet again. And though he tried to speak, all he could do was fall into a fit of moaning and coughing before mercifully falling silent.

In the waiting room Rusty looked up hopefully. "How is he doing?"

Quinn spoke for Cheyenne, who was too upset to say a word. "Right now he's in some pain. Dr. Walton says he needs rest, but she thinks he'll survive."

The building contractor let out a deep sigh of relief. "That's good news." He looked over at Cheyenne. "If you'd like, I could head on up to your ranch. If any of your wranglers come down from the hills, they'll need to know that Micah survived."

She shot him a look of gratitude. "Thank you, Rusty. I appreciate it."

When he left, Cheyenne's fingers worried the edge of her parka as she began pacing the length of the room and back.

After several long minutes Quinn caught her hand and drew her down to the chair beside his. "You're going to wear yourself out."

She avoided his eyes. "I can't stop thinking that I was gone when Micah needed me."

"You had no way of knowing what was happening. For all you knew, he could have changed his mind about staying in the bunkhouse to drive up in the hills with the wranglers."

"I wish he had. Oh, Quinn, I wish he'd gone with Wes and the wranglers."

"It's been a long winter and spring. He said his old bones were aching. He probably figured a night alone would give him a break from the routine."

"But don't you see, Quinn? For the past months he's been worrying about me whenever I've been alone on the ranch. And now, when he was alone, I wasn't there for him." She looked down at her hands. "I was ... with you while he was suffering."

"So that's what's bothering you?" Quinn wrapped his arms around her and gathered her close. Against her temple he murmured, "Listen to me, Cheyenne. You're no more responsible for this accident than Micah is. Despite all that's happened, or maybe because of it, you have a right to get on with your life. Micah would be the first one to tell you that you have every right to be happy."

Tears sprang to her eyes and she pushed a little away to look at him. "How do you know what I'm thinking? Are you reading my mind?"

He gave her a knowing smile. "You're as transparent as glass." He touched a finger to her quivering lips. "I know you're feeling guilty about not being there for him, but when Micah recovers he'll tell you the same thing I'm telling you now. This is not payback for a night of loving. The fates are not going to slap you down every time you find a moment of happiness."

She gave a deep sigh. "My mind tells me that you're right. But my heart says something different. The way my life has been going, I've started to believe that I'm living under some sort of dark cloud. Everything and everyone I love is snatched away from me."

They both looked up sharply as the doctor stepped into the room.

Cheyenne was on her feet at once. "How is he?"

"Resting comfortably. He has a concussion from a huge bump on his head. I'm guessing he was struck by falling timber. The blow was enough to knock him unconscious. But the good news is, his lungs are clearing and I feel certain that by the end of the day he'll be breathing without oxygen. Judging by the bruises and burns on his arms and legs, he was trapped in the burning building for some time before he managed to extricate himself and crawl to safety. This could be the cause of his agitation. Until the sedative kicked in, he was suffering delusions, fighting imaginary demons." She shook her head. "He may be old, but he's as strong as a bull. That man was fighting for his life."

"Oh, thank heaven. I was so afraid—" Cheyenne surprised herself by bursting into tears.

The doctor touched a hand to Cheyenne's shoulder. "If you'd like, you can sit by his bedside. I'll warn you, though, it could be a long vigil. I gave him a strong seda-tive that will keep him asleep for hours."

Cheyenne nodded, struggling to find her voice. "It doesn't matter how long before he wakes, I need to be with him."

The doctor turned to Quinn. "Feel free to stay, too. But you may want to bring something from the diner while you're waiting."

"Maybe later." He caught Cheyenne's hand. "Come on. Let's make ourselves comfortable in Micah's room."

Cheyenne held back. "You don't have to stay with me. You have ranch chores to see to."

"And enough family to pick up the slack while I'm gone." He led her toward the room. "If you're staying, I'm staying."

He paused to turn to the doctor. "Will you be here?"

She shook her head. "I'll be in and out, and so will my assistant, Margie. My office is attached to the clinic, but the buzzer on the desk in the outer office alerts me if I'm needed here. I'll be looking in on my patient from time to time, but whenever he wakes I'd like to know. Just press that buzzer and I'll be right here."

They nodded before heading toward the other room.

Once inside, Quinn drew a chair close to the bed.

When Cheyenne was seated, she took the old man's hand in hers and clung to it the way she had when she'd been a little girl.

Quinn hauled a second chair beside hers and sat qui-etly, watching and waiting. When he was satisfied that she had her emotions under control, he turned to her, keeping his voice low. "I'm going to drop by the chief's office and report this latest fire."

She nodded.

He brushed a kiss over her cheek. "I won't be gone long. Would you like me to pick up something at the diner?"

She pressed a hand to her stomach. "Maybe later. Right now I wouldn't be able to eat a thing."

"Okay." He tugged on a lock of her hair. "Stay strong."

She turned toward the old man, her eyes solemn, her mouth a grim, tight line of concentration, as though willing him her strength.

Quinn walked from the room and went in search of the police chief.

Rusty Perry drove into the yard and parked his truck beside Cheyenne's house. Acrid smoke filled the air, and the charred remains of the bunkhouse still smoldered in the midmorning light.

One of the wranglers could be seen walking gingerly through the ashes, kicking at burned timbers, poking through the debris, as though searching for anything worth salvaging.

When Rusty stepped from his vehicle, the wrangler walked over.

"Hey, Rusty." Austin stuck out his hand before nodding toward the smoking remains of the bunkhouse. "You picked a bad day to stop by."

"Actually I was here earlier."

Austin's brows shot up. "Earlier? While the fire was still burning?"

"Yeah. Though it had pretty much burned itself out by the time I got here."

Austin turned back to study the ruins. "That had to be

"Exactly. So, some of them figure it's easier to forge a dead man's documents than to deal with all the questions."

"But in this case, Austin, or the guy pretending to be Austin, has been living and working at the ranch for the past couple of years. He's become like one of the family."

"So, the question is, why? What's his game?"

Quinn gripped the arms of his chair. "How long will it take to figure out who this guy is and what he's up to?"

The chief pointed to the fax across the room, spitting out pages of documents. "If we're lucky, the state boys may have already sorted things out."

He stood and began retrieving the loose pages before setting them on his desk. As he read through them, his eyes narrowed and his mouth became a grim line of anger.

"This guy is a real piece of work. His real name is Abbott Monroe. His parents were killed in a house fire, and he entered the foster-care system when he was only twelve. His first foster parents managed to escape a fire in their home, and he was evaluated by psychologists working with the state as a sociopath. This guy, they say, fits the description to a T. Charming as hell until he doesn't get what he wants. To him, the end justifies the means. And woe to anyone who refuses him anything he's set his sights on. He'll do whatever it takes."

Chief Fletcher's voice lowered as he added, "He was supposed to be in a mental health facility, but an inquiry discovered that he went missing several years ago and seems to have fallen off the face of the earth."

Quinn got to his feet so quickly he nearly knocked over the chair. "And, while he was there, he got to know Austin Baylor."

The chief nodded. "You got it. Knowing that Austin

some fire to burn down the entire bunkhouse." He shook his head from side to side and stared at the toe of his boot. "Poor old Micah. The way that old man sleeps, I figure he never had a chance."

"Fortunately for him, he woke up."

"What do you mean?" Austin's eyes went wide.

"Well, he may have been asleep when the fire started, but he managed to escape. When I came by earlier I found him in the snow."

"In the snow?" Austin's voice lowered. "Dead? Or alive?"

"Alive. Barely. But I hauled him to town and the doc thinks he's going to make it."

Seeing the stunned expression on Austin's face, Rusty clapped a hand to his shoulder. "I knew you'd be relieved to hear the good news. Since Cheyenne wanted to stay with him at the clinic and I was heading here anyway, I told her I'd let all of you know that the old guy survived, so you wouldn't have to worry. Of course, he isn't out of the woods yet. But at least for now, he's got a fighting chance."

"Good." Austin seemed at a loss for words. "That's … good."

"Now, while you pass the good news to the others, I'll get to the business that brought me here in the first place."

Rusty walked to the door of the ranch house and lifted a hammer from his tool belt before nailing the building permit to the door.

As he walked toward his truck he called over his shoulder, "You'll be sure to tell Wes and the others that Micah survived, won't you?"

"You bet." Austin stayed where he was, watching as Rusty climbed into his truck and drove away.

Chapter Twenty-four

Another fire?" Everett Fletcher pulled up a form on his computer screen and began typing while Quinn fed him the details. When he'd heard enough, he paused to peer over his glasses. "I haven't even received the investigator's results of the first fire, but I'm telling you, a second fire on the same property raises too many red flags. With that first fire at Cheyenne's home, her wranglers started the cleanup the next morning and I was in agreement, because she needed to get back into her house as soon as possible. This time, I'm going to insist that none of the debris gets touched until the fire and insurance investigators sift through everything and make a determination."

Quinn nodded. "I agree, Chief."

Everett rubbed a hand over his brow. "How's Micah holding up?"

"Dr. Walton thinks he'll recover. He received a lot of bumps and bruises and some burns before escaping the

bunkhouse. From the looks of him, he's lucky to be alive. It had to take some pretty fierce determination to make it out with a fire raging and the building collapsing around him."

"I've known Micah Horn for a lifetime. He's a tough old cowboy." The chief looked up as his phone rang. "Excuse me a minute, Quinn."

He spoke into the phone and listened in silence before a look of alarm crossed his face. "You're sure of that?"

Moments later he replaced the phone and shook his head in disbelief. "That was the state police. They ran a check on everyone on Cheyenne's payroll and came up with some pretty shocking news." He waited a beat before saying, "It seems that Cheyenne has a dead man on her payroll."

"What's that supposed to mean?" Quinn's eyes narrowed.

"Austin Baylor was a twenty-seven-year-old inmate in a mental hospital in Laramie. The records show that he died there five years ago."

"If Austin isn't Austin Baylor, who is he?"

The chief shrugged. "That's the million-dollar question."

"So, you're saying that some cowboy decided to use a dead man's name and whatever documents could be forged in order to conceal his own identity?"

The chief nodded. "It's not as rare as you'd think. W[e] have a lot of transients working up here, especially duri[ng] calving season and again during roundup. If someone [has] a criminal background, it's hard to get hired." He pee[red] at Quinn. "Would you want to take on a part-timer w[ith a] criminal record?"

Quinn shrugged. "I'd want to know what the [crime] was and whether he really wanted to work or just w[anted] a place to hide out until he hatched his next big sch[eme]

Baylor was dead, he felt safe using his name and any personal information he could glean." Chief Everett Fletcher checked his handgun before pushing away from his desk. "I'm heading up to Cheyenne's ranch right now to take him into custody."

Quinn started toward the door. "Call me when you've made the arrest. I'll be at the clinic. I'm not leaving Cheyenne's side until you have him under lock and key."

Cheyenne sat stiffly in the chair beside Micah's bed, his hand clutched firmly in hers. Though she told herself that she was willing him her strength, the truth was, she was seeking his. She had a desperate need to touch him, to assure herself that he was truly alive. With every heartbeat, every unsteady breath he took, her own heart rate began to slow and her world to settle.

As long as he continued to live, to grow stronger, she would be content to do nothing more than sit quietly, his big, rough hand in hers.

As the quiet minutes ticked by, she found herself thinking back to her childhood, and the cowboy who had always had time for a joke or a lesson for the little girl who had followed him like a shadow. It was Micah who had put her in the saddle for the first time, who had taught her to groom her horse, to muck stalls, to fetch grain and water for the animals in her care. And always with a smile and a wink, as though what they were sharing was the most important part of his day. He'd made her feel safe. Protected. Loved. Cherished.

"Oh, Micah." She leaned close to kiss his grizzled cheek. He smelled of woodsmoke and leather, familiar scents from her childhood. "Please get better. I need you."

His lids flickered. His eyes opened and she could see him struggling to focus.

The agitation was back. His fingers closed around hers with enough pressure to cause her to wince. His throat, badly injured by smoke and fire, caused his words to be little more than guttural sounds as he struggled to speak.

"It's okay. Don't tax yourself, Micah." She pressed a hand to his shoulder when he tried to sit up. "You're in the clinic now, and Dr. Walton says you're going to be fine."

"Here you are." At the sound of Austin's voice Cheyenne looked over.

He strode across the room and studied the way Micah was twisting and turning in the bed. "Rusty Perry stopped by the ranch and said he'd brought Micah here."

At the sound of his voice Micah went very still before becoming even more agitated.

Cheyenne put her hand on the old man's forehead, hoping the touch of her would have a calming effect. "Thank heaven for Rusty. I don't know what would have happened if he hadn't arrived when he did."

"What's the doc think?" Austin nodded toward the figure in the bed. "He going to make it?"

"She thinks so. He was so agitated she had to give him a sedative."

"It doesn't seem to be working." Austin stepped to the other side of the bed. "Maybe you ought to go find her and ask her to bring something to quiet him down."

Micah stared in horror at the man beside the bed before swiveling his head toward Cheyenne.

"She's in her office next door." Cheyenne sat down and captured Micah's hand in hers. His pulse, she noted, was pumping like a runaway train. He seemed even worse now than when she'd first arrived. "Dr. Walton said that if I needed her, I should press the buzzer on the desk in the outer office. Maybe you could do that now and she'll be here in a few minutes."

"I saw a couple of cars pulling up in front of her office when I got here." Austin glanced at his watch. "Even if she hears the buzzer, she could get sidetracked by her patients and forget all about him. I'd be happy to stay here and keep an eye on him while you get her."

Micah moaned and thrashed about, waving his arm in the air before both his hands closed around hers in a vise-like grip.

Cheyenne felt a moment of panic. Micah was definitely worse now, and so highly agitated, she feared for his heart.

She looked over at Austin. "Something is terribly wrong. I think you're right. The doctor needs to see him right now."

She extricated her hand from the old man's grasp and leaned over him to murmur, "I'll only be gone a minute, Micah. Hold on. Austin is right here."

With the old man making strange sounds she turned and hurried from the room.

She followed the small corridor that connected the walk-in clinic with the doctor's office. Once in the office she had to wait until the receptionist got off the phone with a patient before she could let her know that she was very concerned about Micah and ask that the doctor come immediately.

When the receptionist agreed to send the doctor to Micah's room, Cheyenne started back along the same corridor.

The door to Micah's room was closed.

She knew she'd left it open.

Puzzled, she opened it and stepped inside.

Austin was leaning over the bed, holding a pillow to Micah's face.

"What...?"

Austin's head came up sharply. The look on his face was one Cheyenne had never seen before. A look of pure evil.

All the color drained from her as she realized what he was doing.

With a cry of rage she raced across the room and snatched the pillow from his hand, tossing it to the floor.

Micah lay as still as death.

Austin gave a snarl of fury and slapped her so hard her head snapped to one side. Then with a grunt he shoved her against the wall, pinning her arms at her sides.

She experienced a surge of outrage. "Take your hands off me."

At her words he merely smiled. A terrible, chilling smile. "I'll put my hands on you any time I please. And you can't stop me. Just like that old coot couldn't stop me."

She tried to shake off his hands, and they merely tightened on her until she couldn't move. With her body pinned to the wall, her arms effectively immobilized, she hissed out a breath. "Are you mad?"

His smile disappeared, replaced by a look of cold disdain. "I happen to be the smartest man on earth. And you, you stupid, all-trusting idiot, are about to learn just how smart I really am." His grasp tightened and he pulled her away from the wall before twisting her arms behind her until she cried out in pain.

With one arm around her throat he pressed until she

was struggling for breath. And still he pressed until strange lights began dancing in front of her eyes. She could feel herself slipping into a deep, dark hole and realized that she was about to lose consciousness.

He bent close to her ear. "If you want me to stop, nod once, and I'll relax my grip, as long as you promise to walk quietly ahead of me. If you don't agree to my terms, I'll just keep on until you pass out cold and I'll carry you."

She managed the faintest nod of her head and was relieved when he loosened his grip on her, just enough to allow her to breathe.

As he relaxed the pressure on her throat she sucked air into her starving lungs. Gasping for every breath, she could feel her legs beginning to tremble, and she feared she might fall to the floor.

Austin caught her by her hair and yanked hard enough to have tears springing to her eyes.

"Start walking."

With one arm around her waist, the other firmly grasping her hand in his, he dragged her to the doorway.

She turned for a last look at Micah, who continued to lie as still as death.

With a muttered oath Austin hauled her outside, where one of her ranch trucks was idling.

She stared around wildly, hoping to see Quinn returning from the police chief's office, or someone else who would recognize her. Before she had a chance to call out, Austin shoved her into the cab of the truck and roughly tied her hands behind her back before tying her ankles as well. In a flash he was behind the wheel before taking off with a screech of tires.

As they drove through town, he turned up the radio

and began to sing along with reckless abandon at the top of his lungs.

While Cheyenne struggled to loosen her bonds, her mind was in turmoil.

Austin had smothered Micah. Smothered her dear, sweet old friend.

This was why Micah had been so agitated. Had he known what Austin was planning? But how?

And then another thought struck. A thought her mind could barely accept.

The fire. Had Micah seen Austin start the fire? Was that why he'd fought so hard when Austin had entered the room? Was that why Austin had silenced him?

That had to be what Micah had been trying to communicate to Rusty, to the doctor, to her and Quinn. And instead of at least allowing him to try to convey the truth, the doctor had subjected him to sedation.

Micah. Dear, sweet old Micah. After surviving a raging fire in the bunkhouse, he had now been smothered to death. It was too horrible, too impossible, to imagine.

Even while Cheyenne was overcome with grief for her dear friend she was also terrified.

Where was Austin planning on taking her? And why?

She had no answers. She knew only that in order to have done what she suspected him of doing Austin Baylor had to be completely mad.

He was a killer with no conscience.

Sweet heaven. She was helpless to do more than rage against the painful cord digging into her wrists and ankles. And all the while she was in the hands of a madman.

A madman who was singing at the top of his lungs, as though he hadn't a care in the world.

CHAPTER TWENTY-FIVE

———◆◆◆———

Quinn stepped into Micah's room to find Dr. Walton bending over the old man's bed adjusting an oxygen mask.

With a smile Quinn glanced around. "Where's Cheyenne?"

The doctor's usually placid bedside manner turned brisk. "That's what I'd like to know. She told my assistant that she was worried about Micah, but when I got here she was nowhere to be seen. And my patient is in a terrible state. Look at him. He looks like he's been in the fight of his life. When I walked into his room that first thing I saw was the pillow from his bed tossed clear across the room. If he did it, he must be Superman. He was hyperventilating, his breathing so labored you'd have thought he'd been mountain-climbing instead of lying quietly in a bed. And if that isn't enough, look at the marks on his wrists. Like somebody locked his hands together and was holding him down."

"Have you asked him what happened?"

"Of course I didn't. Look at him. He's exhausted, and fighting for every breath."

"Is he too sedated to hear me?"

At Quinn's question the doctor shook her head. "I'm sure he can hear. He just can't speak over that smoke-damaged throat."

Quinn leaned over Micah, bringing his face into the old man's line of vision. "Micah. It's Quinn Conway. Do you know what happened to Cheyenne?"

The old man's eyes went wide and once again he tried to tear off the mask.

When Dr. Walton tried to hold the mask in place, Quinn laid a hand over the doctor's, to still her movements. "Could you remove the oxygen for a minute?"

"I don't under—"

"This is critical. I'm talking about life and death, Dr. Walton."

With a sigh of frustration the doctor removed the mask, and Quinn leaned closer as Micah struggled to make himself understood.

"Aus..." Micah began coughing.

"Austin. Was he here?" Quinn demanded.

The old man nodded.

"Did Cheyenne go with him?"

Again, Micah nodded.

"Did she go willingly?"

He shook his head. "She...fought."

Quinn's heart sank. "Do you know where he's taking her?"

The old man's eyes turned bleak, and he made a low, moaning sound.

Quinn squeezed his arm. "Don't worry, Micah. I'm calling the police chief now. We'll find her."

Micah clutched Quinn's sleeve. "He's..." A series of wracking coughs left him gasping for breath.

Dr. Walton brought the mask to his face. "I can't wait any longer. He needs this now."

"No." The old man continued clutching Quinn's sleeve, eyes wide and pleading, as he struggled to get the words out. "Austin's...evil."

"I know that now. And believe me, Micah, I intend to see that he doesn't hurt Cheyenne." He patted Micah's arm. "Rest now. Do what the doctor says, and get yourself strong enough to get out of here. I swear to you, I'll find them, and see that Cheyenne is safe."

Quinn turned away and dialed the police chief. As he stepped from the room and sprinted toward the front door he said, "Are you at Cheyenne's ranch yet?"

"Just driving up." The chief gave several loud, savage oaths at the scene of carnage unfolding before him. "There's nothing left of the bunkhouse but ashes. It's a wonder old Micah made it out."

"What about Cheyenne? Is her truck there?"'

"I thought she was at the clinic."

"She's gone. Micah said she left with Austin. And not willingly."

The chief swore again. "I'll look around here. There are plenty of barns and outbuildings where he could hide."

Quinn heard the slam of the chief's car door. "I'm not seeing any vehicles around. Can you think of any other place they'd go?"

"He could be taking her anywhere." Quinn climbed into the truck. As he pulled the door shut, he had a flash of memory. Cheyenne had told him she'd had a feeling of being watched in the night.

"My cabin." He put the truck in gear and started along the main street. "Chief, I have a cabin in the northernmost section of our ranch. In high country. I'll give you directions as I drive. If I'm right, Austin, or whatever his name is, may have followed us there last night."

"What reason would he have for taking Cheyenne there?"

Quinn's tone was grim. "I have no idea how a madman's mind works. But if I'm right, he wants me to find them."

"I'm calling in the state police. I don't need to warn you, Quinn. You're dealing with a sociopath. If you get there ahead of the law, you need to be extremely careful."

"Right." He dropped his cell phone into his shirt pocket and, as he drove away from town and hit the main highway, floored the gas pedal.

He had no plan in mind. No idea what he would do if he found Cheyenne with Austin at his cabin. He knew he ought to be plotting what to do when he got there. But he couldn't seem to wrap his mind around anything except the fact that the woman he loved was at the mercy of a crazed gunman.

The woman he loved.

The realization hit him with all the force of a bullet.

Whatever doubts he'd had before, there was no doubt now. He knew with absolute certainty that he loved Cheyenne. Loved her as he'd never loved anyone.

He prayed that he wouldn't be too late to tell her.

As the truck roared along the highway, Cheyenne struggled against the bonds at her wrists, securely fastened behind her back. The cord cut into her. The more she struggled, the more it tore at the tender flesh of her wrists, until blood began to run in little rivers down her back.

Each time a vehicle approached from the opposite direction, she stared hungrily at the people inside, hoping someone would catch her eye. If only she could wave her arms or kick her feet through the windshield, she thought. But all she could do was stare silently and pray.

Beside her, Austin seemed to be enjoying her misery. The more she struggled against her bonds, the louder he sang along with the music on the radio.

When their truck veered off the highway onto a stretch of woods, she went very still.

"Recognize this, Cheyenne?" His voice was exceptionally happy.

Her heart nearly stopped.

"Answer me. Do you recognize this?"

"Yes." She swallowed. "The road to Quinn's cabin."

"Your little lover's hideaway in the mountains. Cozy." He hummed as he maneuvered the truck between low-hanging branches of trees that brushed the windows and scraped against the roof of the cab.

"How do you know about it?"

"I was there last night. Watching you. You woke up and looked around." He gave a low rumble of laughter. "Oh, it was so much fun watching you trying to see in the dark. Afterward you climbed back in the bed and you were all snug in Conway's arms. Snug as a bug."

He seemed to like the phrase and repeated it over and over. "Snug as a bug. Snug as a bug." He smiled over at her. "My little bug. I'm going to squash you. You and Conway."

"Why?"

"Because I can."

As they bumped along the rutted trail, she began to feel more and more desperate. Her last hope of attracting attention from passing vehicles was gone. There would be no one here to see or hear. No one to find her.

"Why did you smother Micah?"

"Honestly?" He turned with a smile. "I hate that old man. I've always hated him."

"But why? What has he ever done to you except feed you and make you feel welcome?"

"Oh, gee. You're breaking my heart. What do you care? He's nothing." Austin snapped his fingers. "Less than nothing. I don't want to talk about him. Let's talk about you. Micah said you're in love with Conway. That you're going to marry him and give up the ranch. That true?"

She went very still, weighing his words. "When did Micah say this?"

"Yesterday, when you and Conway left your ranch. The old man said you had the look of a woman in love."

"And that's why you followed us? This is all about me, and my feelings for Quinn?"

"You don't get it, do you? It's all about me. Let's just say I'm curious." He glanced over, but this time he wasn't smiling. "This happened awfully fast. One day you're staying at his ranch; the next you're sleeping with him in his"—his hand swept the cabin looming before them in the woods—"his little love nest."

Her throat went dry as he brought the truck to a sudden halt. He was out the door and around to hers before she could blink. He dragged her roughly out of the truck and up to the front of the cabin.

With his booted foot against the door he shoved it inward and pulled her inside before kicking the door shut.

He caught sight of the blood soaking the sleeves of her shirt. "You wasted all that effort for nothing. You think you can break through those?" He gave a short laugh. "The harder you fight against them, the more you hurt yourself. Go on. Try all you like. All you'll get is more pain."

He pushed her into a chair before crossing to the bed, where he opened a backpack and began removing things from it. A handgun. A knife.

Whistling a tune, he walked to the kitchen area and began making a pot of coffee. When it was ready he poured himself a cup.

"Sorry you can't join me, but it's kind of hard drinking without a free hand."

He laughed at his little joke, and Cheyenne wondered how she could have ever thought of him as normal. Even his laughter sounded manic. Especially when she could see the spark of madness in his eyes each time he looked at her.

"Let's get nice and comfy." He sat, tilting back his chair, propping his feet on the table, and sipping his coffee. "We have to wait for the second act."

"Josh?" Quinn maneuvered the truck with one hand while shouting into his cell phone.

The rutted pathway had his truck rocking from side to side as he took each twist and turn at top speed.

"Yeah, Bro. You sound excited about something. Did you get that pretty woman to finally kiss you?"

"I'm in trouble, Josh."

"Nothing new for you."

Quinn swore.

Hearing the change in his brother's tone, Josh was instantly alert. "Okay. Spill it."

As quickly as possible Quinn laid out what he'd learned from Chief Fletcher.

"Where are you now?"

"Just coming up to my cabin. I can see one of Cheyenne's ranch trucks parked out front."

"You going to just charge in there like the U.S. Cavalry?"

"There's no way to hide. We're in the middle of wilderness. They could hear my truck coming a mile away. Besides, with only one way in or out, he's bound to be watching me driving up this path."

"Okay. You got your rifle?"

"Yeah. But I have a feeling he's not stupid enough to let me walk through the door with it."

Josh's voice began to fade in and out, and Quinn could tell he was running through the barn. "I'll have Big Jim take up the plane."

"There's no place to land it here."

"We'll find a spot. It's the fastest way I know to get there. So do whatever you have to do to keep this crazy guy from killing both of you until we can get there."

"I'll do my best." Quinn took a breath as he brought his truck to a stop. "Tell Pa and Big Jim—"

"You tell them yourself when this is over, Bro." Josh rang off.

Quinn opened the truck door and grabbed his rifle before striding toward the cabin.

When he was halfway there the door was flung open

and Cheyenne was framed in the doorway. Her hands and ankles were bound, and blood dripped from her wrists, causing Quinn to suck in a breath of horror at the sight of her. It was one thing to imagine her in peril. It was another to witness the real thing.

From behind her came the familiar, too-pleasant voice of the man who'd called himself Austin Baylor.

"Come on in. We've been expecting you. But before you take another step, you'd better toss that rifle this way. It just isn't neighborly of you to bring a weapon into our little lovefest."

CHAPTER TWENTY-SIX

Quinn paused at the foot of the steps, his rifle at his side. It took all his willpower to tamp down the wave of fury he felt at the sight of Cheyenne looking so wounded.

He fought to keep his tone level. "Are you okay?"

"Yes. I'm—"

Austin's voice broke in. "No small talk until you toss that rifle."

Cheyenne's head came up sharply. "Don't do it, Quinn. He's already killed Micah. Now he's going to kill us, too."

"Micah isn't dead."

She shook her head. "He is. I saw Austin smother him."

"He may have tried to, but he didn't succeed. I just left the clinic, and Micah's going to be fine."

At the news Austin swore savagely. "I said toss me that rifle and be quick about it unless you want to watch your precious woman die right now."

Quinn tossed the rifle and Austin caught it in midair

before yanking Cheyenne viciously by her hair and dragging her backward into the room.

As Quinn stepped into the cabin, Austin shouted,
"Close the door and lock it."

"Afraid of visitors?"

"I just don't want any surprises."

Quinn pulled the door shut and set the lock. Before he
could turn around he heard Cheyenne's cry of alarm and
felt a blow to his head that staggered him and had him
dropping to his knees. He shook his head to clear the stars
that were dancing before his eyes, only to find Austin
standing over him, the rifle held like a club in his hands.

"That was just to let you know who's in charge here.
Unless you do exactly as I say, you'll get something
worse." He pointed with the butt of the rifle. "Sit over
there, next to your woman."

Quinn crossed to Cheyenne and touched a hand to her
cheek. "Stay strong, baby."

"I didn't say you could touch her." A shot rang out and
Quinn heard Cheyenne's scream just as a searing red-hot
pain shot through his arm. In the same instant his limb
dropped uselessly to his side while blood spurted from the
wound like a fountain.

The pain had him clutching the edge of the table,
struggling to hold on.

When he turned, Austin was smiling that bright mega-
watt smile he could turn on and off like a switch. "Told
you. I'm in charge. Bet you won't forget it again."

With her hands behind her back, Cheyenne was helpless to do more than watch as Quinn absorbed wave after
wave of pain. "Oh, Quinn, I can't bear to see you hurt like
this."

"That's nothing to what you'll both get if you don't pay attention. Now," Austin said as cheerfully as though he were talking about the weather. "Sit next to your lady love where I can keep an eye on you."

"There's no reason to do this," Cheyenne cried. "You can see he's wounded, Austin."

"His name isn't Austin. It's Abbott. Abbott Monroe." Quinn's steely gaze bored into his opponent, pleased to see that he'd caught him off-guard.

"How do you . . . ?" Abbott's mouth opened and closed while he struggled to regain control of the situation.

Seeing it, Quinn knew at once that control was very important to this madman.

Abbott brandished his weapon. "What do you know about Abbott Monroe?"

Quinn dropped into the chair beside Cheyenne and ripped aside the sleeve from his plaid shirt, using his teeth and his good hand to tie off the wound. It didn't really help ease the pain, but it helped slow and absorb a good deal of the blood. "Only what the state police have said. They know all about your little charade."

Cheyenne stared from one man to the other. "I don't understand. What are you talking about, Quinn?"

"Our friend here assumed the identity of a dead man, so that his own criminal history couldn't be traced."

"Criminal history?"

"When you gave your personnel records to the state police, they learned that Austin Baylor has been dead for years. He died in a mental facility."

"But how did you . . . ?" She turned to Abbott. "How could you know about a dead man in a mental facility?"

When he said nothing, Quinn gave a dry laugh. "He

knew because he was there, too. He was one of the mental patients."

"Shut up!" Abbott lifted the rifle and swung it at Quinn's head.

Quinn's ears were ringing from the blow, a strange, faraway buzzing, and he wondered how much longer he would be able to remain conscious. He knew that he needed to buy some time. Time enough for Chief Fletcher and the state police to get here. Time for his family to fly here. But how long would it be before this crazed animal would lose control completely and kill him? Not that his life mattered right now. His only thought was saving Cheyenne. He had to distract Abbott until someone could get here in time to save her life.

Now that he was face-to-face with this monster, he realized just how dangerous Abbott Monroe was. He'd never before dealt with a psychopath. Charming as hell one minute, a vicious, cold-blooded killer the next.

Quinn made a vow to himself. He would save Cheyenne at any cost. And that meant that he had to keep Abbott talking, even if it meant bearing the brunt of his fury to do so.

"It seems Abbott has a history of getting rid of people that get in his way. He likes to set fires. Isn't that right, Abbott?"

Instead of the angry response he'd expected, Abbott surprised Quinn by puffing up his chest. "I set my first fire when I was six. You should have seen my baby brother's face get all red and twisted when his blanket started to burn." He threw back his head and chuckled. "When my mother found us, I went into my innocent act and actually helped her put out the flames. That night I was hailed on TV as a little hero." He began to laugh, that high, wild sound that scraped on nerves already stretched to the breaking point. "Nobody would ever believe that a sweet little kid like me could do something like that on purpose. When I realized I'd managed to get away with my little lie, I decided to try it again. That time my stupid parents and little brother didn't survive. Poor me. A little orphan at the age of twelve." His eyes went flat. "But then I got a foster family, and they weren't any better. So..." He shrugged. "I figured I'd take them out the same way I'd taken out my family. And it worked. Only that time, the shrinks and government agencies got into the act and put me in a mental hospital for 'evaluation.'" His voice lowered. "I knew I had to get away for good, or I'd rot in that stinking place. So, when Austin died, with no family around to mourn, I decided to be him if I ever managed to slip away and get another chance. I watched and waited, and one day the opportunity came. And here I am."

"The fire at my ranch. It wasn't an accident. You set it." Cheyenne couldn't keep the horror from her voice.

"That's why he insisted on the quick cleanup, isn't it, Abbott? To hide the rags you'd used to start the fire?"

"Clever, wasn't I? By the time the insurance investigator got there, the evidence had disappeared."

"And now you tried to kill Micah in a fire, too." Cheyenne's tone was one of disbelief.

Abbott swaggered across the room and tossed the rifle onto the bed before picking up the handgun and knife, as though preferring his own weapons to Quinn's.

He turned to her. "Micah should have died. I gave the old guy a whack on his head that would've killed most men. Then I set the fire and left, thinking he was a goner."

His smile faded as he tucked the pistol into the waistband of his pants. "If I'd thought for one minute that he'd manage to crawl away from that inferno, I would've stayed and finished him off."

"But why target Micah?" Quinn asked.

"In case you haven't noticed, he's as close to Cheyenne as her father and brother were. After eliminating them, I realized he had to go, too."

Quinn went very still as the words sank in. This went so much deeper than he'd first thought.

He fought to keep his tone even. "Eliminated? Are you saying that Cheyenne's father and brother didn't die in accidents?"

The smile was back, and Quinn realized that Abbott was enjoying himself. This madman relished the opportunity to brag about the unspeakable things he'd done.

"Buddy was so easy. He was like a big, dumb puppy. I knew exactly how to play him. I hadn't planned on taking him out like that, but it had to be done quickly after he ran into Deke Vance at the bar and the two of them went off to a booth in the corner to talk. I knew, by the look on Buddy's face, that Deke had managed to persuade him that he hadn't stolen that money."

"You set Deke up?"

At Cheyenne's gasp his evil smile grew. "That part was easy. All I had to do was accuse that poor dumb fool of stealing, then to prove it, I stuck the two hundred-dollar bills I'd stolen from the drawer into his parka pocket, carried it in from the utility room, and poof." He clapped his hands together. "Deke became a thief, convicted in the eyes of the whole family. Once I had all of you believing that, the rest all fell into place. Until that night at the bar.

Then I knew that Buddy had to go, because he no longer believed me."

"You said my brother was drunk." Cheyenne's voice was little more than a whisper as she tried to take in all that he was saying. It was simply too much to absorb.

"Buddy never drank more than a beer. But I made sure that everybody in the place saw me buy him three more. The waitress delivered them to his booth. He probably left them there, or maybe Deke drank them. When we left, Buddy said he wanted to talk, and I put him off, saying we'd talk at home. I stayed close behind him in my truck and waited until we reached a stretch of deserted road. Knowing Buddy, and that strict code of honor, I figured he was distracted and probably beating himself up over the fact that he'd misjudged his best friend, and that had him driving faster than he usually did. It was so easy to pull alongside and slam him as hard as I could. His truck went out of control and spun around before hitting that tree and exploding." He shook his head before adding, "Now there was a ball of fire. A really great blaze. I made sure the flames did the trick before calling for help."

Cheyenne couldn't bear the pain. With her hands still tied behind her back she lowered her head to the table, hoping to blot out his words.

Quinn's voice was a low growl of fury. "Untie her hands."

Abbott whirled on him. "Did you just try to give me an order? What did I tell you?" He lifted the rifle and took aim at Quinn's head. "I'm in charge here."

Quinn didn't flinch. "Shoot me if you want. But untie her hands. She's just learned that you killed her brother. Or aren't you man enough to let her mourn in peace?"

"I'm more man than you'll ever hope to be. Man enough to kill anyone in my way." Instead of pulling the trigger, Abbott used his knife to cut through the cords on her wrists.

Cheyenne buried her face in her hands and slumped forward at the table, unable to absorb all that she'd heard. It was simply too much for her mind to accept.

"What about Cheyenne's father?" Quinn kept his tone level, to hide the fury that was raging through him. Now that he'd managed to persuade Abbott to free Cheyenne's hands, he needed to find a way to get her out of harm's way.

Abbott snagged a chair, turned it around, and leaned his arms on the back of it. The knife rested in his lap.

"Her father's death took a little more finesse." Abbott had the satisfaction of seeing Cheyenne's head come up sharply, her eyes wide with stunned surprise.

A big smile split his lips. "You heard right. After Buddy was gone, I persuaded your dad to keep me on at the ranch and consider me part of the family. I started calling him Dad, because I could see that he liked it. While we were in the hills with the herd I asked him for your hand in marriage. And he said I was putting the cart before the horse. He actually laughed at his little joke." Abbott shook his head, as though still unable to believe what her father had told him. "He said he knew his daughter as well as he knew himself and he'd never seen any sign that you thought of me as anything except a friend. He expected that someday he would recognize that you were wildly in love with some cowboy and only then would he give his blessing." His smile was wiped instantly from his lips. "I knew what I had to do. That night I told him about some of the herd splitting off from the rest and getting trapped in a box canyon. I suggested that he take an all-terrain vehicle up there to drive the herd back down. It was an easy matter to follow him up into the hills on horseback, so he wouldn't hear me above the sound of his engine. I watched when his vehicle flipped, after hitting a rope."

Cheyenne looked startled. "A rope?"

"Yeah. A rope I'd strung earlier along the path, knowing it would be invisible in the dusk. Then I stuck around to make sure he was trapped under his vehicle and wasn't going to make it out of there before I pocketed the rope and headed back to the ranch, so I'd be there when his body was found."

"You left my father all alone in the hills to freeze to death?" The pain in her heart was so deep, so all-consuming, she could hardly speak. "Why? We took you in and treated you like family. Why would you kill the people who had opened their hearts and their home to you?"

"Why?" His voice took on a whine, like a petulant child. "I'll tell you why. Now that I was free of that hateful mental prison, I vowed to live the life I wanted. And what I wanted was to be like Buddy. Part of a real family. When he invited me to his ranch, I met you, and realized that you were the key to everything I'd ever wanted. You and I would marry, and I'd be part of a real family and living the dream."

"But you never...We never..." Cheyenne paused, struggling to find the words. "My father spoke the truth. I didn't feel that way about you."

"You would have. Once you were alone, I figured

you'd have nobody else to turn to and you'd lean on me. The night of that first fire, when Micah arrived up in the hills and said you were alone, I figured I'd ride back and turn on the charm. Instead"—his voice turned to ice—"I found you alone with a stranger."

"And you set fire to my home?"

"He was reverting to type," Quinn said quietly. "It's how Abbott has always eliminated anybody who crossed him."

Abbott actually smiled at Cheyenne. "I toyed with the idea of letting Quinn die and saving you. But at the time, I was so furious, I wanted you both dead. But when you survived, I decided that I'd take you back."

"Take me...?" She couldn't believe what she was hearing.

"What about the fire at my ranch?" Quinn asked.

"I saw the way Deke reacted when he ran into you in town. Hell, half the town saw it. Nobody would question whether or not he was guilty of setting that fire. I figured it was a good way to get back at Deke and at you, for taking Cheyenne away from me."

"How could I take away someone who was never yours? She's already said she didn't want to be with you."

Abbott turned a blinding smile on Cheyenne. "Oh, I knew you'd come around. I just needed time alone with you to persuade you."

Watching him, hearing the wild sort of joy in his voice as he boasted of his prowess, left Cheyenne no doubt that he was utterly, completely mad. She wondered why she had missed the signs of it all this time. How could she have been so blind?

"You're crazy." She shook her head in disbelief.

"Don't call me that." His attitude went from wildly happy to unbridled fury in the blink of an eye.

With the knife raised threateningly, he started across the room.

Quinn's mind raced, determined to keep him distracted. "What will you do now that the police are on to you?"

Abbott stopped dead in his tracks. "Yeah. Now that's a problem. But I've always been good at solving problems. In case you haven't noticed"—he tossed his head in a gesture of supreme pride—"I'm a genius. The shrinks said I tested off the charts. So, for now, I may have to abandon my plan of creating a family here, but there are plenty of other places where I can start over. In the meantime, you have to die."

"Another fire?" Quinn taunted.

"Why not? We're far enough from civilization that nobody will notice the smoke until this cabin is nothing but a pile of ashes. And the two of you with it." He pointed to the pile of papers spilling out of his backpack and removed a container of gasoline. "There won't be enough left of either of you to identify for months."

"I don't understand why you didn't use a fire to eliminate Cheyenne's father."

Abbott's eyes flashed. "Don't think I didn't want to. There's something so satisfying about a really hot blaze. But I had to act quickly, before he told Cheyenne what we'd talked about. So I improvised."

When he heard the drone of a plane, his head came up sharply.

"Did I forget to tell you?" It was Quinn's turn to smile. "I contacted the state police and my family on the way here. Sounds like they've finally made it."

As the sound drew nearer, Abbott raced to the window to watch as a low-flying plane appeared to be pointed directly at the cabin.

At the last moment the nose of the plane lifted and it passed directly overhead, then turned and made another low pass.

Directly behind them a helicopter, clearly marked with the state police logo, came into view over the hills.

Abbott turned from the window and saw that Quinn had used that moment of distraction to race across the room and snatch the rifle from the bed.

Before Quinn could take aim, Abbott dragged Cheyenne from the chair and held his knife to her throat.

"Okay, hero. Let's just see what kind of gambler you are." With a high-pitched laugh he pressed the blade to her throat, drawing a thin line of blood that trickled down the front of her shirt.

At her cry of pain his smile grew. "Now you have a choice. You can drop the weapon, knowing you'll have to die, or watch your woman die right this minute."

Quinn tossed the rifle aside. "Let her go, Abbott."

"Now why would I do a stupid thing like that?" He withdrew a lighter from his pocket and dropped it onto the papers in his backpack, watching with satisfaction as the flame caught.

They could see the flames grow, the line of fire moving slowly toward the container of gas.

Abbott's voice was jubilant. "Once it hits, there'll be this exquisite explosion, and this entire log cabin will burn like tinder."

He dragged Cheyenne across the room toward the door. "Sorry we have to leave your lover behind. With the law this close, I'll need to use you as my ticket out of here. Even the law's best marksmen won't risk the life of an innocent woman."

When he realized the door was locked, he lowered the knife and gave her a shove. "Unlock the door and be quick about it."

Quinn knew that this was his last chance. Calculating the distance, he leaped at Abbott and managed to take him down.

"Run, Cheyenne. Get out. And don't look back."

The two men rolled across the floor, grunting, exchanging blows, breathing hard each time a fist made contact with flesh. Each man fought like a demon, neither willing to give an inch.

Even while he was pummeling his weakened opponent, Abbott struggled to free the gun from his waist. As he slid it loose, Quinn's fist connected with his nose, sending up a fountain of blood.

With a scream of pain Abbott pressed the pistol against Quinn's chest. "Now you're going to—"

Quinn brought his head up under Abbott's chin with such force, he could hear bone scrape against bone at the same instant that the sound of the gunshot reverberated through the room. With a cry of pain at his broken jaw Abbott dropped the pistol. But the bullet had already shot into Quinn's body with enough force to send him slamming against the wall before slumping to the floor.

Clutching his broken jaw, Abbott began frantically searching for his fallen weapon. Just as his fingers closed around the cold steel, he felt a boot clamp down hard, crushing his hand. He looked up to see Cheyenne standing over him.

"Don't try it," he hissed.

"Try to stop me." In one quick motion she bent and snatched up the handgun before straightening and taking aim.

Abbott rolled aside and knelt over Quinn's motionless body, the knife in his hands pointed directly at Quinn's chest.

"Well now. It's your turn to gamble." His smile was back and, with it, his too-cheerful confidence. "I'm betting that before you have time to pull that trigger, I can plunge this knife so far into his heart, he won't have a prayer of a chance of surviving."

Cheyenne hesitated.

That was all Abbott needed. He gave a high-pitched laugh. "Just as I thought. Coward. You're all a bunch of—"

A single shot rang out and Abbott went rigid, staring at Cheyenne with a look of shock mingled with pure hatred as she prepared to fire again.

"You...can't..." The knife slid from his nerveless fingers. His mouth worked, trying to speak, but no words came out.

His eyes went suddenly blank and he slumped forward.

Cheyenne tossed aside the pistol and pulled Abbott's deadweight off Quinn.

"Oh, Quinn." Seeing so much blood, she began feeling for a pulse. "Oh, sweet heaven. Please stay strong. Please don't die."

"Get...out," he managed to mutter. "Fire—"

"No!" She began dragging him through the open doorway. "I'm not leaving without you."

His body, pure muscle, was massively heavy, and she had to use every ounce of her being to drag him to safety.

Just as they reached the porch there was a deafening explosion as the flame hit the gasoline and erupted in a fireball that tore off a piece of the cabin's roof.

Cheyenne and Quinn were thrown down the steps by the force of the blast and landed in the grass.

"Oh, Quinn." Cheyenne's tears were now sobs as she felt for a pulse. "Please stay with me. Please."

"Don't . . . cry."

Hearing his voice, she wrapped her arms around him and rocked him like a baby. "Oh, God. There's so much blood. You've been shot. Stay with me, Quinn. Please, please don't die." She couldn't stop the tears that flowed like rivers.

Quinn tried to lift a hand to her face, but the effort was too great and his arm fell heavily to his side.

Suddenly the scene around them erupted into chaos.

The Conway men raced forward to gather around Cheyenne and Quinn, followed by Chief Everett Fletcher and a team of state police officers.

For the space of several seconds they simply stared at Cheyenne, sitting on the ground, cradling Quinn's body in her arms, her tears mingling with his blood to form a mottled puddle in the grass around them.

"Is he alive?" Cole demanded, dropping to his knees beside Cheyenne.

"He is. But barely. He's been shot."

Cole felt his son's feeble, thready pulse and took a deep breath, knowing nothing else mattered as long as Quinn's heart continued to beat.

Big Jim, needing to do something, anything, began shouting orders. "We need an ambulance. Our boy needs a medic."

Cole's next thought was the madman. "Josh. Jake. We need to make certain that scum doesn't get away."

"Don't worry, Cole." Chief Fletcher put a hand on his arm and pointed to the line of uniformed officers swarming about the burning cabin.

Minutes later they emerged carrying Abbott's lifeless body while others raced around bagging evidence before it could be swallowed by the raging fire.

A team of medical personnel began strapping Quinn to a gurney and administering an intravenous to ease his pain.

Through it all, Cheyenne refused to let go of Quinn's hand.

"Sorry, ma'am," a burly medic said. "We need to load him into a copter for a flight back to town."

"I'm going with him."

One of the officers started to refuse until Quinn said, "She...goes...or I stay."

The officer gave a nod of his head and the medic smiled. "This way, ma'am."

Minutes later, as the police helicopter lifted off, scattering a mix of dirt and snow, Cheyenne huddled beside Quinn, her head resting against his chest, her heart taking comfort in the steady beat of his.

It was, she thought, the very best sound in the world.

The world? It no longer mattered. For now, for as long as she could be with him, all that mattered was this man. He was, she thought contentedly, her world, her universe, her everything.

CHAPTER TWENTY-SEVEN

$\blacklozenge$

Dr. April Walton walked through the doorway connecting her office with her walk-in clinic to discover a mob scene.

Quinn lay in the examining room, surrounded by family. Because he had steadfastly refused to be airlifted to a hospital in Casper, insisting that he would go no farther than Paintbrush, the Conway family had completely taken over the little building.

"Drink," Ela said, lifting a spoon to his lips.

The old woman, her gray hair perfectly braided, her native dress covered with a white apron, held a bowl of homemade soup that perfumed the room with its steam. "It will heal you."

To keep her from fussing, Quinn accepted several spoonfuls from her before lifting a hand to refuse any more.

"Enough."

"But I made a pot of it."

Quinn pointed to Micah, seated in a wheelchair in a corner of the room. "Feed the rest to him."

Quinn expected her to give him an argument. Instead, the old woman waddled across the room and planted herself beside Micah.

Big Jim settled into a chair by the bed and propped his feet on the edge of the mattress. "This reminds me of the time Clementine had to haul me into town after a bear attacked me up in the hills." He looked over at his grandsons. "Have I ever told you this story?"

Josh and Jake exchanged knowing smiles.

Jake muttered, "Probably a hundred times or more. But what's one more time among family?"

"It was the spring of '46, and this old bear must have just come out of his den after a long winter of hibernation. Probably hungry, and mad as a hornet," he added, chuckling. "I turned around and there he was. I dropped my rifle and started up the nearest tree, but he was quicker, and he grabbed me by my leg and hauled me back down. Luckily, as he started dragging me on the ground, my rifle was close enough to snag, but by the time I got off a shot he'd put his teeth through my thigh, and I knew I'd bleed to death if I didn't get help fast. I tied a tourniquet and rode my horse down the hill. Clementine tossed my hide in the truck and drove through a spring thunderstorm into town, where old Doc Walton, Dr. April's daddy, sewed me up good as new."

Dr. April took one look at Big Jim's feet on the bed and gave him her best hairy eyeball until he dutifully slid them to the floor and straightened the bed linens.

Cole walked in with a tray of burgers and shakes from Flora's Diner. As he began passing them around, Phoebe Hogan shook a finger in his face.

"Don't you even think about eating all that grease and sugar, Cole Conway."

He was about to argue until he saw the glint of anger in her eyes. Adopting a contrite tone, he said, "Hell, I was just trying to stave off starvation. Why, my poor old father—"

"Can still outwork, outrun, and outtalk everyone in this family, and you know it. It was just an excuse for you to sneak over to Flora's and have a piece of her coconut cream pie."

He gave her a pained expression. "How can you even accuse me of such a thing?"

"How?" She touched a finger to the corner of his mouth before holding it up. "Here's the evidence. Whipped cream. Oh, Cole, how could you?"

He looked truly contrite. "I didn't mean anything by it, Phoebe. It's just—"

"While you two argue, would you mind passing over those burgers and shakes?" Jake took the tray from his father's hands and began handing the food and drinks around.

Quinn looked at Cheyenne, who sat silently beside him, holding his hand in hers.

"Feeling a little smothered yet by my crazy family?"

She managed a laugh. Oh, it was so good to be able to laugh, after all they'd been through. "Not at all. I just love watching all of them, and listening to all their crazy stories. They're really special, you know."

"Yeah." He motioned her to come closer.

She inched her chair closer and leaned over him. "What is it? Are you having some pain?"

He gave a slow shake of his head. "With all the painkillers Dr. April gave me, I probably won't come down until next week. Believe me, I'm high as a kite. I just want you close."

"What can I do to make you feel better?"

"You've already done it. You saved my life."

"And you saved mine."

"I guess that makes us even."

She shook her head. "Hardly. When I think about all the trouble you and your family suffered because of me. I never dreamed that Austin...I mean Abbott...was a cold-blooded killer."

"Chief Fletcher called him a textbook sociopath. Perfectly charming, until anyone got in his way. Then he could kill without a second thought."

She shivered. "All the same, your beautiful family shouldn't have had to deal with it."

"Look at them. They're none the worse for it." Quinn couldn't stop grinning. "They're treating this more like a family reunion than some kind of medical emergency."

"Like I said, you have a very special family."

"They think you're special, too. And I happen to agree with them. So, how about joining us?"

"Joining?"

He paused. This wasn't at all how he'd planned on asking her. The painkillers must have loosened his tongue, as well as his brain. But now that he'd blurted it out, there was no going back. He decided to soldier on. Especially since it was such a great idea. "I guess what I'm saying is, how would you like to become a Conway?"

It took her a moment to get his meaning. She cocked her head to one side, regarding him. "Are you... proposing?"

"Yeah. Are you accepting?"

She let go of his hand and stared hard at the floor. "This wasn't at all what I was expecting in this madhouse. It wasn't a very romantic proposal."

Quinn experienced a slice of razor-sharp fear. "I know the timing's all wrong. And it wasn't at all romantic, but it's the best I can do under the circumstances." He paused a beat, his smile fading. "Maybe I should have waited. I know my timing isn't always—"

She put a hand over his mouth. Just a touch, but they both felt the rush of heat.

She had to nearly shout to be heard above the din. "Actually, I was just thinking how much I'd like to join your crazy family. But I was figuring I'd have to ask your father to adopt me."

Quinn shook his head. "Not a good idea. That would make you my sister. And that would really mess with my plan."

"Just what is your plan?"

"The first part is having you accept my unromantic proposal."

She pretended to consider for long, silent moments. Finally, unable to keep from laughing, she said softly, "Even though it will probably get the award for the most unromantic proposal of all time, I accept. Call me crazy, but I want to be a part of your life, Quinn."

He gave a long, deep sigh. "Thank heaven." With his good arm he gathered her against his chest and kissed her until they were both sighing.

When the kiss ended, they became aware of an ominous silence. When Cheyenne lifted her head, the entire family had gathered around the bed.

As if on cue they broke into cheers.

Big Jim and Cole were laughing and slapping each other on the back. Josh and Jake came around the bed to hug Cheyenne while old Micah began wiping away tears.

Ela bent over the bed to kiss Quinn while Phoebe hurried around to embrace Cheyenne.

"All right." After this went on for several more minutes, Dr. April used her most authoritative tone of voice. "You will all clear this sickroom at once. I need to change my patient's dressings."

After more hugs and handshakes, the entire Conway clan began moving toward the hallway.

Cheyenne bent to brush another kiss on Quinn's lips before starting away.

The old doctor put a hand on her arm. "Not you, Cheyenne. You can stay."

"But—"

The old woman winked. "I've had a lifetime of dealing with the Conways. Sometimes, until you get used to them, they can be a bit overwhelming. I just figured you and Quinn deserved some quiet time. As for me..." She crossed to the door. "I've got appointments in my office. Folks in town will want to know the latest Conway gossip. And I have an inside track on it." She winked. "I'll be back in an hour or two. I'm sure you'll find something to do with the time alone."

With a mischievous grin she walked out, closing the door firmly behind her.

Quinn caught Cheyenne's hand in his and drew her close. "Now, let's see. Where were we?"

She lay down beside him in the bed, curling against him. "I believe we were about to plan a life together."

"Yeah." He kissed her, lingering over her lips, and felt a deep welling of contentment settle over him. When he could finally find his voice, he said against her lips, "I'm not sure one lifetime will be enough."

She laughed, low in her throat, before wrapping her arms around him. "Then we'd better start putting whatever time we have left to good use." She paused a moment before asking, "Just how much pain are you in at the moment?"

He gave a deep rumble of laughter. "What pain?" He reached for her. "Come here, woman. Let's get a head start on our future together."

EPILOGUE

———◆———

"Come on, Cheyenne honey. Time's a wasting. If we don't get going, the preacher will be there ahead of us." Micah leaned on his three-pronged cane and stood at the bottom of the stairs, staring at his watch.

In honor of the occasion, the old man had gone to town and bought himself a new suit and string tie, while insisting that he couldn't possibly replace his comfortable weathered boots that had seen him through years of ranch chores. Instead, he'd polished them until he could see his face in them.

When Cheyenne started down the stairs toward him, he had to swallow the lump that threatened to choke him.

She'd insisted on keeping things simple. No lacy bridal gown for her. Instead she'd chosen a fluid column of supple bleached cowhide that kissed her slender body and swirled about her ankles. The hem was scalloped and bore intricate Arapaho symbols.

"Is that your mama's wedding dress?"

Cheyenne nodded. "She once told me she'd made it herself."

She wore her thick, dark hair long and loose, the way Quinn liked it, pulled to one side with a diamond and pearl clip, leaving it to spill down her breast in a riot of curls. The effect was stunning.

"What do you think?" At the foot of the stairs she paused to twirl. When she turned back, she saw the tears in Micah's eyes. "That bad, huh?"

"Oh, Cheyenne honey, you're absolutely perfect." He caught her hand and led her toward the kitchen table, where a small white box lay. He picked it up and handed it to her. "I didn't want to give you this in front of everybody. It's...personal."

She opened the box to find a sparkly bracelet of woven bands of delicate silver and gold filigree.

"This was my mother's. It's the only thing I have of hers, and"—he smiled through his tears—"since you're the daughter I never had, I've been saving it for you."

"Oh, Micah." She held out her arm and he fastened it about her wrist.

She turned it this way and that, allowing the delicate bands of precious metal to catch and reflect the light. "I love it. I'll treasure it always. Thank you."

He lifted her hand to his lips. "I couldn't believe it when you said you wanted me to give you away. I figured you'd give that honor to Cole or Big Jim."

"They're my new family, Micah. You're my always family."

The old man turned away to keep from embarrassing himself. "Come on. Time to get going."

She followed him outside, to find Wes Mason and the wranglers seated on horseback in a semicircle around the truck. When they spotted her they tipped their wide-brimmed hats and began applauding.

Seated among them was Deke Vance.

She had arranged to meet with him to let him know all that she had learned about the man who had assumed the identity of a dead man named Austin Baylor. After her apology, which Deke had graciously accepted, he'd expressed relief that the truth had finally been uncovered and regret at the price her family had been forced to pay for their trust of a stranger. And then he'd surprised her by saying that he was still in need of a job and, since she would need a few extra hands while she settled into married life, he was more than willing to help out.

She paused to extend her hand. "Thank you again, Deke."

"No, Cheyenne." He winked at her. "Thank *you*. I'm just happy to be working here again."

She looked around at the circle of cowboys. "My thanks to all of you. You don't know how much it means to know that all of you are willing to spend this special day working while I'm off getting married."

Wes spoke for all of them. "Chey, you've earned a day all to yourself. Don't you worry about a thing here on the ranch. We'll take care of it like it's our own."

"I know you will. You always have." As she stepped into the truck she blew them a kiss, before putting the vehicle in gear.

Quinn had suggested that they live at his family ranch only until her own house was restored, after which it would be her decision whether to keep it or sell it. The fact that it would be her choice was the best gift he could have given her. She would take her time, weighing everything, before making a decision.

As she and Micah drove along the curving gravel driveway, she watched in the rearview mirror as the wranglers headed up into the hills to see to the never-ending ranch chores. Already her house, only partially restored, was rising from the ashes.

Like her life, she thought.

Big Jim climbed to the windswept hillside and paused beside the headstone, as he did nearly every day.

Earlier, Phoebe had filled two tall marble urns on either side of the graves with masses of fragrant white roses and trailing ivy and had tied white satin ribbon to the wooden bench, giving it a festive air.

"It's a grand day, old girl. Your grandson Quinn is about to take the big step." Big Jim touched a hand to the smooth marble. "If he's even half as happy as we were, he'll be the luckiest man in the world."

Big Jim watched as Cole and his three sons came strolling up the hill to join him.

When had these three become men? It seemed as though one minute they were those bold, brash little boys following him around like shadows, questioning everything, wanting to know the why and how and where of things. In the blink of an eye they had changed into tall, muscular, take-charge men capable of running this ranch, with all its complexities, with no trouble at all.

Quinn held up the bottle of aged Irish whiskey his grandfather had requested. Josh carried five tumblers. Jake had a box of cigars tucked under his arm.

"Well. Here we are." Big Jim cleared his throat. "About to celebrate a day I'd always hoped I'd live to see."

Quinn filled the tumblers and passed them around.

Big Jim had to swallow back the lump that lodged in his throat. "Every man dreams of seeing his children grow and prosper, and to see his children's children. There was a time when I thought I'd been cursed." He clapped a hand on his son's shoulder. "But Cole here defied the odds and lived to adulthood. With every year that passed I grew more proud and hopeful. And now, the first of my grandsons is about to add to the Conway history."

He touched his glass to Quinn's. "It's about time we welcomed a female into our family. You chose well. Your bride is not only beautiful; she's smart, and tough, and as brave as they come. So here's to you and your bride-to-be. May you live and prosper and be blessed with all good things."

"Hear! Hear!" The others touched their glasses and drank.

Jake passed around the box of cigars and Cole held a lighter to the tip of each one.

As rich clouds of smoke dissipated into the air they turned at the sound of a truck's engine and watched as Reverend Cornell started toward them, followed by Phoebe and Ela, who had been working all morning in the kitchen. Throughout the house the rich aroma of slow-cooked roast beef filled the air. It, along with garden vegetables and mashed potatoes, promised a wedding supper fit for a king. Ela's chocolate layer cake, with a filling of sweet cherries and frosted in mounds of soft, gooey whipped cream, was topped by a bride and groom holding wolf pups. It was, Phoebe had told the old woman, absolutely inspired.

Several bottles of champagne were on ice, in anticipation of the wedding supper.

Cheyenne's truck came to a halt beside the minister's, and she stepped down before hurrying around to loop her arm through Micah's.

"Wow." Josh gave a whistle. "Forget smart, tough, and brave. That is one gorgeous woman, Bro."

Quinn looked as though he'd just had a glimpse of heaven.

As Cheyenne and Micah approached, the others gathered around, giving her no chance to speak to Quinn.

"Oh, just look at you." Phoebe, caught up in the moment, gathered Cheyenne into her arms and hugged her.

When the two women stepped apart, Ela touched a hand to Cheyenne's gown. "This was your mother's."

"Yes."

"I helped her make it. She wore it with pride when she married her rancher. And now, it suits you as it suited her."

"Thank you." As Phoebe and Ela started to step aside Cheyenne stopped them. "I brought you each something."

They looked startled.

Cheyenne handed each of them a single white rose. "These are from my mother's rosebush. They were her favorites."

Phoebe dipped her face into the fragrant flower to hide her tears while Ela regarded Cheyenne with a piercing look.

"What's wrong?" Cheyenne asked the old woman.

"I gave your mother just such a flower when she married her rancher. I told her to plant it in her garden. If it grew, it would bring her many blessings."

Now it was Cheyenne's turn to hold back her tears.

The minister cleared his throat. "Would you folks like to begin the ceremony?"

As Quinn stepped up beside the minister, his brothers formed a line beside him.

Micah offered his arm and Cheyenne kissed his cheek before placing her hand on his arm. Together the two walked closer until Quinn stepped forward to claim his bride.

With the breeze tossing their hair and the perfume of roses all around them, the two spoke their vows before the minister and their family.

When they were finished, old Ela stepped forward. "This is the blessing of our people."

She placed a gnarled hand on each of their heads and said in a strong voice, "Now you will feel no rain, for each of you will be the shelter for the other. Now you will feel no cold, for each of you will be warmth for the other. Now you are two persons, but there is only one life. May your days be good and long upon the earth. May you remember always what brought you together." She touched their faces and smiled. "Go now to your dwelling place, and enter into the days of your togetherness."

Except for the whisper of the breeze in the trees, there was silence as her words washed over all of them.

Quinn gathered Cheyenne into his arms and kissed her, and the two remained locked in an embrace, the world around them forgotten for the moment.

Finally, Big Jim cleared the lump from his throat and broke the silence.

"I know that Phoebe and Ela have been working their magic in the kitchen all day. Let's head on back to the house and enjoy that wedding supper."

As their little group headed down the hill Quinn suddenly caught Cheyenne's hand and started sprinting toward his truck.

"Where are you going?" Cole shouted.

"Sorry, Pa. I have something important to take care of. We'll be back in time for that supper."

"What is this about?" Cheyenne was more than a little surprised by how quickly Quinn had hustled her into his truck. "I thought I'd lend a hand to Phoebe and Ela—"

"They have everything under control. There's something I want you to see." Quinn drove as fast as he could until he suddenly veered off the highway and headed along the familiar trail into the woods.

As they came to a halt he hurried around to open her door and take her hand.

"Oh, Quinn." Cheyenne stepped out of the truck and stared around in surprise.

The shell of a new cabin now stood in the spot in the woods where his old cabin had burned to the ground. All trace of the fire was gone. Even the charred ground was now beginning to be covered with fresh new life. Tiny evergreen seedlings had sprung up among the tangled growth of vines and wildflowers.

"So this is where you've been working every day when you leave my place."

He nodded. "I wanted to get it framed in before I showed you." He led her around the outer perimeter of the building. "I thought I'd add a big wooden deck back here, so we can leave our ranch chores behind and sit outside on a summer evening to watch the wildlife."

"It's the perfect spot for it."

"There's something else."

She could tell, by the tension in his voice, that he was about to say something of the utmost importance. "Having second thoughts so soon after the wedding?"

"You must be kidding." He gathered her close and kissed her lips. "You're the one who insisted on a proper ceremony. If I'd had my way, we'd have met with Judge Bolton weeks ago and made it legal."

"I know." She smiled up at him. "I'm glad you were willing to wait. I could see how much it meant to your family to make this into an occasion. I'm glad I thought of gifts for Phoebe and Ela. And look what Micah gave me." She lifted her arm to show off the sparkly bracelet at her wrist. "It belonged to his mother. I was so touched and he was so happy, we both cried."

"Happy tears." Quinn kissed her again. "They're the best kind."

"Yes, they are. All right." She looked around. "Now tell me that 'something else' you mentioned."

He nodded toward a stand of trees some distance from the cabin. "While I was working, I heard a few yips and spotted a wolf family. Their den is in that woods. I'm thinking of tagging the young male."

"Oh, Quinn. You've found your next wolf to study."

"Only if you agree. It means a lot of time on the trail, in the wilderness, following wherever they lead."

"You think I'd object to your life's work? Quinn, I don't mind how much time you're gone, as long as you always come home to me."

He gave her one of those dangerous grins that always did such strange things to her heart. "I guess I haven't made myself clear. I wouldn't dream of hitting the trail alone anymore. The loner you met has been transformed.

The thought of leaving you, for even a day, is too painful. I was hoping you might want to tag along."

Before she could open her mouth he added quickly, "I know it's a lot to ask. The life is pretty primitive. Sometimes we'd be out in the wilderness for a week or more, without ever seeing another human. Just us and the stars at night, and our wolf pack, howling at the moon."

She shivered and wrapped her arms around his waist before tipping her face up to his. "You just described paradise."

He paused to stare down into her eyes. "You're sure? You wouldn't mind leaving your ranch in the hands of your wranglers to spend time in the wilderness?"

"Quinn. You're just asked me to share not only your life but your dream. And you ask if I'm sure? Oh, my darling, I've never been so sure of anything in my life."

She brushed her mouth over his and felt the thrill that coursed along her spine at the thought of all that had happened. She'd been lost, without family, and unaware of the danger living under her very roof until this man had come along to change everything. With Quinn Conway she had found all the things she'd thought lost to her forever. Love. Laughter. Family. And, best of all, a renewed purpose in life.

He gathered her into his arms and held her close, feeling the way her heartbeat kept time with his. They were perfectly suited. They shared the same love of hard work. The same sense of wonder at the beauty of the countryside around them. The same passion for the wildlife that thrived in this land.

Quinn still couldn't believe his good fortune. He'd walked headlong into a raging storm and emerged with the great love of his life.

Whatever dark cloud had been hovering over his family for generations, it had been dispersed. He wouldn't question the wonder of it. It was enough to know that he loved, and was loved by, the only woman who would ever tame his wild heart.

"Come on." He caught her hand. "We've kept the family waiting long enough. I don't want to be late. You realize we're about to start on the adventure of a lifetime."

The adventure of a lifetime.

As they headed toward the ranch, Cheyenne felt a tingle of warmth on her cheek and lifted a finger to the spot. As though, she thought, her father and mother and Buddy had touched her in a blessing.

Her heart felt as light as air.

She couldn't wait for the journey to begin.

Josh Conway can rescue
anyone, anywhere.
But nothing can save him
from his attraction to
photographer Sierra Moore.

———◆———

Please turn this page
for a preview of

Josh

Available in October 2012

CHAPTER ONE

Hoo boy." Josh Conway, fresh from morning chores in the barn, shook the rain from his dark, shaggy hair before hanging a sodden rain slicker on a hook in the mudroom. He bent to wash his hands at the big sink and stepped into the kitchen of the family ranch. "Rain's coming down out there like the storm of the century."

"That's what it looks like to me, boyo." Big Jim was standing by the window sipping coffee and watching dark clouds boiling around the peaks of the Grand Tetons in the distance. Jagged slices of lightning illuminated the ever-darkening sky and turned the leaves of the cotton-woods to burnished gold.

Though it was early autumn in Wyoming, there was a bite to the air, hinting at what was to come.

"Do I smell corn bread? Now that ought to brighten my day." Josh made a beeline for the counter beside the oven, where Ela was cutting a pan of her corn bread into squares.

"Wait for the others." The old Arapaho woman rapped his knuckles with her wooden spoon but couldn't help grinning as he stuffed a huge slice in his mouth before turning away to snag a glass of orange juice from a tray.

Josh's father, Cole, who had been going over financial papers in his office, paused in the doorway just as his oldest son, Quinn, and his new bride, Cheyenne, came striding in, arm in arm.

"Good," Quinn said in a loud stage whisper. "They haven't finished breakfast yet."

"Haven't even started." Phoebe, the family's longtime housekeeper, hurried across the room to hug them both.

After the disappearance of their mother, she had been hired to help Ela with the household and to help raise the three boys. A young widow herself, Phoebe had sold her hardscrabble ranch and moved in to become their trusted friend and confidante, and their biggest supporter as they'd made the difficult journey through childhood and adolescence. Now, looking at the grown men she'd helped raise, she felt as proud as a mother hen.

"And you just happened to be in the neighborhood," Josh deadpanned.

"That's right." Quinn helped himself to a cup of steaming coffee. "After morning chores at Cheyenne's ranch, we figured we'd amble over here and see if you needed any help."

"Amble? Bro, you had to drive a hundred miles an hour to get here in time for breakfast." Jake, their youngest brother and the family prankster, stepped in from the mudroom, his sleeves rolled to the elbows, his hair wet and slick from the downpour.

Cheyenne shared a laugh with her husband. "I told you

they wouldn't buy the story that we just happened to be in the neighborhood."

"The only thing that happens to be in this neighborhood is Conway cattle," Big Jim said with a laugh. "And maybe a few of Quinn's wolves and Cheyenne's mustangs."

"I'm betting they'd start a stampede for some of Ela's corn bread."

At Quinn's remark they all laughed louder.

"That's one of the reasons we're here." Quinn turned to Ela. "Cheyenne and I have used your recipe, but it never turns out like yours."

Josh winked at his new sister-in-law. "I bet she left out a key ingredient, just so you'd always have to come back here to get the best."

"You see, Ela?" Jake was grinning from ear to ear. "I told you it would work."

They all joined in the laughter.

"Sit down, everybody."

At Phoebe's invitation they gathered around the big wooden trestle table and began passing platters of ham and eggs, potatoes fried with onions and peppers, and Ela's corn bread, as well as an ample supply of wild strawberry preserves, a favorite of Big Jim's.

Phoebe circled the table, topping off their cups of coffee.

Jake filled his plate before handing the platter to Josh.

"Big Jim and I are heading up to the hills after breakfast."

"You're heading right into the storm," Josh remarked.

"Yeah. I've been watching those clouds." Jake nodded toward the window, where the sky had been growing murkier by the hour. "Want to come along, Bro?"

Josh helped himself to eggs. "Sure. A little rain doesn't bother me. I can lend a hand. You doctoring some cattle, Doc Conway?"

Jake nodded. "Pretty routine stuff. But the work goes a lot faster with an extra pair of hands."

When Josh's cell phone rang, he idly glanced at the caller ID. His voice took on a businesslike tone: "Josh Conway."

He listened in silence before saying, "Okay. I'm on it."

As he tucked his phone into his shirt pocket he turned to Jake with a grin. "Guess I'll have to take a pass on going along with you and Big Jim. I'm needed on the mountain."

Cole shook his head. "I wouldn't want to climb those peaks in this storm. How come they never call on you to climb on a sunny day?"

"I guess because no fool hiker ever gets himself lost in good weather, Pa." Josh drained his cup and pushed away from the table. "I think it's some kind of rule of the universe that every careless hiker in the world decides to climb the Grand Tetons just before the biggest storm of the century blows through."

He left the room to fetch his gear, which he kept always packed and ready for just such emergency calls. Through the years Josh Conway had built a reputation as a fearless, dependable climber who could be counted on to locate lost hikers who couldn't be found by the rangers.

When he returned to the kitchen, Phoebe handed him a zippered, insulated bag.

At his arched brow she merely smiled. "Something to eat on the drive to your mountain."

"Thanks, Phoebe." He brushed a kiss over her cheek

before giving a salute to the rest of his family. "See you soon."

"Take care, boyo." Big Jim listened as his grandson's footsteps carried him through the mudroom and out the back door.

The old man glanced at his family gathered around the table. Though their conversation resumed, it was muted. And though they never spoke of it, every one of them knew that there was no such thing as a routine climb. Not when the one doing the climbing was there because the professionals had already tried, without success, to find a missing hiker.

Josh was their last resort. The strong, capable loner who would never give up until the one who was lost was found.

See you soon.

Josh's parting words played through Big Jim's mind.

Funny, he thought, that ever since Seraphine disappeared all those years ago, none of them could ever bring themselves to say good-bye.

Maybe it was just as well.

Good-bye seemed so final.

"The missing hiker's named Sierra Moore." Mitch Carver, a ranger who had been working the Grand Teton range for over twenty years, tipped back his chair and tensely tapped a pen against the desktop, the only sign of his agitation. "A professional photographer and veteran hiker. When she filled out the required backcountry use permit, she was warned of possible storms in the area and said she was hoping to capture them on film. I didn't think much of it, until she failed to check in with our station.

I tried her contact number, and she never responded. It could mean that she simply forgot to power up her cell. Or the storm may have knocked out any chance of a signal. But her lack of response could mean she's in trouble. And, since she didn't fill out the names of any friends or family to contact, I decided to send Lee to track her. But she wasn't found in the area where she'd said she was heading." He glanced at the papers she'd filled out. "Midlevel, possibly climbing as high as the western ridge."

"Lee knows his stuff." Josh had worked with rangers Mitch Carver and Lee Haddon for years and was comfortable that neither of them would ask his help unless they were convinced that they had chased every lead they could.

Mitch returned to his pen tapping. "Lee found no trace of her. None of the rangers spotted her. So far she hasn't taken advantage of any of the rest areas or campsites, though they're all on alert to watch for her. It's like she just vanished."

Vanished.

Josh felt the quick little shiver that passed through him and resented the fact that even now, all these years later, the word could have this effect on him.

"Okay." He forced himself to relax. "We know she's somewhere on the mountain. And with the storm, she's probably hunkered down somewhere until it's gone. Mark all the places that Lee hiked, and I'll chart a different route."

Mitch handed over the map with a highlighted overlay.

Seeing Josh's arched brow, he grinned. "After so many years, I'm pretty good at anticipating what you'll ask for."

Josh studied the trail taken by Lee Haddon. It was the

logical path to the area the missing hiker had indicated. That meant that she'd been sidetracked along the way, or had chosen to climb higher than she'd first planned. The latter seemed unlikely, considering the fierce storms she'd have had to deal with. But he had to consider every possibility.

He began making a mental trail of his own. Though most hikers came to these mountains once or twice in their lives, this was Josh's home turf. He didn't need a physical map to tell him where every peak, every dangerous dip, curve, and valley lay.

The storm, however, changed everything. Here at ground level, it was merely thunder, lightning, and heavy rain he had to contend with. If he was forced to climb to the higher elevations, that would change to snow and sleet and tremendous winds.

Josh picked up his gear and strode to the door of the ranger's office. "I'll be in contact."

"I know you will." Mitch Carver lifted his hand in a salute as the door closed.

Josh had been climbing steadily for hours. And though he'd found no trail, or even a trace of another human being, he continued on.

As he'd suspected, the rain had turned to sleet in the higher elevations, and now had turned to a bitter snow driven by an even more furious, blinding wind. It whistled up the face of the mountain, flinging a sudden spray of ice and snow in his eyes, like a slap in the face.

He needed to stop for the day and make camp. His muscles were beginning to protest the extra effort it took to climb over slick ice-and-snow-covered rock. His fingers had long ago lost all feeling. Despite the protective glasses, his eyes burned from the constant buffeting of wind and snow.

When he arrived at a flat stretch of snow-covered space between two towering peaks, he lowered his pack and used it as a seat while he fumbled with his cell phone.

Hearing Mitch's voice, he said, "Good. At least I have service here. I was afraid I was too high to get through."

"You're fading. I'll probably lose you any second now. Any sign of our hiker?"

"Not yet. I'm at the North Ridge."

"That high? You've been doing some serious climbing, my friend."

Josh laughed. "I'm going to call it a day. Make camp here, then start a horizontal tomorrow before deciding if I want to go any higher."

"Okay. Stay in touch."

"You do the same."

He tucked away his cell phone and began looking around for a spot to set up his small tent.

The wind had picked up to nearly gale force, kicking up snow in little funnels that were nearly blinding.

He blinked, wondering if his eyes were playing tricks on him. When he looked a second time, he knew that what he was seeing was real. A small white bubble tent was snugged up against a snow-covered peak, making it almost invisible. Had it not been for the extreme wind, causing the tent to shimmer with each sudden blast, it would have been impossible to see. Almost, he thought, as though it had been deliberately set up that way to deceive the eye.

At the same moment, a strange thought leaped unbidden into his mind.

Was this how his mother had been able to leave without a trace? Had she yearned for a new life, far from the demands of a husband and sons and the loneliness of ranching, using camouflage to make her escape across the mountains?

The instant the thought took form, he banished it from his mind. His memories of his mother, though distant and scattered, were happy ones. Seraphine had been a loving, though unconventional, mother. She neither cooked nor cleaned, but she had happily read to her sons and played classical music and directed them in plays and musicals for hours on end. When her boys grew weary and insisted on doing the things boys loved, playing outside or riding their ponies, she would simply take her books and music outdoors and watch them from a nearby hill.

Though she was athletic, with a lithe, sinewy dancer's body, she never took part in any of their outdoor activities that Josh could recall. That told him that she would have never resorted to climbing these mountains.

Josh had never seen her unhappy or moody or less than exuberant about life. She would often tell her boys that, though she missed dancing onstage and receiving the adulation of the audience, she didn't miss the gypsy lifestyle, living in dingy hotel rooms, traveling from town to town. She seemed to genuinely love being a rancher's wife, and their mother, and had treasured the anchor of their big, comfortable home and sprawling land to call her own.

But there had never been an explanation for the fact that she vanished, without a trace. There had been only theories.

The code of silence that had descended upon her family prevented any of them from knowing just what Cole

Conway believed to be true. Did he suspect desertion by an unfaithful wife? Foul play? An alien abduction?

Josh pulled himself back from the thoughts that had plagued him for a lifetime. Forced himself back to the present, and the job at hand.

If, as he suspected, this was the tent of Sierra Moore, his task had just become a lot simpler than he'd imagined.

Josh hoped the saga of the missing climber would have a happy conclusion and by this time tomorrow he would be enjoying another helping of Ela's corn bread.

THE DISH

Where authors give you the inside scoop!

♥ ♥ ♥ ♥ ♥ ♥ ♥ ♥ ♥ ♥ ♥ ♥ ♥ ♥ ♥

From the desk of Stella Cameron

Frog Crossing

Out West

Dear Reading Friends,

Yes, I'm a gardener and I live at Frog Crossing. In England, my original home, we tend to name our houses, and the habit lives on for me. Some say I should have gone for Toad Hall, but enough said about them.

Things magical, mystical, otherworldly, enchanting— or terrifying—have occupied my storytelling mind since I was a child. Does this have anything to do with gardening? Yes. Nighttime in a garden, alone, is the closest I can come to feeling connected to the very alive world that exists in my mind. Is it the underworld? I don't think so. It is the otherworld, and that's where anything is possible.

At night, in that darkness, I feel not only what I remember from the day, but all sorts of creatures moving around me and going through their personal dramas. I hear them, too. True, I'm the one pulling the strings for the action, but that's where the stories take root, grow, and spread. This is my plotting ground.

In DARKNESS BOUND, things that fly through tall trees feature prominently. Werehound Niles Latimer and widowed, mostly human, Leigh Kelly are under attack from every quarter by fearsome elements bent on tearing them apart. If their bond becomes permanent and they produce a child, they can destroy a master plan to take control of the paranormal world.

The tale is set on atmospheric Whidbey Island in the Pacific Northwest, close to the small and vibrant town of Langley, where human eyes see nothing of the battle waged around them. But the unknowing humans play an important part in my sometimes dark, sometimes light-hearted, sometimes serious, a little quirky, but always intensely passionate story.

Welcome to DARKNESS BOUND,

Stella Cameron

♥ ♥ ♥ ♥ ♥ ♥ ♥ ♥ ♥ ♥ ♥ ♥

From the desk of R.C. Ryan

Dear Reader,

Ahh. With QUINN I get to begin another family saga of love, laughter, and danger, all set on a sprawling ranch in Wyoming, in the shadow of the Grand Tetons. What could be more fun than this? As I'm fond of saying, I just love a rugged cowboy.

There is something about ranching that, despite all its hard work, calls to me. Maybe it's the feeling that farmers, ranchers, and cattlemen helped settle this great nation. Maybe it's my belief that there is something noble about working the land, and having a special connection to the animals that need tending.

Quinn is all my heroes wrapped into one tough, rugged cowboy. As the oldest of three boys, he's expected to follow the rules and always keep his brothers safe, especially with their mother gone missing when they were children. In tune with the land he loves, he's drawn to the plight of wolves and has devoted his life to researching them and to working the ranch that has become his family's legacy. He has no need for romantic attachments...well, until one woman bursts into his life.

Fiercely independent, Cheyenne O'Brien has been running a ranch on her own, since the death of her father and brother. Cheyenne isn't one to ask for help, but when an unknown enemy attacks her and her home, she will fight back with everything she has, and Quinn will be right by her side.

To me, Cheyenne is the embodiment of the Western woman: strong, adventurous, willing to do whatever it takes to survive—and still very much a beautiful, soft-hearted, vulnerable woman where her heart is concerned.

I loved watching *the sparks* fly between Quinn and Cheyenne.

As a writer, the thrill is to create another fascinating family and then watch as they work, play, and love, all

♥ ♥ ♥ ♥ ♥ ♥ ♥ ♥ ♥ ♥ ♥ ♥ ♥ ♥

From the desk of Jami Alden

Dear Reader,

Who hasn't wished for a fresh start at some point in their lives? I know I have. The urge became particularly keen when I was starting high school in Connecticut. Not that it was a terrible place to grow up, but an awkward phase combined with a pack of mean girls eager to point out every quirk and flaw had left their scars. Left me wishing I could go somewhere new, where I could meet all new people. People who wouldn't remember the braces (complete with headgear!), the unibrow, the glasses (lavender plastic frames!), and the time my mom tried to perm my bangs with disastrous results.

In RUN FROM FEAR, Talia Vega is looking for a similar fresh start. Granted, the monsters from her past are a bit more formidable than a pack of snotty twelve-year-olds, and the scars she bears are physical as well as emotional. But like so many of us, all she really wants is a fresh start, a new life, away from the shadows of her past.

But just as I was forced to sit in class with peers who remembered when I had a mouth full of metal and no idea how to wield a pair of tweezers, Talia Vega can't outrun the people unwilling to let her forget everything she's tried to leave behind. Lucky for her, Jack Brooks, the one man who has seen her at her absolute lowest point, will do anything to protect her from monsters past and present.

And even though I got my own fresh start of sorts